Flashback

Gabriele,

I hope you enjoy my
Low Country adventure!

D. A. Welch

Flashback

A Low Country Novel

D. A. Welch

iUniverse, Inc.
New York Lincoln Shanghai

Flashback

A Low Country Novel

Copyright © 2007 by DAWELCH, LLC

iUniverse books may be ordered through booksellers or by contacting:

iUniverse
2021 Pine Lake Road, Suite 100
Lincoln, NE 68512
www.iuniverse.com
1-800-Authors (1-800-288-4677)

This is a work of fiction. All of the characters, names, incidents, organizations, and dialogue in this novel are either the products of the author's imagination or are used fictitiously.

ISBN-13: 978-0-595-41271-6 (pbk)
ISBN-13: 978-0-595-67886-0 (cloth)
ISBN-13: 978-0-595-85627-5 (ebk)
ISBN-10: 0-595-41271-8 (pbk)
ISBN-10: 0-595-67886-6 (cloth)
ISBN-10: 0-595-85627-6 (ebk)

Printed in the United States of America

In memory of Bill Roth, an honorable man.
Semper Fidelis, Dad.

In memory of Eileen Evans, a Low Country angel.
Watch over us.

We have just enough religion to make us hate,
but not enough to make us love one another.

Jonathan Swift

Hate and force cannot be in just a part of the world
without having an effect on the rest of it.

Eleanor Roosevelt

ACKNOWLEDGMENTS

All cover photos are attributed to my talented husband, Pete Welch. During the writing of *Flashback*, Peter prepared wonderful dinners, tolerated late nights, and patiently edited several drafts of this book. He's been my partner in life, strongest critic, and biggest champion for over thirty years. I'm a lucky woman.

Thanks to the avid readers: Lila Konecny, Marty Layman, and Grace Roth. In the earlier stages of *Flashback*, they gave me valuable feedback and words of encouragement.

Thanks to Josh Wartchow, USMC. After serving in Afghanistan and Iraq, he educated me on weaponry and other stuff.

Thanks to iUniverse for making it possible to break through the publishing barriers. Your staff has been incredibly honest, helpful, and supportive.

PROLOGUE

The sound of an explosion jolted him out of a fitful sleep. Naked and drenched in sweat, he raked his fingers though his damp hair and clawed his way out of a nightmare. The red digits on the nightstand clock glared 4:00 AM. In two hours, he could be on a military transport headed south. He had escaped the Middle Eastern deserts with his life. He had walked away from Bethesda doctors on his own two feet. Now, he would leave the District of Columbia on his own volition. It was time to go home, to a place where life was simpler, to a place where he could find some sanity—maybe his own.

I

As the plane dipped a wing and banked right, the pilot began his landing approach, putting the Atlantic Ocean behind them and taking a northerly course over the Port Royal Sound. Nate sat behind the copilot and looked in both directions. On his left, he saw Hilton Head Island. On his right, Parris Island came into view. He thought about the contrast. Hilton Head was a large resort community where people lived and vacationed, some in extreme luxury. Wealthy people played there and had people pamper them. Parris Island was a boot camp where young recruits got their first taste of hell and learned to survive it. It toughened them and made them stronger. As the plane crossed the Broad River, Nate looked down and saw Beaufort, South Carolina. They would be landing at the Air Station soon and he would be back in the Low Country.

He remembered growing up in the small town of Beaufort; life had been predictable and safe. His mother had chosen the location when his father announced his transfer to Parris Island. She moved there with her five-year-old son and infant daughter while her husband completed his last tour of duty overseas. The small, southern town was steeped in history, with antebellum homes and majestic oak trees that had stood for well over two hundred years. Unlike most of the south, Beaufort had escaped the worst ravages of the Civil War. The Union saw its strategic value early, and with an aggressive naval assault, they took control of the town. The army converted homes to hospitals and quarters for Union officers instead of burning them to the ground. From this key position, the Union would plan, prepare, and move against major Southern strongholds in Charleston and Savannah. His parents had taught him to appreciate the rich history that formed the quiet towns, charismatic cities, and diverse barrier islands throughout the Low Country. When they landed, Nate looked forward to seeing his father.

She stood on the sidewalk in front of his boyhood home. Nate looked at the house and wondered why she was taking photos of the aging Victorian. The home had always been a sanctuary for him, but it constantly needed repairs or repainting. He shifted his focus back to her. She had a long, slender figure and wore a form-fitting top with a knee-length skirt. The light wind swirled the flowered fabric around her legs and tousled the blond hair that fell to her shoulders. Although there was nothing sinister about it, her presence bothered him. She might be a realtor or a reporter; the thought of either one made him uncomfortable. As he approached her, he asked, "Do you mind telling me who you are and why you're taking pictures of this house?"

Her head spun in his direction and she looked up at him, raising her hand to block the sun. "Do you mind telling me who *you* are and why it's your concern? Which one of us goes first?"

Nate studied the face of a beautiful woman with deep blue eyes, high cheekbones, and a mouth made for a man's enjoyment. When he extended his hand, her demeanor remained cautious and unsmiling. "I'm Nate Dunlevy." He glanced at the house. "I grew up here."

Her expression changed and she smiled as she accepted his hand. "You have John's eyes. I'm Eve O'Connor, and I adore your father. It's a genuine pleasure to meet you."

Before Nate could respond, the front door of the Victorian opened and John Dunlevy walked onto the porch. "Nate, I can't believe you're here. I see you've met Eve. Don't just stand there. Come inside. Are you done taking those pictures, sweetheart?"

Nate had only heard his father use that expression with two other women—his mother and his sister. What was his connection with this beautiful young woman? Nate guessed her to be in her late twenties. At fifty-eight, John Dunlevy was handsome, healthy, and single. He also had a twenty-nine-year-old daughter. Nate had been away for three months, but they had just spoken on the phone two weeks ago. His father never mentioned a woman in his life.

Despite the breeze, the sun felt hot and his dark-colored shirt absorbed enough heat to cause a thin trickle of sweat to run between his shoulder blades. He remembered his days in the Arabian deserts, where the air was so dry that the sweat would evaporate before it even poked through your pores. He didn't mind the moisture on his skin.

Eve took his hand and walked toward the house. "John, you didn't tell me your son would be here today?"

"Because I wasn't expecting him. Did I miss something in our last conversation, Nate?"

"No. I made a last-minute decision and left Washington early this morning on a military transport. I should have called from the base before I barged in on you. Sorry."

The two men embraced. "Don't apologize. I'm glad you're here. Last time we spoke, you didn't know when you'd be heading back to South Carolina. How'd you get here from the air station?"

"My car was at the base. I'm parked around the corner."

Nate felt awkward as he followed them into a house he knew better than his own. They walked past the living and dining rooms and into the kitchen. Eve went to the refrigerator and took out a pitcher. "I'll bet you've missed one of our southern staples, Nate. I made iced tea earlier." He watched her move around the kitchen with ease. She walked to a cabinet, took out three tall glasses, put them on the counter, and began to pour.

John reached for two glasses and handed one to Nate. "Are you home for long?"

"For a while. I want to finish the work on my house in Charleston."

"That's great. Eve and I made plans for lunch today. We're finalizing an agreement. You must be hungry and I'd like your input, so come with us."

Nate stood in the family kitchen with his father and a woman named Eve and could not come up with a single intelligent thought. Then he heard an urgent scratching sound at the back door. When Eve opened it, a large, hairy critter bounded across the kitchen floor. Nate thanked God for dogs and small miracles. "Rufus!" The dog trotted to him, circled twice, and plopped his hindquarters on Nate's left foot. When he squatted down to scratch behind the dog's ears, Rufus looked at him with large, soulful eyes. His wet tongue lolled out the side of his mouth, and then it lapped Nate's chin. "How've you been, old boy? I've always said you are so ugly that you're downright cute." Rufus drooled on the floor while Nate continued to scratch the dog's ears.

John commented, "That dog needs a bath as much as this kitchen floor needs one. I'll deal with it when we get back from lunch. Are we ready to go?"

Wanting to avoid another awkward moment, Nate spoke. "Listen, Dad, I don't want to intrude on your plans. I'll head back to Charleston and catch up with you later in the week. The two of you don't need me tagging along."

Nate walked to the sink with his glass and his father gripped his arm. "I think you have the wrong impression."

Eve blushed when she made eye contact with John. Then she turned to Nate. "We had planned to discuss a project over lunch. I'm an artist. Your father asked me to do a painting of this house. I took pictures to study the architecture and the lighting."

Nate looked at his father and then at Eve. The thought of having an affair had clearly embarrassed both of them. Nate found himself at a loss for words again. John reached for his son's empty glass and refilled it, giving everyone a moment to regroup. Nate took several large swallows and shook his head. "You called her sweetheart." He paused. "The two of you acted so natural with each other, I just thought …" He trailed off then added, "Can I go outside and start over again? I'm sorry if I offended either of you."

Eve smiled at Nate. "You haven't offended me. Your Dad's quite a catch for any woman. But I'm not in the market right now."

They had lunch at a local restaurant overlooking the Beaufort River. During the meal, Nate watched his father with Eve and concluded they had developed a good friendship. She told John about several commissions for her work and he suggested ways to protect both parties in the contracts.

John practiced law in Beaufort, South Carolina. Before that, he had served as a Marine Corps lawyer—a JAG. Colonel Dunlevy's reputation on Parris Island made Nate's decision to enter the Marine Corps easy. That's where the similarities in their military careers ended.

John directed the conversation to Nate. "Eve belongs to a group that owns a gallery in Charleston. It's on East Bay Street, a few blocks from the open market. That's where I first saw her work. It made me want a painting of our house on Craven. Your mother loved that house."

Memories of his mother stirred emotions. "Mom loved the whole town and decided we'd grow up there. But she died of cancer twenty years ago, before she could finish with us."

Eve said, "I'm sorry you lost her, Nate. How old were you when she died?"

"Fifteen."

John continued, "Nate was fifteen and Olivia was ten. Within a year, Devon became part of our family. He had lost his parents and only sister in a car accident when he was fourteen. He went through a very difficult time before he came to us. Since then, Devon has become a son to me and a brother to Nate and Olivia. We couldn't imagine our lives without him."

Eve's face reflected the tragedy John just described. "I live far from my parents and my sister. I miss them every day and I can't imagine losing them."

John nodded in agreement. "Time has helped, but I miss Sophia. I still talk to her, especially when something comes up with the family." He smiled. "We had a long discussion when Olivia moved to New York last year. I knew it was good for her career, but I couldn't imagine our baby girl all by herself in that big, crazy city."

By the time they finished a long lunch, Nate warmed up to Eve O'Connor. She had grown up in the south, but he wouldn't label her a socialite. Over the years, Nate had met several women who liked to flaunt their place in southern circles. Often, their pedigree outweighed their intelligence, and they valued bank accounts more than personal character. Eve came across as a smart and sincere woman. He thought about asking her to dinner when he got better.

Back on Craven Street, Eve said good-bye to John and promised to contact him about the painting soon. Nate followed Eve to the metallic tan BMW parked across the street. As he opened the car door, he said, "Thank you for being a friend to my father. I apologize for my misunderstanding earlier. At lunch today, I realized how much he misses Olivia since she moved to New York."

"If I've fulfilled a need for your father, he's done the same thing for me. He's a very good man. You're lucky to have him in your life."

He agreed. "I want to spend more time with him this afternoon, and then I'll head back to Charleston. I have a house on Tradd Street, one that I'm renovating." He hesitated. "Would you mind if I called you sometime?"

"Nate, thank you for asking, but I can't go out with you. Please don't take it personally."

He thought about his own problem. Tired, cynical, perhaps crazy—that's how he felt. He lifted his hand to brush a wisp of blond hair from her cheek. The touch of his fingertips caused her to flinch. He apologized and waited for her to settle behind the wheel before he closed the car door and watched her drive away.

John stopped mopping the kitchen floor when he saw his son standing in the doorway. "I'll be done here in two minutes. I just want to clean up a little dog spit." Rufus perked up his ears but remained horizontal under the kitchen table. "The Braves game is on in the living room; they're up three to one. I'll grab a couple beers and be right there."

Rufus skittered up from beneath the table and followed Nate into the next room. When Nate stretched out in a comfortable armchair, Rufus circled at his feet then flopped down with a grunt. John came in with the beers. "I hope you're clear about my friendship with Eve. You surprised me when you thought of me as a dirty old man."

"I never thought of you that way, Dad. Plenty of men fall in love with women half their age and most of them would appreciate a woman like Eve." Then he thought about her remark. "I asked if I could call her and she blew me off. Is there something else I should know?"

John shrugged. "I can't tell you much. She dated a man for several months. His father owns a large car dealership on the west end of Charleston. He was top salesperson there. Apparently, he became serious about religion and expected her to share his enthusiasm. Something happened that she wouldn't discuss. She only told me she doesn't date anymore."

Nate listened with interest and remembered how she had reacted when he brushed at her hair.

John went on. "I worry about her, but I guess it's my nature, because I worry about your sister, too. Eve lives by herself on Sullivan's Island. Her parents moved to Ireland a few years ago. They left a large house to her and her sister, but her sister is gone most of the time. She's a musician, and her work keeps her on the West Coast."

Nate decided to shift the conversation away from Eve O' Connor. He didn't need any other complications in his life right now. "Did I mention that Dev's driving down from Washington in a few days? He and Max are finishing a proposal for a new DMG contract and then he's taking some time off. I had planned to drive down with him, but I decided to get out of Washington sooner."

Nate, Devon, and Max Gibb formed DMG, Inc., a security company, around the time they accepted an early retirement option from the vice-admiral of the United States Navy. After four years in the Marine Corps and eight years as Navy SEALs, they chose to leave active duty. During the three years since, DMG had fulfilled various contracts and their business thrived. One of their best clients was the United States Government. Some contracts forced them to disappear from time to time and the government would claim total ignorance if they were discovered in certain parts of the world.

John asked Nate if he could discuss the new DMG project. Nate nodded. "Believe it or not, it involves consulting for the Secret Service. You remember when Dev took a temporary assignment during the last presidential election."

"I do. The terrorist threats were quite serious. I didn't know he wanted to do it again."

"He's doesn't, but the Secret Service asked us to bid a project. The agency may hire someone from the outside to look for holes in their security."

"Why the sudden willingness to let others see where you're vulnerable?"

"It's fallout from the Homeland Security task force. You know how they publish sweeping directives. The last one involved sharing information among the various agencies and tapping resources outside normal channels. They release feel-good rhetoric to the press, mostly to placate the voters, but the director of the Secret Service approached DMG. We can thank the admiral and Devon's history with the agency. The director may be playing the game. Hire us, report to Homeland Security, one directive followed." He shrugged. "Or maybe he wants input from people who have recently seen a terrorist eye to eye, people who know how they think."

"Are you sure you want to juggle the politics?"

"If we get the contract, we won't make it a career."

"Must you go back to Washington soon?"

"The wheels of bureaucracy turn slowly. Dev will present the proposal this week. While I'm here, I'll do some research on the Port of Charleston that might pan out in the future. Right now, I'm going to hang drywall in a neglected house. I'll call you when Dev gets to Charleston and we'll have dinner together."

"I'm looking forward to seeing him. Just let me know when and where."

Nate drove north on Route 21 toward Charleston. Despite his weariness, he looked forward to the next hour on the road. From Hilton Head Island to Myrtle Beach, the entire coastal area of South Carolina is known as the Low Country. It's named for the topography—the region is flat, and much of it is wetland that gently melds into the sea. The terrain includes marshes, tidal basins, and estuaries flowing eastward toward the sounds that separate the barrier islands from the mainland. During late afternoons, the lowering sun casts light on the *Spartina* grass, giving it a golden glow. Summertime brings a grayish-green color to the water, which teems with life, but it becomes a jewel-toned blue as the weather cools and the microscopic animal life start to die off. It remains that color until the following spring when new fauna emerges. The dolphins that inhabit the local waters depend on the cycle; so do the men who still eke out a living with their shrimp trawlers. Nate had seen many changes occur in the Low Country and worried how long the cycle could last.

When he arrived in Charleston, Nate gave his two-story row house a thorough search. He found no signs of entry during his absence and no devices hidden in or around his home. Such paranoia had kept him alive more than once. Hoping for a good night's sleep, Nate took a hot shower and went to bed. Hours later, a deafening blast and a flash of blinding light caused him to bolt upright in his bed.

Sweat poured off his skin and his head pounded. He looked around the room and tried to steady his heart. Within seconds, he knew nothing had happened. The shock that woke him was only in his mind.

He groped his way through the blackness into the bath and flicked the wall switch. The bright light made him squint hard. After splashing cold water on his face, he looked in the medicine cabinet for aspirin and found none. He took his jeans off a hook and stepped into them, cursing as his foot caught and he almost toppled over the commode. Then he made his way down the stairs and found aspirin in a kitchen cabinet. As he opened the refrigerator, he remembered it was bare—so much for the cold milk his throat craved. After filling a glass at the faucet, he tossed the pills into his mouth and chased them with the tepid water. He climbed the steps to his bedroom, lay across the bed, and prayed that a few hours of peaceful sleep would come.

II

Four days later, three tall, fit men reached the corner of Tradd and East Bay and turned left. The temperate climate made the walk from Nate's house to Grill 225 pleasant. Taking long strides, they quickly covered the fifteen blocks. John pointed out the Morning Light Gallery on the other side of East Bay Street. "That's Eve O'Connor's gallery. It's closed right now, but the two of you should stop in some time. Her paintings are very impressive."

Devon asked, "Who is Eve O'Connor?"

Nate responded, "A new lady friend of Dad's who happens to be young and very beautiful."

Devon's interest perked up. "I didn't know you were seeing someone."

"I'm not dating her, and Nate knows better. But she is a friend, and I agree with his description. She's also very talented."

They sat at a table in the corner near the window and looked forward to the best steak dinner in Charleston. When the bartender spotted them, he poured three beers and signaled their server. Devon waited until the server handed them menus and walked away. "So, what's up with this Eve O'Connor? When did you meet her?"

"She was at Dad's house the day I got back from Washington." The story of Nate's mistaken impression amused Devon.

"Have you got dibs on this lovely lady?"

"I don't have dibs on anyone. Besides, she says she's sworn off men."

"And when have you paid attention to everything a woman says?"

"Whenever they come crying to me about your poor excuse for a pecker, Dev."

John chuckled quietly as he listened to the exchange. He had missed the camaraderie and the banter that went on between them.

After exchanging a few insults, Devon announced his plans for Mexico. "I want to spend a few days on a warm beach with scantily dressed women. You want to come along, Nate?"

Nate shook his head, wondering why he didn't share Devon's enthusiasm for fun in the Mexican sun. "I want to get the drywall hung in the room next to the kitchen. It's time I got serious about setting up an office in Charleston."

"Tell you what, big guy. I'll help you hang drywall for the next few days and then we'll go to Mexico."

John thought back to the time when the two gangly teenagers had grown into strong, virile men. At six feet two inches, Devon stood within an inch of Nate and outweighed him by almost ten pounds, but since they met in high school, Nate had always been taller. "Big guy" had been his nickname from the first day they met.

Nate shrugged. "I'll think about it."

During their meal, Devon updated John and Nate about business at DMG. "I finished our proposal three days ago. By the way, the bureaucrats like to call it a 'white paper.' I never could understand that term. It sounds like they sit around and read papers that tell you nothing."

"Some people call it the *Washington Post*, Dev."

He chuckled. "You're right. And our capitol is a place where people get paid gobs of money to put meaningless pages of drivel on the desks of elected officials. Guess who's paying for it?"

John laughed. "I've been telling you that for years."

"Yes, you have, Dad. The work we did on this last proposal made that clear to me. Christ, maybe I'm meant to carry an automatic weapon for the rest of my life."

"Did you deliver the proposal?" Nate asked.

"I delivered it to the director's secretary two days ago. Yesterday, I met with the director. The meeting was brief but he told me he wants to find holes they can plug and wants people who think outside the box." Devon shrugged. "Who knows? Maybe he's sincere. The critique of their training program got his interest."

Nate Dunlevy and Devon McLean had endured intensive and often brutal training. Navy SEALs were culled from the top echelon of young applicants, most were active duty soldiers who had already excelled mentally and physically. Both men had high IQs. Along with special warfare and survival skills, they were experts in explosives, electronics, surveillance, and intrusion.

John asked, "What do you think of their training?"

"They should put more emphasis on explosives and more focus on terrorists … people who will blindly sacrifice themselves and how they're trained to do it."

While they discussed the Secret Service, John mentioned agents he had met years earlier during training seminars at Quantico. Devon told him at least two were still active with the agency. The topic shifted to the power struggles in Washington—not just those involving the two parties but also the political versus military influence on policy and the war. The waiter cleared the meal and asked the men if they wanted coffee, dessert, or another drink. John ordered coffee. Nate had been silent for a while.

Devon frowned at his glassy eyes and sweaty forehead. "Nate, do you want anything?" He remained silent and unfocused even after Devon gripped his shoulder.

John spoke in a firm voice. "Nate! Are you with us?"

The sound of his father's voice and the pressure on his shoulder brought Nate back to the present. He shook his head and winced. A few seconds later, he excused himself and went to the men's room.

John put his coffee cup down and started to get up from his chair. Devon stopped him. "Stay here and finish your coffee, Dad." Then he got up and walked to the men's room.

Nate stood at the sink with his hands under the cool water faucet. He didn't bother to look up when Devon entered the room. "Sorry. I went off on a tangent—I'm okay now."

"Bullshit! We're going to deal with this, and we're going to do it soon." Devon left the restroom, walked back to the restaurant, and asked the waiter for the check.

The three men said very little as they walked back to Nate's house, each preoccupied with his own thoughts. When they reached the front door, Devon said, "I'm going to make a pot of coffee and put a bottle of bourbon on the table. Choose your poison before we sit down. Then we're getting things out in the open."

John remained silent as the two younger men stood eye to eye.

"Why are you doing this, Dev?"

"Because I saw the episode you just had in that restaurant. I thought someone drove steel spikes into your head. You look like shit and it's time to let someone help. Who can you trust more than Dad and me?"

Nate went through the front door and walked to the stairs. "I'll be down."

Devon made coffee and put glasses, ice, and bourbon on the table. "What can I get for you, Dad?"

"I'll stick with coffee for now. I might have bourbon later."

"Don't feel you have to drive back to Beaufort tonight. I'll crash on the sofa and you can use the second bedroom."

"We'll see."

Nate came back into the kitchen, walked to the table, put ice in a short glass and filled it halfway with bourbon. He looked over at Devon. "You want a drink?" Devon nodded and Nate made another drink to match his own. He looked at his father and asked, "Dev tell you anything while I was upstairs?" John shook his head.

The three men pulled out chairs and sat down at the kitchen table. No one spoke for several seconds. Nate rubbed his temples and looked at his father. "Dev's right. There's no reason not to tell you what happened. Hell! When I think about the stuff we've been through, it's not that big a deal; but I can't put this one behind me. I thought time would help, but the nightmares and flashbacks are getting worse."

"Tell me what you can, son. Just start with that."

"According to our government, the mission never took place and the specifics don't matter—we were in a desert in a country that was neither friend nor enemy. There was no engraved invitation. We eliminated a camp, one that brainwashed young men and trained them to become suicide bombers. We found plans that listed London, Madrid, Sydney, Los Angeles, and Washington as targets. We killed the trainers and the recruits, took the plans, and destroyed everything else. Then we got out."

Nate sat back in his chair and paused. Devon began to speak, but Nate stopped him. "Let me finish here. There's something I have to say about the trip out of there."

"It's one I won't forget, Nate."

He nodded. "Six of us had parachuted into the area. We got out using three of their vehicles to get back across the border. We kept some distance to avoid a cluster fuck. The sand made the travel difficult. Max and I led the group and I rode shotgun. Ahead of us, someone moved out of the brush—a boy. He started running toward us, so Max pulled to the left. The sand bogged us down. While Max threw the vehicle into reverse, I sighted my weapon on the boy. He hadn't seen his first whisker and wasn't thinking about virgins in heaven. I saw that his chest was too big for his frame—he was wearing a shirt packed with explosives. Max yelled for me to shoot as the boy reached toward his shirt. After squeezing the trigger, I saw the hole in his forehead, then an explosion. That's the last thing I remember."

Devon took a swallow of bourbon. "You had no choice. He was going to die whether he took you with him or not. He triggered the bomb. I was behind you and didn't see him that clearly, but I knew why he was there. I hauled your ass away from that wreckage. If he had gotten any closer, you wouldn't be sitting here."

"I know, Dev, but his face still haunts me. He was scared! He was scared shitless, but he kept on coming!" His voice quieted. "He didn't want to die, but he didn't know what else to do. He was just a little boy."

John tried to suppress the shudder that went through his body. "Were you badly injured?"

Devon spoke up before Nate could respond. "Max had already opened the driver's door when Nate's body slammed across the front seat and knocked him ten feet from the vehicle. Nate was hanging out of it, and he was out cold. I carried him to my vehicle. The debris had caused superficial injuries, but his gear had protected most of his body from any real damage. We found out later that he cracked two of his ribs when he hit the steering wheel. It took us two hours to get to a chopper because the sand slowed us down and we had to reach the border. Nate started to come around, but he couldn't see or hear. It was temporary, thank God. After two days in a field hospital, he was functioning close to normal."

Nate saw the genuine concern on his father's face. "Dad, I got back to the States and went directly to Bethesda. Trust me when I say they were thorough. Other than the ribs, I left with a clean bill of health."

"When did these other symptoms start, Nate?"

"About a week after I was released from the hospital. Dev found me crashed out in the Washington apartment one day. He woke me from a nightmare. I started getting headaches, which isn't common for me. Then the flashbacks began. I thought about seeing a shrink at Bethesda but ruled that out."

"Hell no!" Devon stood up from the table. "The next thing you know some medical mucky muck will be stamping 'unfit' on your folder. It's happened to some of the best men who fought next to us over the years."

"I know, Dev. That's why I haven't done anything." Nate looked back at his father. "So that's it ... all I can tell you. Got any advice?"

John steepled his hands together, leaning the two index fingers against his chin. The younger men knew this gesture well and remained silent. "I know the ugliness of war and terror. Your generation isn't the first to see children used as pawns by cold-blooded, ruthless people. Atrocities happened in Vietnam and other places—other wars. That doesn't make it acceptable, and the incident you survived must have brought the horror that much closer."

Both Devon and Nate stared into their drinks and John continued, "When you became soldiers, you took an oath to fight for your country, to do battle and to kill when ordered. But you didn't agree to kill children. That could be at the root of what's troubling you, but I don't know how to fix it."

Nate added ice to his glass then poured more bourbon. "Dev's right about the military shrinks, Dad. I don't want to go that route."

"I know, son. I've been there, too." John finished his coffee. "I know someone at MUSC. He's a psychiatrist on staff, but he takes private cases as well. I've used him for consultations. He's well respected, he's discreet, and he treats military personnel." John looked closely at his son. "I'm asking you to make an appointment with him." He finished his coffee and added, "You should also take Devon up on his suggestion. Get away from everything for a few days. Don't read the newspaper and don't watch the television. Go to Mexico, string up a hammock, get drunk, have sex, whatever. Then see this doctor when you get back." He glanced over at Devon. "I'm ready for that bourbon now. Got another glass?"

III

Nate and Devon sat on barstools under a thatched roof on a Yucatan beach. Devon referred to the place as the Butt Hut, because most of the women who gathered there wore thongs—and only thongs. Devon and Nate watched women walk up and down the beach. Nate signaled the bartender, "*Corona y Tequila, dos mas, por favor.*"

Since they arrived the day before, Nate seemed to relax and both men enjoyed the local scenery. From behind his sunglasses, Devon scanned the beachfront. "Did you notice the one in the red thong?"

Nate turned his gaze back toward the water. "I saw them. She bought those puppies."

"I think you're right, big guy. They sit right up there even though she's flat on her back. Still a great pair of tits."

"Hmmm." Nate took another draw from his bottle of Corona and tossed back a shot of Tequila.

Devon finished his beer and got up from his stool. "It's getting hot. I'm up for a quick swim and then the pool bar."

Nate said to the bartender, "*La quenta, por favor.*" He finished his beer and reached for the check before Devon could grab it. "I'm paying for this round." Minutes later, they left the bar and walked toward the pool.

Several women watched them as they stopped by a small table. One woman nudged her friend on the chaise next to her. "Lori, wake up or you'll miss Yum and Yummer!" Devon stripped off his T-shirt and walked to the edge of the pool.

Lori opened her eyes, slid her sunglasses lower on her nose, and followed Carol's gaze. "That's USDA prime." They watched Devon dive into the pool, swim two laps, and stroke his way to a submerged seat at the pool bar.

Carol glanced at Lori. "I suddenly have a mighty thirst. How about you?"

Lori looked toward the pool. "I'm parched."

The two women watched Nate slice cleanly through the water as they lowered themselves into the pool. They waded toward the bar and sat on stools next to Devon. The bartender looked in their direction as he pulled two Coronas from a cooler of ice. Carol ordered, "*Dos margaritas con rocas, por favor.*" The bartender nodded.

Devon had watched the two attractive bikini-clad women as they approached the bar. He had traveled enough of the world to know they were Americans. When the bartender served their drinks, he lifted his bottle in a salute. Both girls raised their drinks and smiled. Devon feigned uncertainty. "I'm taking a chance here, but I'm guessing you're from the States."

Both women nodded then Carol responded, "I'm Carol, and this is Lori. We flew down from Seattle to soak up the sun for a few days." Devon introduced himself and gestured toward Nate, who finished his swim and waded toward the bar.

Nate saw Devon talking to the two women and wondered if his brother had cast the line or bitten the one they tossed in his direction. "Nate, this is Carol and Lori. They're from Seattle."

Nate reached for the towel offered by the bartender, "*Gracias.*" Then he looked in the direction of the two women. "Nice to meet you. Are you enjoying your time in Mexico?" Devon handed him a Corona and the girls lifted their margaritas.

"We are now," Carol replied. Then she frowned. "But we're flying home tomorrow."

The men learned that Carol and Lori worked at a hospital in Seattle. They were lab techs and had been close friends for the last four years. Devon told them that he and Nate had been friends since high school and entertained them with stories of their past. Nate mostly listened. Time went by as the conversation and drinks flowed.

Carol got up from her immersed seat to reach for a napkin and lost her footing. She grabbed Devon's shoulder for balance and he instinctively wrapped his arm around her waist. "Steady as she goes there, Carol."

"Sorry about that." She did nothing to free herself from his hold.

She looked down at his strong arm and focused on his watch. "I've seen that exact watch before, when I drew blood from a Navy SEAL. She looked at Devon, then at Nate, who wore a similar watch, then back at Devon. Are you a SEAL? Are you both Navy SEALs?"

Devon glanced at Nate. Then he told Carol they were SEALs but that they had gotten out of the Navy three years earlier.

Lori seemed fascinated by this revelation. "I've seen movies about Navy SEALs." She looked over at Carol. "Do you remember the one called *G.I. Jane* starring Demi Moore? Is it really that brutal, the training and all?"

The two men studied their beers for a second. John Dunlevy had no tolerance for racism or sexism. He instilled the concept of equality in Nate, Olivia, and Devon long before they reached adulthood. But the idea of a woman becoming a Navy SEAL was pure Hollywood fantasy. The Ground Combat Exclusion Act made it illegal and the physical demands of the program made it impossible.

Devon glanced up. "The movies hype that stuff, don't they, Nate?"

"Hmmm." Nate nodded and picked up his beer.

Carol was fascinated by the topic. "I've read stuff about survival training. I know this is gross, but do they really make you drink urine?"

The question amused the two men. If that had been the worst part of the program, the country would be swarming with Navy SEALs. "That part is true, Carol. We did have to drink our urine." Devon paused for a second then grinned. "Most of us struggled not to toss our cookies. But not Nate, he liked it so much, he drank mine!"

Nate choked on his beer while everyone else, including the bartender, cracked up. After a final cough, he was able to speak. "Goddamn it, Dev, you swore not to tell!"

Devon tossed his head back and laughed harder.

That night they met in the lobby for dinner and walked through the small beachside town where local vendors filled the streets, hawking everything from shoeshines to fake Rolexes. Devon kept his arm around Carol's waist, and Nate gently gripped Lori's arm as they worked their way through the narrow, crowded sidewalks. They enjoyed a meal of Mexican fare served on Mexican time—slowly. After dinner, they navigated more streets, looking at the colorful wares. Music poured from several lounges, and when they walked past one with live entertainers, Devon leaned in against Carol's ear. She nodded. He looked back at Nate and Lori. "Carol and I are going to stop in here for a nightcap. Want to join us?"

Lori responded that she'd had too much sun and wanted an early night. As she hoped, Nate offered to walk her back to the hotel. A few blocks later, Lori's foot hit an uneven slab of pavement and her ankle buckled. Nate sensed her balance shifting and tightened the grip he had on her arm while reaching around with his other arm to steady her. She held on for a second then gingerly took another step. She looked up at Nate. "I think I sprained my ankle. How far is the hotel?"

Nate looked down at her foot, which she held just above the pavement. "It's not far, but we'll ride the rest of the way." He looked around and saw a cab approaching from the opposite direction. He shouted and waved to the driver, who pulled toward the far curb of the busy street. Nate scooped up Lori, quickly crossed the street, and then helped her stand next to the waiting cab. He opened the door of the vehicle and Lori got into the back seat, sliding over to make room for him. As he got in, he instructed the driver, "*Casa del Sol, por favor.*" Minutes later, Nate paid the driver and helped Lori walk into the hotel lobby. He held her firmly around the waist to keep as much weight as possible off her injured foot. The desk clerk saw them and asked, "*La Senorita dañar la pie?*"

"*Si,*" Nate responded, "*Algun hielo para la senorita, por favor.*"

"*Si, senor. Un momento.*"

The clerk walked away from the desk as Nate guided Lori to a nearby chair. "He's getting us ice for your ankle." Nate reached into his pocket for a tip as he walked to the desk. The clerk returned with a large champagne bucket full of ice. Nate handed him the folded bill as he reached for the bucket.

"*Muchas gracias.*"

"*Con placer, senor. Buenas noches.*"

"*Buenas noches.*" Nate walked back to Lori. He carried the ice in one arm and used the other to help her hobble to the elevator. When they reached her room, Nate took the key from her and opened the door. He put the ice bucket on a small desk and helped her to one of the beds. "Sit back and keep your feet up. I'll get a towel for the ice."

"There are clean glasses and a bottle of Stolichnaya on the sink, Nate. Bring them in and we can put this ice to more than one use."

"Sounds like a plan." Nate returned with the glasses, the vodka, and a hand towel. He used the towel to ice down Lori's ankle then made the drinks. "Your ankle is sprained but not badly. It's slightly swollen around your anklebone and there's a little bruising. If you keep it iced and elevated it should be much better by the morning."

An hour later, Lori had forgotten all about her ankle. Her back arched as another orgasm ripped through her. She expected Nate to move on top of her, so she reached down to touch him and bring him toward her.

Lori's responsiveness aroused Nate mentally, but his body would not oblige him, and he couldn't stay hard. After several minutes, he rolled onto his back and stared at the overhead ceiling fan. "I'm sorry, Lori. I don't think this is going to work for me tonight. Maybe the tequila I drank earlier is punishing me." He knew better.

"You don't need to apologize, Nate. I certainly enjoyed it. Am I doing something wrong for you?"

Nate rolled toward her again and lay on his side. "It's not your fault. You're a delightful woman. Let me hold you." He put his arm around her and pulled her closer. Moments later, he felt her drift into a peaceful sleep. The neon hotel sign cast an orange glow through the window as Nate stared into the darkness. Without realizing it, his thoughts drifted to Eve O'Connor. He felt a strong pang of guilt lying in bed with one woman while thinking of another. An hour later, he slipped quietly out of bed and got dressed. Lori never stirred.

Nate stopped by the front desk before going to his room and wrote her a brief note. It reminded her to keep her foot elevated on the plane trip home and wished her a happy life. On the way to his room, he passed Devon's door and smiled when he saw the "*No Molestar*" sign hanging on the knob. He opened his door, stripped, climbed into bed, and hoped sleep would come soon.

IV

A tropical storm had settled over the southeast coast. Clouds darkened the skies, palm trees bent, and wind buffeted the live oaks laden with Spanish moss. Rain fell in torrents, flooding the tributaries throughout the Low Country. Local news stations warned residents to stay away from the swelling creeks and broadcast pictures of rescue teams pulling people from partially submerged vehicles. Forty-eight hours later, a high-pressure system pushed the storm out to sea. The weather returned to normal, sunny and seventy-five degrees.

They had driven the drywall screws before they went to Mexico. Now they taped, spackled, and sanded. "This room looks a lot bigger, Nate. It's going to make a decent office. We may be ready to paint before I head back to Washington."

"I appreciate the help, but you've got better things to do before you leave. The storm passed and the weather's great. Wash off the compound dust and get out of here for a while."

"Since you mentioned it, I planned to knock off early today. I want to stop by Eve O'Connor's gallery this afternoon."

Nate stopped sanding a seam and turned to face Devon. "What do you have in mind?"

"You've met her, and Dad's told me more than once how much he likes her." He smiled. "I want to meet her before I leave town." He scooped up more drywall mud. "Remember, you suggested we give the painting to Dad as a gift. I want to see what kind of talent we're buying and find out when she'll have it done. Are you coming with me?"

Nate went back to his sanding, but his mind went elsewhere. "We don't even know if she'll be there today. I doubt she's there every day. When would she find time to paint?"

"It's simple enough to find out. Do you want to call, or should I?"

Nate stopped sanding, walked into the kitchen, picked up the phone, and punched in the number. He had phoned the gallery two other times and knew the number by rote. As Devon watched him make the call, he knew it was hands-off with Eve O'Connor. His brother had her within range—real men didn't poach.

Eve answered the phone, and Nate told her that he and Devon wanted to stop by so they could learn more about the painting their father had commissioned. They had planned to make it a gift to him.

Their interest in her work surprised Eve. "As a matter of fact, I've had been thinking about my approach to John's request, and you'd make a good sounding board for my ideas. And I'd like to meet Devon." Nate and Eve agreed they'd meet at the gallery at four o'clock.

That afternoon the two men walked to the Morning Light Gallery. When they opened the door, Eve stood behind a glass-enclosed display case at the far end of the room and a man leaned toward her from the other side. Nate observed the good-looking, impeccably groomed man wearing an expensive European-cut suit with a silk tie and matching handkerchief in his breast pocket. This man was the type who would attract a woman like Eve. He and Devon scanned the room full of paintings and sculptures, both with their hands in their trouser pockets as though they were afraid they might accidentally touch something.

Eve scrutinized the two men standing in her gallery … both were strikingly handsome yet rugged. Nate's light gray eyes reminded her of his father. His dark hair had grown since they met in Beaufort and now it fell below his collar. The sleeves of his shirt were rolled almost to the elbows and her eyes were drawn to the black hair covering his tan forearms. Devon was just shy of Nate's height and had a build just as muscular. His hair was shorter than Nate's and neatly squared off above his collar. The shade was a light brown with hints of red and blond that showed up under the bright gallery lights.

As Eve made her way around the counter, Nate admired her grace. The emerald green dress draped her figure in a subtle, flattering way and the color complimented her fair skin. Today, her blond hair was swept back from her face and she wore just enough makeup to highlight her beauty. He wondered if a woman like her would ever accept a man like him.

Eve smiled has she extended her hand. "It's good to see you again, Nate."

She reached out to Devon as Nate introduced him. "Meet Devon McLean. He's a legend in his own mind."

Eve laughed. "I'm Eve O'Connor, and it's a pleasure to meet you."

Devon smiled warmly and enclosed her hand in both of his. "The pleasure is mine, Eve. Pay no attention to Nate. He feels very inadequate when I'm around."

Still laughing, Eve turned to the man who smiled at them from his position near the glass case. She waved her hand in his direction. "This is Randall Harrison." She paused, smiled, and added with a flourish, "The Third." Randall bowed as Eve presented him as the gallery manager.

Randall moved forward when Eve completed her introduction. "Well, don't the two of you make a powerful impression as you darken a person's door?" He extended his hand to Nate and Devon. "Are these the two men you've been expecting?"

"Yes, Randall, they're new clients of mine. Their father is John Dunlevy, and they want to pay for the painting he's commissioned."

"You mean Colonel Dunlevy? I remember him well from the last time he stopped by the gallery. He bought that copper and turquoise bracelet for his daughter. What a lovely man." The phone in an adjacent room started to ring and Randall excused himself to answer it. Nate and Dev glanced at each other briefly and shared the same thought. No one had ever described John Dunlevy, a retired Marine Colonel, as a lovely man.

Eve took both men on a tour of the gallery, explaining that she shared the location with three other artists, all of whom were investors. They sold other goods purchased by Randall, who also had an ownership interest. "This gives us, the artists, time to work. You don't create art by staying inside the same four walls all day long. And Randall knows how to merchandise. He has an excellent eye for unique pieces and work done by local artisans."

Nate admired a large marsh scene signed by Eve. "Where do you do most of your painting?"

"I work on site to do landscapes like the one in front of you. It depends on the subject. I do a lot of preliminary sketches, or entire paintings, in a studio I have at home. I live on Sullivan's Island."

Nate pointed to her signature. "It must feel good when you can put your name on a painting like this."

"That piece took me over six weeks to complete. I headed to Edisto before five o'clock every morning so I'd be set up before sunrise. I'd paint nonstop for two or three hours, then stop when the lighting changed too much for the mood of the painting. I loved watching the egrets and herons leave the rookery each day."

Nate looked back at the painting and nodded. "I hope Edisto stays that way."

Eve smiled and agreed with him. "I'd like to show you some sketches I've done of your father's home. I'll be right back."

Devon looked at the small sign next to the painting. It read,

Eve Marie O'Connor
Original Oil
Edisto Sunrise
$9500.00

"She gets a decent buck for her work, doesn't she? I've got to admit it's good—if you want to spend that kind of money on art."

Nate agreed and looked at several other paintings bearing Eve's signature. Several depicted houses he knew from Charleston and Beaufort. They appeared more muted than the landscapes, and when he looked at the signs identifying them, he saw they were watercolors.

Eve returned with a sketchbook in hand. "We can use the viewing room over there. It has comfortable seating. Or we can walk two blocks and get a table at Cypress. It won't be crowded yet. Since you're both going to be clients, I should at least offer to buy you a drink."

Randall had walked back into the gallery. "Why don't you just skedaddle? I'll wrap up here for the day, princess."

Just inside the door to the gallery, Nate stopped and stared at a painting of two women sitting at a small table. It had drawn his attention earlier when Eve showed them around the gallery. Eve noted his interest. "We're lucky to have that piece; it's on loan from another gallery. The artist is Pino; he's from Italy, and he's amazing."

Devon and Nate both agreed as they studied the two women in the painting. Eve continued, "Pino has an extraordinary ability to capture the essence of womanhood. When I look at them, I see several traits—they're very feminine, but you see an inner strength. Their faces are demure and sensual at the same time. I'd give anything to recreate that look."

Nate opened the gallery door for her. "You can. Just look in a mirror." Eve blushed as she walked past him. Silently, Devon gave his brother high marks for the line. Then he saw the look on his face and knew it wasn't a line at all.

Cypress is a restaurant and bar frequented by the young professionals that work in the historic downtown Charleston area. The first floor functions as the main dining room, and there are additional tables and smaller rooms on the second floor. The upper floor also contains an art deco bar and cocktail tables that sit against glass partitions overlooking the dining room and the open kitchen below. A two-story glass enclosure on the outer wall houses hundreds of bottles of wine, and it is accessed by a metal spiral staircase.

Eve ordered a chardonnay; Nate and Devon ordered beers. While they waited for the drinks, Eve explained her ideas for the painting of the Dunlevy home. She showed them several different views, using her photos and the sketches in her book. "You can cluster three smaller pieces with portrait orientations in the same space as one large painting with a landscape orientation." She used her sketchbook to illustrate the concept. "The house has such interesting angles that I'm having difficulty picking a single focal point. I want to do a grouping of three paintings instead of one. I know where John wants to hang the painting and I can use that space very well with this approach. And here's the kicker." She looked at Nate. "I'd like to see family photos so I can add people to the scenes. They won't be obvious—like a snapshot—more impressionistic. But I need a feel for how you lived in that house."

Devon looked up from her sketches. "Like a picture of Dad reading the newspaper on the porch?"

"That's right, or one of Sophia in the garden." She looked at Nate. "The work will have more meaning if it tells a story. I know your parents loved each other very much. I want the result to be something special for your father." Nate found himself stirred by the idea and the woman who presented it.

The bartender served their drinks and they talked about more ideas for the paintings. Nate told Eve stories about growing up in the house. When Eve excused herself to use the restroom, Devon said to Nate, "I like the idea, but we should ask about the cost and the timing. Do you want to bring it up, or should I?"

Nate picked up his beer and took a swallow. "I'll do it."

Eve returned to the bar area and shook her head when the bartender asked if she wanted another glass of wine. She also gave him a silent signal that she wanted the tab brought to her. Nate stood as she approached the table and held her chair while she sat down. "We have two questions: how much do you want for the paintings and when will you be finished?"

"I'll answer the easy one first. I told John I would do a painting for five thousand dollars, mounted and framed in a nice hardwood. Actually, I suggested doing it for less if he gave me permission to do a limited edition of prints for resale. He felt strongly about keeping the painting private. Since it's my idea to do three smaller paintings, I'll do them for the same price. If you want prints for the family members, you can have them at my cost."

Nate said, "After seeing the prices in your gallery today, I have to ask why you aren't charging more. The paintings will be originals, and we'll have the only reproductions."

"Nate, your father is a friend, a good friend. I'd do the paintings for nothing, but he wouldn't let me. I'm charging a fair price for my time—which leads me to your other question. I'm guessing you had Christmas in mind when you mentioned a gift." Devon and Nate both nodded. "I hope this doesn't make me sound like a temperamental artist, but I can't guarantee a completion date. I'm excited about the project and eager to start work, but inspiration isn't the only skill I'll need. The translation from brain to canvas is the hard part. Sometimes I'll work on a piece for days and toss it because it's all wrong. I know writers go through the same experience. I don't want to rush the project just to get something done and not like the end result."

Nate and Devon agreed with her. The bartender came by the table and asked the men if they wanted another beer. When they declined, he came back and handed a leather folder to Eve. Before she could reach it, Nate took the folder from the bartender. "I've got this. The price you've given for those paintings is fine. Do you want a deposit?"

"No. I'll collect my fee when the work is complete. Can you get me some family albums? Soon?"

"I'll come up with a reason to borrow them and bring them to you next week. We'd like to make this part a little surprise for Dad."

The two men stood as Eve got up from her chair. Devon suggested they have dinner together, but Eve insisted on getting home before nightfall.

As they walked to her car, Devon said, "I'm going back to Washington in a few days, but I enjoyed meeting you."

"The feeling is mutual, Devon. When will you visit us again?"

"I'm not sure, but I stay in touch with Dad and Nate."

Whey reached her car, Nate opened the door. "Good night, Eve."

She slid into the driver's seat. "Good night to both of you, and thank you for the drink."

After they watched her drive away, Devon turned to Nate. "That is one fine lady and you could use a good distraction right now."

"I know, Dev, but I don't want to pressure her. She's afraid of something and I have my own baggage."

"Have you called that doc Dad mentioned?"

"Yeah, I've got an appointment next week."

V

Throughout the following week, the Low Country enjoyed bright skies and temperatures in the low eighties. No hurricanes or tropical storms threatened the area. Sailboats and cabin cruisers traveled past Charleston, taking advantage of the calm waters and good forecasts. Despite the great weather, Nate felt as though a large black cloud loomed over him as he walked toward the Outpatient Medical Building at MUSC. Inside the building, he looked at the directory and found the suite number for Dr. Joseph Reynolds. After a moment of hesitation, he stepped into the elevator.

He entered the reception area, found it empty, and wondered where all the people were. Then a grim thought entered his mind—maybe this doctor didn't have any patients. His father's words popped into his mind. *He's discreet.* Nate told himself to relax. He scanned the magazines on the table and picked up a copy of Sports Illustrated. As Nate turned to take a seat, the door across the room opened. A tall, slender man with graying hair and eyeglasses stood in the opening. He wore a sport coat, but no tie. "Commander Dunlevy?" He extended his hand.

"Yes, but just call me Nate." The two men shook hands.

"Okay. Call me Joe. Please come in."

Nate followed him through the door, past a desk scattered with files, and into a sitting area with a small sofa, two chairs, and an occasional table.

The doctor gestured toward one of the roomier-looking chairs. "Have a seat. Would you like something to drink—coffee, water, soda?"

"Water's fine."

Joe moved to a small refrigerator and took out two bottles of water. He put one on the table next to Nate's chair. Then Joe walked to his desk and picked up a pen. "I've known your father for several years. He's a good man."

Nate nodded. "Yes, he is. He's the reason I'm here right now. He recommended you."

"That's why I'm bringing this up, Nate. I want you to know that anything we talk about stays strictly between us. I don't discuss our conversations with anyone. Is that clear?"

"It's clear."

Joe sat in a chair across from Nate and picked up a file from the table next to him. "This is the copy of your medical record that you sent me. I understand why you didn't want it to come directly from Bethesda. When you walked through that door, you looked as though you'd rather face a firing squad than a psychiatrist."

Nate propped one long leg on his knee. "You're very observant, but don't take it personally."

Joe smiled. "You aren't alone in your aversion to head doctors. Most men dread their first appointment with me more than a prostate exam. I never look forward to those."

"Given a choice, Joe, I'd rather just bend over and be done with all this."

"Then tell me why you're here?"

For the next twenty minutes, Nate described his symptoms: the headaches, the nightmares, the flashbacks. He told Joe about the incident that led to his recent hospitalization and the discussion he had with his father and Devon. Nate reached for the bottle of water as he depicted, in vivid detail, the young boy's face the moment before his bullet hit and the explosion occurred.

Joe listened intently and took notes. When Nate paused, the silence hung heavy in the room. He wanted Nate to take a few minutes to regroup his thoughts and relax a little. Joe reached for his water and looked at his patient. "Is there anything else you want me to know about?"

Nate stared at the bottle in his hand and watched the water move inside as he slowly circled the bottle in the air. "I don't know if this problem is related." He thought to himself … *This has to be a man's worst admission.* He took another drink from his bottle of water and decided to suck it up and get it over. "The last two times I was in bed with a woman, I couldn't keep it up." He paused again. "It happened in Washington about four weeks ago. I had the same problem two weeks ago in Mexico." Nate looked directly at Joe. "It's never been a problem for me."

Joe looked up from his notes and asked casually, "Do you get nocturnal erections?"

"I've woken up with hard-ons."

"Have you had one recently?"

"Yes." Nate's face flushed … he hated speaking about such a private subject. He looked at his water bottle and laughed quietly to himself. "I've found it at full attention in the middle of the night. But the last two times I've given it a direct order, it's been insubordinate. Maybe it should be court-martialed."

Joe smiled. "I appreciate the soldier's analogy, Nate." Then he silently reviewed some notes. "You chose your words to help get past an awkward moment. Think about them. A court-martial investigates a wrong deed in the military and often results in punishment. Do you think your mind is punishing your body? Or could it be the other way around?"

Nate shrugged. "I guess either's a possibility."

Joe continued, "I want to put your mind at ease about something. If you're getting erections, especially strong ones, that's a good sign. You're in excellent physical condition. Although we can't rule out a physical problem entirely, your dysfunction is probably psychological. It might be your brain's way of punishing you for putting a bullet into that boy's head."

"I see your point. Can you tell me how to fix it? Can you tell me what's causing the headaches and flashbacks and how to get past them?"

"I think you have post-traumatic stress disorder. It would account for several of the physical symptoms you've been experiencing. What you describe as flashbacks others would call anxiety attacks. They're very similar. Unfortunately, there is no instant cure."

Joe got up and walked to his desk. "I'm going to give you samples of the little blue miracle pill. It might help the next time you crawl between the sheets with a warm, soft body." He reached into a desk drawer and pulled out a sample drug packet. "Don't be embarrassed to try these. I can prescribe other medications, such as mood enhancers, sleeping aids, anxiety blockers …"

Nate shook his head. "I'd like to avoid that route as much as possible."

"That's fine as long as you aren't a danger to yourself or anyone else. From what I've heard, that doesn't seem to be the case. Can you see me at the same time next week?"

"I can." Nate reached for the packet and put it in the pocket of his slacks. He extended his hand. "I dreaded coming here today and I'm still uncomfortable about our discussion. You made it less difficult. Thanks."

Joe took his hand. "You're welcome. I'll see you next week." Joe opened the door and Nate walked out. The waiting room was still empty.

On Saturday, Nate drove to his father's home. When he entered the house, Rufus sprinted to the front door, circled twice, and sat on Nate's left foot, his eyes upward and his tongue lolling. The unconditional affection made Nate feel good inside. He bent down and returned the greeting, scratching the dog behind the ears.

John heard Nate come in and shouted from the kitchen, "Back here. I'm making us Dagwood sandwiches."

Nate and Rufus walked side by side into the kitchen. Rufus took a position in front of the counter next to John. His eyes stared longingly for a dropped morsel. "I'm even more honored by the hound's greeting considering the sacrifice he must have made."

"He knows whatever he gets is from his bowl. I've worked hard to keep the beggar out of him, but I suspect Olivia had a soft heart when she worked around this kitchen."

"Have you heard from Liv recently?"

"Spoke to her last week. She's going to England—combination work and pleasure."

"She'll enjoy it there. I heard you bought her a special bracelet recently."

John looked at Nate as he put the top piece of bread on the two large sandwiches. "You must have gone by Eve's gallery. I've been wondering when you'd make a move in that direction." He carried the two plates to the kitchen table and went to the refrigerator for beers.

"I wouldn't call my visit a 'move.' Dev and I went by the gallery before he left for Washington. I met Randall. He's impressive."

"Don't get the dueling pistols out just yet. Randall's a good-looking man, and his tastes are expensive—he comes from old Charleston money—but he's a little light in the loafers."

"Gee, Dad, thanks for the heads up on that one."

John hid the smile. "Not so long ago, that kind of sarcasm earned a slap upside the head. He does dote on Eve, you know."

"I could tell. He has a good eye. I saw the type of bracelet you bought for Liv and the look is right for her … sort of upscale bohemian." Nate smiled when he thought of his sister's eccentric flair with fashion and color.

"When I described her, Randall suggested it, so I bought it for her birthday."

Randall had made another sale to Nate and Devon the prior week. "Dev and I bought a Christmas present for Liv, but we need your help with something."

"How's that, Nate?"

"Randall sold us an antique gold locket and convinced us to put a hand-painted porcelain miniature in it. He knows an artist who is very good at reproducing one from a photo. We thought of a miniature portrait of Mom."

"That's a great idea and Olivia will treasure something like that. What can I do?"

"Let me borrow a few photo albums. Do you still keep them in the guest bedroom chest?"

"I do. Help yourself to whichever ones you need. Just be sure I get them back."

They spent the afternoon watching the Braves and the Phillies play ball. Rufus sprawled on the carpet between them, jumping up only when John and Nate boisterously contested an umpire's call. During the seventh-inning stretch, Nate told John he had seen Joe Reynolds the previous week. "It's not my comfort zone, Dad. But he's down to earth and doesn't fit my biased impression of a shrink."

John respected Nate's privacy and didn't ask about the appointment. "I've always liked Joe. I hope he can help."

Nate got up from his chair. "You ready for another beer?" John nodded. When he returned from the kitchen, Nate handed John a beer and sat down. "What do you know about post-traumatic stress disorder?"

John looked at Nate. "Only that it's real and that people in all walks of life can get it after they've been through an extraordinarily stressful situation."

"That's what Joe thinks I have."

"What do you think?"

Nate shrugged. "He's the doc. My symptoms point in that direction. I'm still getting them, but the flashbacks haven't been as frequent since I talked with you and Dev. The headaches still come and go. Joe wants to see me every week for now."

"Keep a positive outlook, son. Accept his help and trust that this will pass."

Nate nodded. After the game, Nate went for a run before driving back to Charleston.

VI

In the early-morning hours, shore birds flock to the beaches along the barrier islands of the Low Country. Large clusters of sandpipers, laughing gulls, terns, and plovers scurry to and from the surf in search of a meal along the Atlantic Coast. Just offshore, pods of dolphin roll gracefully through the ocean swells, their dorsal fins appearing intermittently among the gentle waves. Pelicans glide with outstretched wings floating on air currents rising from the water. Eve watched as one dove, landing with a big splash, bending its large wings in awkward directions. The contradiction between its graceful flight and crash landing made her laugh. Then she turned and walked back to her home on the other side of Sullivan's Island.

Nate drove to the Morning Light Gallery hoping Eve would have lunch with him. She had declined an invitation by phone the previous week. He had the photo albums she needed, so he had a legitimate reason for them to spend time together. If she considered it a date, he would explain otherwise. If she refused lunch, he would just spend time with her in the gallery.

When Nate found a parking space on East Bay Street, he decided the fates were smiling down on him today. He walked into the gallery and saw Randall showing one of Eve's paintings to a prospective client. Randall signaled Nate toward the back room. Nate walked into a private office and found a young woman he had never met using a computer.

"I'm sorry, Randall's busy, and he pointed me in this direction. I expected to find Eve here."

The woman appraised Nate thoroughly as she spoke. "I'm Jenny. I work here part-time when Randall needs extra coverage. Eve's not here. Do you want to leave a message for her?"

"Do you expect her back soon?"

"Not today. She called this morning and said Mother Nature spoke to her when she woke up. Eve's spending the day digging in the dirt. I'll tell her you stopped by if you tell me your name." She added silently … *and your phone number and your address and what you like on your pizza and …*

Nate held out his hand. "Nate Dunlevy." Jenny reached up and shook his hand. She would have to find out why Eve had kept this one a secret.

Well, hell! Nate thought. Eve typically spent Wednesdays at the gallery. His mind switched gears—time for a ride to Sullivan's Island. "There's no message, Jenny. I'll catch Eve another time. Nice meeting you."

Jenny saw a man on a mission and wondered if she should call Eve. *Nah! Women need a nice surprise every now and then. It keeps us on our toes.* "Bye, Nate."

After crossing the bridge to Sullivan's Island, he turned left at Dunleavy's Pub and considered the name of the small restaurant another positive omen, despite the difference in spelling. Nate looked at his watch—the lunch invitation was still valid. He carried the photo albums up the brick stairway that led to the front door, rang the bell, and waited. No one answered. He rang it again and listened carefully to ensure it was working. He heard the faint tone of the door chime and music in the distance. He waited a few more seconds then decided to walk toward the source of the music.

The music became clearer as he neared a large raised wooden deck area attached to the rear of the house. The structure encompassed a small pool built into the deck, an enclosed cabana, benches around the perimeter, containers overflowing with flowers, a few chaises and chairs, and a table shaded by a Cinzano umbrella. The yard around the decked area had two live oak trees that had survived Hurricane Hugo and a smattering of palmetto trees. Stairs at the rear of the deck led to a walkway and a long wooden dock that spanned the marsh and ended at the deeper water of the Intracoastal Waterway. Two squirrels chased one another down a long twisted oak branch; a cardinal zipped out of the dense foliage and perched briefly on the top rail of the deck.

Eve emerged from the far side of a cabana carrying a tray of bright flowers. Nate stood still and eyeballed the electric blue bikini that revealed much of her lightly tanned skin. She had tied her blond hair loosely at her neck and there were smudges of dirt on her hands and knees. He watched her bend to place the flowers near a row of large pots that appeared ready for the new stock. Turbulent classical music played from the outdoor speakers. Lost in her own world and unaware of him, she carefully lifted a plant from its slot in the tray.

He didn't want to frighten her. On the other hand, he would not turn around and walk quietly away. "Eve," he called out just loud enough to be heard above the music.

Her head whipped in his direction, she dropped the plant, and her hand instinctively moved to cover her heart.

Nate felt awful about scaring her. Her hand left a large splotch of dirt on her chest and another on her forehead when she used it to brush a stray strand of hair that blew into her face. "I'm sorry. I didn't mean to frighten you. I have the photo albums for you."

Eve held up a finger signaling Nate to wait. She walked to the cabana, reached up on tiptoes to a speaker mounted on the eave, and turned a volume control to soften the music. "Come around to the stairs at the back." She walked around the edge of the pool to meet him. He watched her as she moved and thought of the line in old war movies about women with legs that could sink a fleet. She waited near the railing as he climbed the steps to the deck.

"I tried the doorbell, but I guess you couldn't hear it. When I heard the music, I wandered around the side to see if you were home." He smiled and reached out to brush the dirt from her forehead. "I caused a real mess, didn't I?" He couldn't help but look at the dirt on her chest.

"No, I'm perfectly capable of making my own mess." Eve looked down at her body and the several parts of her anatomy that were speckled with potting mixture. "I get so carried away when I've got flowers and music that I'm oblivious to the world around me." She looked at the albums. "Let me get cleaned up." She turned and walked to a hose at the side of the cabana.

"Don't stop on my account. This is the second time I've shown up unannounced."

"You have a way of popping up, don't you?" She smiled as she rinsed the dirt from her hands.

"I stopped by the gallery and Jenny told me you were working at home today. I should have called before driving here. You can look at these photos another time."

Eve looked at the sky. "The sun is at its peak for the next three hours and I've been in it since nine this morning. I should give my skin a break ... and I'm getting hungry." She pointed toward the colorful flowers. "You can do me a favor by moving that tray into the shade. I'll finish planting them later."

Nate put the albums on the table in the far corner and walked to the flowers Eve had been planting. She bent over and used the hose to rinse dirt off her knees. Nate moved the tray to a spot that would remain shaded by the cabana. Eve turned the hose toward the tray of flowers. Once again, his eyes focused on the dirt just above her bikini top and the cleavage it left exposed. "There's still some dirt right here." Nate pointed toward the center of his chest.

Without warning, Eve pointed the hose at Nate and let the blast of water soak him thoroughly. She doubled over with laughter at the expression on his face.

Eve was still laughing as she turned to shut off the water. Then she found herself lifted off her feet, in his arms, and suspended over the pool.

"Put me down."

Splash.

He stood on the side of the pool and waited for her to surface. "Did I misunderstand?"

She waded to the steps, climbed out, and suppressed a smile. "Some day … somehow, you'll pay for that."

Eve opened the door to the cabana and reached inside for two towels. She handed one to Nate and wrapped the other around her body. "Want me to toss that shirt in the dryer?"

Nate looked down his sodden shirt and pants. "If you want to dry me out, I'll have to go down to the skin. I'll use the towel then just air dry out here."

The last thing Eve wanted was Nate Dunlevy wandering around in a towel, so she didn't argue. "Stretch out on a chaise? I'm going to change clothes and then we can raid the fridge. I want to get my hands on those albums."

Nate took a chance. "While you rummage through your clothes, pick out something to wear when we have dinner this weekend."

"It's not going to happen, Nate. And don't consider this afternoon a date."

Nate hid his annoyance and held up his hands as though surrendering.

Eve shook her head and went into the house. After a quick shower, she put on a pink terrycloth romper. It was short and sleeveless but covered more than her bikini. Eve wasn't shy about her body, but she chose not to flaunt it. She called to Nate from the screened porch of the house. "Have you dried out?"

"Yes, thanks to the weather, I'm just damp now." He got up from the chaise and walked to an enclosed porch that separated the deck and pool from the main house. Eve opened the door inviting him inside. Nate gave her a quick appraisal as he entered. "That's cute, but I liked the other outfit better."

"Color me surprised." Her tone signaled that Nate had best move to another topic. "I can toss a few things together for a salad. How does that sound?"

"I had hoped to buy you lunch today. Since that's not happening, whatever you have is fine with me. How can I help?"

The porch led to a big country kitchen. Eve went to the refrigerator and pulled out a variety of vegetables, lettuce, and cheese. "I'd offer you a beer, but

I'm no longer in the habit of keeping it on hand. I have a bottle of Sauvignon Blanc. Would you like a glass?"

"Are you having some?"

"Yes, I think I will."

Nate spotted wine glasses behind a glass-enclosed cabinet. "Tell me where your opener is and I'll do the honors."

Eve handed Nate the chilled bottle of white wine and pointed to a drawer in the island counter behind her. Nate was opening the wine when he felt several needles stab him a few inches above the knee. He looked down and found a very furry gray feline stretched against his leg with its claws imbedded into his slacks. "Nice kitty. Try to leave a little skin behind."

Eve had just put the food on the cutting board and looked down. "Bootsie, let go." The cat looked at Eve and blinked two green eyes but didn't retract its claws. "Bootsie, stop that." The cat delighted in Eve's attention and started to purr. At the same time, it began mashing its claw-laden paws against Nate's thigh. Nate winced. Eve giggled and feebly apologized.

Nate put the wine bottle on the counter and reached down toward the cat. "I'd say we've bonded enough your way." He gingerly extricated the cat's claws from his leg and lifted the feline into his arms. Long fine gray hair covered the animal from snout to tail, but each paw had white fur. "Let me guess why they call you Bootsie." Nate rubbed the feline around the neck and ears; the cat purred loudly in appreciation.

They had their lunch on the screened porch, a room that could be closed off with jalousies when the weather got nasty. Two large ceiling fans circled slowly. Today all the windows were cranked open and the breeze felt tropical but cool. The large room accommodated a cozy sitting area furnished with comfortable wicker pieces and overstuffed cushions. It also held a glass-top pedestal table with four side chairs, a smattering of occasional tables and lamps, and several pieces of Eve's artwork on the back wall. Nate and Eve ate lunch at the table while flipping through the photo albums of the Dunlevy family. When Eve pointed to a particular picture, Nate described its significance. Pictures of his mother brought back bittersweet memories. So did other old photos.

Eve stood to clear the lunch plates and Nate got up to help. When the phone rang in the kitchen, Eve told him to relax and pour more wine. To avoid eavesdropping, Nate moved to a wicker sofa and picked up a sketchpad from the coffee table. There were dates on the cover indicating the contents of the book were probably six to twelve months old. Nate started flipping through the pages and

Bootsie jumped into his lap. This time, the cat kneaded gently against his leg before curling into a ball. The sketches portrayed people, plants, and animals. "Here's a flattering one of you, Boots." Nate looked down and stroked the cat's fur. He came across one that he guessed was Eve's sister. She had a strong likeness to Eve and looked to be a few years younger. Nate flipped past sketches of egrets and herons. Then he came to a sketch that made him pay closer attention—it was a man's face, a handsome face with a strong jaw and a pleasant smile. But the eyes didn't coincide with the composition; they looked mean. The man bore no resemblance to Eve, and no one had ever mentioned a brother in the family.

Nate looked up from the sketch when Eve came back from the kitchen with a big smile. "That was my sister, Katie. She'll be home next week, and I can't wait to see her." Then she saw the sketch Nate had in his hand.

He watched her expression change. "The book was on the table. I hope you don't mind me looking at the sketches. I saw the one that must be Katie; it's obvious the two of you are sisters. This one doesn't look like a relative."

Eve had forgotten she had the sketch of that man. She tried to sound nonchalant. "No, he isn't a relative, just a past acquaintance. I haven't looked through that book for some time." She cursed herself for not finding the sketch and destroying it months ago.

"Is this the man who hurt you, Eve?"

She watched Nate stroke the cat. The motion of his hand appeared soothing. But you couldn't always trust appearances, she reminded herself.

Nate gently moved the cat from his lap to the sofa cushion, closed the sketchbook, and placed it on the table. He stood, walked to Eve, and put both hands on her shoulders. She remained silent and avoided eye contact. "Eve, tell me what happened. How did he hurt you?"

She looked up at Nate. "I can't explain it very well."

"Just tell me what he did."

She put her hands over her face and shook her head. "I need you to stop touching me." Nate opened too many emotions in her, ones she had worked hard to lock away.

Nate dropped his hands. "Sit down. I'll get our wine from the table." She began to argue, but he cut her off. "Eve, please just go sit down."

Eve sat in a chair next to the sofa. Nate put two refilled wine glasses on the coffee table and took his same seat on the sofa. The cat crawled into his lap and started kneading. It made Eve smile. "You've got a way with animals. Bootsie usually doesn't warm up that fast to strangers."

"Animals have that sixth sense that let's them know who they can trust and who they can't." He looked down at the cat. "So, Boots, how much longer before *she* will trust me?" The cat responded by rolling on its back and exposing its belly for Nate's hand. He looked over at Eve. "You should take that as a sign."

"I'm not one to pour my heart out, Nate." She thought for several seconds. "The man in that book caused me to lose confidence in myself ... in my decisions. By the time things ended, I felt scared and vulnerable. I don't like feeling that way. No one does."

Nate nodded but remained silent, a trick he learned from his shrink.

"He acted very charming at first. I can honestly say that I was wined and dined in style. We went to the theatre and the symphony; we exchanged books. When I look back, I realized he had started to pick away at things, little things, eroding my self-confidence. He wanted to move the relationship to another level of intimacy, but I didn't want to go there yet. He was good at manipulating words and actions. I started to feel inadequate as a woman and he started to drink more heavily. He blamed me for his frustration and his drinking problem." Eve took a sip of her wine and collected her thoughts.

"I tried to back off at that point, but he wouldn't let it go. He went back to being Prince Charming. He stopped drinking around me except for the wine we shared at dinner. I felt especially lonely after Katie went back to the California last January, and he came on strong at a very weak moment. We had a nice dinner together and he was very solicitous. We came back to this house and ended up in bed together." Eve paused and drank her wine. She looked Nate directly in the eyes and her tone changed. "He was lousy—a really lousy, selfish, rotten lay."

Her vehemence took Nate by surprise. "Don't sugarcoat it, sweetheart."

"I wasn't a naive virgin when I climbed between the sheets with that bastard. And I knew I should have trusted my instincts and never gotten there in the first place." She slapped the closed sketchbook. "That man got me into bed, got his rocks off, rolled out of bed, walked downstairs, and started drinking my vodka. I stayed in bed for a full minute asking myself what just happened. I didn't even get a 'thank you, ma'am'! I got up, put on a robe, and went down to find out what he was doing. He had the balls to tell me I was frigid!"

Watching her temper flare mesmerized him. She wasn't beautiful when she was angry. She was spectacular!

Eve raised her wine glass. "This is doing me a world of good. I'd almost forgotten how angry I was that night."

"I'm happy to help."

"Let me be blunt here." Eve leaned forward and focused her eyes directly on his. "I am not *frigid*!" She paused. "I don't want to get specific, but I shared more than one bed before that night. I had to be attracted to the man and enjoy his company. When I felt that physical pull—you know the one—I didn't need trumpets and flower petals to enjoy sex. Before him, I was accustomed to a nice give and take. The pleasure was always mutual."

Nate nodded. He knew exactly what the physical pull felt like and imagined mutual give and take with her. Even if his pecker didn't join the party, he would have loved to give her as much pleasure as she could take.

Eve reached for the wine bottle and emptied it into her glass. "Sometimes sex is fun. Sometimes it's intense. Whatever it is, it should be good for both people."

"You're preaching to the choir."

Eve snapped. "Don't say the word preach!" Then she shook her head. "Sorry, you hit a nerve. Do you want more wine?"

"No, thank you. I've still got plenty."

"Anyway, he's standing in my house buck naked, drinking my liquor, and accusing me of being frigid. I went back upstairs, bundled up his clothes, came back, and threw them at him. Then I told him go to hell and get out of my house."

"Good for you. I hope he got the hint."

"You'd think so, wouldn't you? But wait until you hear this! The bastard tells me I am irrational and starts quoting scripture. *Neither was the man created for the woman: but the woman for the man.* Well, I told him this woman wasn't created for any man and I didn't want to hear any more about it!"

Eve sipped her wine and spoke softly. "He wouldn't leave until I picked up the phone and threatened to call the cops. He got dressed then called me a whore and stormed out."

Nate looked concerned, "It's over now, right? You ended it and he moved on?"

"God, I wish that had been the end." Eve shook her head and looked down at an invisible spot on the coffee table.

"What do you mean?" He became concerned. "Is the bastard still harassing you?"

"Not anymore, but he kept coming around and calling. He went into the remorseful stage first—sent flowers, apologized, blamed his behavior on the booze, promised to stop drinking, begged me to see him. I stood my ground and told him our days and nights together were over. I didn't like him and never wanted to see him again."

"Did you contact the police?"

"I'm getting there, Nate. I guess he decided the nice-guy act didn't work anymore, and he started drinking heavily again. In retrospect, I think he always had a drinking problem. He just hid it well. His calls started getting abusive. He'd leave messages on my answering machine calling me all kinds of filthy names. I hesitated to get the police involved, so I called his father and told him I would if he didn't convince his son to leave me alone. His father responded by blaming me for the man's drinking problem. Sounds like the apple fell close to that tree. You know the scenario. It's not their fault … someone else makes them do it."

Nate nodded. "So, when did this harassment finally stop?"

"He didn't bother me again until last May. His father convinced him to attend a program run by their church. I don't think the treatment stopped his drinking, but it made him meaner and more zealous about his religious beliefs."

Eve had no more feistiness. She lowered her voice and chose her words deliberately. "I came home from the gallery one evening, and it was almost dark. I unlocked the front door, and before I had it fully opened, he charged up the entry steps and pushed me through the door. I never saw him waiting for me. He must have been crouched down near the side of the house." Eve covered her face with her hands for a moment then looked up. "I tried not to appear frightened and told him to leave immediately. I was very firm with him. He had a tight grip on my arm and wouldn't let go. I thought about gouging his eye with the keys I still held in my other hand. Before I could, he hit me hard enough to stun me and throw me off balance. Then he told me he would rather cast his seed in the belly of a whore than spill it on the ground. That was the only reason why he did me that night. Those were his exact words, Nate. He warned me not to call the police or he'd haunt me to my grave and spit on it. Then he left, and I haven't heard from him since."

Nate regretted the scare he had given her earlier. "I gather you never went to the police with this. How badly were you hurt?"

"Not bad physically, a cut lip and some bruises. But he made me feel vulnerable. I think that was his goal all along. He could not accept the idea of a self-assured woman, one who could manage her life without depending on a man. To make matters worse, my life did not revolve around his religion and I did not want him preaching to me. That bothered him greatly. When we first started dating, he would joke about saving my soul."

"Is he still in Charleston?"

"No, he's not. I had Randall make discreet inquiries right after he threatened me. He moved to Columbia and works at a car dealership. He also became an assistant to a minister at a church there."

"I'd still feel better if the police knew about his threats, Eve."

"I've thought about it, especially during that first month. I bought a small canister of pepper spray and attached it to my key ring, which I still carry. Randall stayed with me for a few days, and then he followed me home when I went to the gallery. By July, I told him to stop, but I still stay home after dark. It's been four months now. I have to believe I no longer matter to Wade Simmons."

Nate hoped so. "I'll be sure to thank Randall the next time I see him. Who else knows what with this guy did to you?"

"Katie knows a little. I didn't want her worrying about me from the West Coast."

"Eve, I've got experience and connections that might be helpful. Let me make sure he never bothers you again."

"Until now you've done a great job listening and being a friend. But I don't want anyone taking charge of my personal life."

Nate shook his head. "That isn't my intention."

"I know, but that will be the result. I'm regaining my balance. Otherwise, you wouldn't be sitting here right now. It felt good to let go of the anger, but I need you to back off from this." She stood. "Right now, I should finish planting. Katie will be here next week and I want the place to look cheerful."

"I'd be glad to help."

"You've done enough. I'd like to scan some of the photos we looked at today. Do you mind if I keep those albums for a few days?"

"Not at all. Are you sure there's nothing else I can do?"

"Yes, I'm sure."

Nate reached into his back pocket, pulled out his wallet, and removed a business card. He picked up a pencil from the table and wrote a phone number on the back of the card. "This card has my home phone, cell phone, e-mail, and all that. The number on the back is one that you can call any time you're frightened. When you call that number, I'll know about it, no matter what. Okay?"

Eve nodded. "Thanks. I hope I never have to use that number." She got up on tiptoes and kissed him on the cheek. "Bootsie has good instincts."

Again, Nate held his feelings in check. He wrapped his arms gently around Eve's body and held her close for a second. "Olivia always told me hugs were the ult." Then he kissed the top of her head.

When he released her, Eve backed away from him. "You'd better go now." She opened the porch door. "An Irish tradition … you leave through the same door you entered." He smiled then walked past the pool and down the back steps. When he turned, she was nowhere in sight.

VII

With little warning, the Low Country can spawn a severe thunderstorm full of lightning bolts. When two opposing weather systems meet along the southeast coast the skies light up, the heavy rains come, and the locals take cover. Nate and Randall sat at Grill 225's dark mahogany bar while the storm lashed out its fury on downtown Charleston. Randall had proved helpful to Nate in many ways. Besides his advice on Olivia's locket, he was a fountain of knowledge concerning a man named Wade Simmons. Nate took notes and quizzed Randall about names, locations, relatives, and other pertinent facts. Then he let Randall vent.

"I never liked him from the first day I met him. I told Eve how I felt. She would kid me about being overprotective and how no man she dated would be good enough for her in my eyes. That just isn't true, but I was very relieved when she broke up with him. I knew the things he said hurt her deeply. When I heard he returned that night ... how frightened she was ... that he actually hit her ... I just wanted to smack the daylights out of him."

"I know how you feel, Randall, and I appreciate all the information you've given me. But I think Eve might be angry if she knew about our conversation today. Can we keep this between us?"

"Nate, I've had to develop good instincts about people. If I thought you'd harm Eve in any way, I wouldn't be sitting here. I won't mention our discussion."

Later that night, Nate went on an Internet expedition. Wade Simmons was indeed living and working in Columbia, South Carolina. Since his parents and a brother lived in Charleston, Nate surmised that he still visited the area frequently.

He confirmed that Simmons served as a deacon in a religious organization and found a Web site for a *The Sovereign Church of God*. Its philosophy preached white male supremacy and the founder, Reverend Dodd, interpreted the scriptures to suit his agenda. Unlike other religions, the teachings of this group contradicted mainstream beliefs. Nate understood the difference between religion and fanaticism. For the past fifteen years, he had spent time in the Middle East fighting fanatics, people who brainwashed others to strap on bombs, including innocent children.

The reverend twisted biblical passages to justify abuse of women, even to the extent of condoning rape. Adam, Eve, and the eviction from Eden were tenets. The site expounded on the role of woman in the downfall of humanity and supported the premise that painful childbirth was women's punishment for inherent evil. Another page on the site was dedicated to William Jennings Bryan and his role as prosecutor during the Scopes trial of 1925. In some areas, the battle between creationists and evolutionists still raged eighty years later. The followers of this church were adamant proponents of creationism.

The church's theories caused his head to pound. After taking aspirin, Nate accessed the DMV and discovered that Simmons had three moving violations over a period of two years. That would be enough to hike up his insurance rates but not enough to suspend his license. He wondered if any of the violations had started as DUIs that he had bargained down to lesser offenses. His family came from old blood, so they probably had several connections with local politicians. They had plenty of money available for campaign contributions.

Nate thought about calling his own father to help locate any civil or criminal complaints against Wade Simmons. Then he thought better of the idea. If Eve had wanted John to know the details of her ill-fated relationship with this man, she would have told him. Nate decided he shouldn't divulge the history without Eve's consent. He had other ways to run a check on the man, but it would take a little longer. So far, what he had learned did not set off alarms with respect to Eve's safety.

Although his research had been discreet, he knew the type and frequency of certain inquiries could raise a flag. He had no doubt that the Simmons family was well connected. To avoid drawing attention, he decided to move slowly through the next layer of information about Wade Simmons. With that thought, he shut down his computer.

The next morning, Nate had just stepped out of the shower and picked up a towel when he heard the doorbell. "Shit!" At first, he wanted to ignore the intrusion. Then he remembered his recent order from an electronics company. After tossing the towel aside, he grabbed sweatpants off a hook and quickly pulled them on. He tied the waist cord loosely as he trotted down the steps and to the front door.

When he yanked open the door, Eve was looking down at the step, preparing to turn around. She found herself staring at his bare feet. Then she lifted her gaze to long legs covered in worn-out gray sweats hanging loosely on his hips. She saw a trail of soft black hair grow up from the waistband and cover a firm, flat abdomen. The hair disappeared a few inches above, revealing smooth skin over a muscular torso. The trail of hair resumed a narrow path upward between his rib cage and ended its journey across a powerful chest. Sporadic drops of water clung to flesh and follicles. Her eyes took in broad shoulders, powerful arms, a smiling mouth, and a disheveled crop of dark, wet hair. "I'm sorry, Nate." She blushed and fought the urge to scan his body again. "I ... um ... caught you at a bad time."

Her unease amused him. For an instant, his brain wanted to toss her over his shoulder and carry her to bed. Instead, he reached for her hand and gently pulled her into his house. "I thought it was the UPS man, but I'd much rather find you at my front door." He answered the unspoken question on her face. "I'm expecting a package that requires my signature, so I ran from the shower."

"It's Saturday. Unless you have it overnighted, they don't deliver on weekends."

"Hmmm."

"I took a painting to the gallery this morning. You live nearby, so I wanted to return these." She held out the photo albums. "Where should I put them?"

Nate took the albums under his arm, led her into the kitchen, and steered her to a peninsula counter with stools. "I started the coffee just before I headed for the shower. Why don't you pull up a stool and pour?" Nate took two mugs and a bowl of sugar from a cabinet and set them on the counter next to the photo albums. "I'll be right back."

Eve felt a little relief when he left the room. She had never responded so strongly to the physical appearance of a man. *Well,* she thought, *at least I know I'm still alive.* After pouring two cups of coffee, she went to the refrigerator for milk. She put sugar and milk in her coffee but didn't add any to his.

He had gutted and redone much of the house, but the kitchen looked like work in progress. Although the cabinets were new, they had an aged finish that suited the older home. He'd chosen solid granite for the countertops and stainless steel for the sink and appliances. The wide plank heart of pine that covered the floor had yet to be refinished, and the walls had not been painted.

Nate came back to the kitchen a few minutes later. He had combed his hair and put on jeans and a T-shirt, but he was still barefoot and unshaven. Eve nodded at the second cup. "I don't know how you like your coffee."

"Black." Nate picked up the mug. "I got used to drinking it that way in the marines. We usually didn't have a choice."

"No, I don't suppose you did. This kitchen is taking shape. Are you doing the work yourself?"

"Mostly. I did the big stuff last spring. Dev helped me move walls and hang cabinets. The space over there is going to be an office. Both rooms need paint, but I don't know what color to use."

Eve peered through the large opening and studied the room beyond. "With that much space, you could use cabinetry for work and storage and still add comfortable seating."

Nate thought about the idea. "You're right. What about the paint?"

Eve scanned the kitchen and picked up a towel with muted green piping. "Try something along this line, Nate. A light sage would help the cabinetry pop out without making the rooms dark. Use a creamy white glossy paint on the woodwork."

He laughed. "I'm out of my league with colors. Since you're the artist, you'll come to the paint store with me."

"If you can wait a week, maybe I will. I've got a lot on my plate and I'm not getting anything done sitting here."

Nate took a gulp of hot coffee. "Before you go, help me pick out the right photo of my mother for Olivia's locket."

Eve remembered the gold locket he and Devon had bought and Randall's suggestion to insert a porcelain miniature. Miniatures weren't her forte, but she knew the artist Randall had suggested. "Sure, I can think of several she can use. You should take two or three of your favorites." She reached for one of the albums and flipped through the pages. She opened it to a large photo of Sophia sitting in a chair. Nate stood next to the chair, his mother's arm wrapped affectionately around his waist.

Nate recalled the photo. "Mom had bought Dad a new camera for his birthday. It came with a special lens and he spent hours taking pictures that day. There's a similar one with Olivia on the next page."

Eve turned the page. "You and Olivia look like siblings, but she favors your mother and I'll bet she's become just as beautiful."

"You're right. Those pictures were taken about two years before Mom got sick." Eve turned back to the picture of Nate and his mother.

Nate stared at the picture. Life had been very good to him. He was approaching thirteen, and his biggest concern was winning his next baseball game. He had loving parents and a little sister who was only a mild pain in the ass. He continued to stare at the picture—into his boyhood eyes. He became transfixed. The eyes and the face were no longer his. They belonged to a different boy entirely. His mother's arm held a boy with a bullet hole in his forehead. There would be an explosion any moment. His mother and the boy would disappear. He had to stop it right now, but he didn't know how ...

"Nate! Are you okay? Nate! Look at me."

Someone grabbed his shoulder and shook it. Something shattered. He reached up and pressed his fingers against his temples—they throbbed. Sweat beaded on his forehead. If he closed his eyes, maybe the explosion wouldn't come. Maybe his mother and the boy would live. Someone put something cool on either side of this face. It felt good. Some of the heat went away.

"Dunlevy, snap out if it!"

It sounded like an order. Nate knew he should pay attention. The drill sergeant would kick his ass. He struggled to concentrate. Eve's face came into focus. She stared into his eyes and her hands pressed against both sides of his face. They felt cool and soft, like his mother's hands when she would cover the cheeks of a young boy who had a fever.

Nate snapped back to reality. The kitchen came back into focus. He reached up and drew Eve's hands away from his face. "Sorry. I took a little side trip."

Eve went to the sink. She dampened a towel with cold tap water, carried it back to the counter, and handed it to him. He took it and wiped the sweat off his face. Then he looked down and saw the coffee stains on his clothes. Eve started to pick up pieces of broken ceramic off the floor. She needed a minute to settle and thought Nate would need the same.

"That was some out-of-body experience you just had." Eve placed the shards on the counter. "Are you okay now?"

He nodded. What could he say to her?

"Does that happen to you often?" She looked at his face and then reached up and ran her fingers through his damp hair, brushing it away from his forehead.

"I came away from a bad episode last July. I still get flashbacks. I'm sorry you had to witness one of them."

"I'm sure witnessing one isn't nearly as bad as having one. It came on very fast. You had me worried for a minute."

He shook his head and got up from the stool. His legs were still a little shaky, but they held. After picking up the other broken pieces of mug, he tossed them into a trash container. Nate opened a wall cabinet near the sink, reached for the aspirin and a glass, then tossed back four pills with water. He braced his arms on the front of the sink and looked out the window.

After fixing another cup of coffee, Eve sat down on a stool and waited.

"I knew I had problems before we met, Eve. I should have been smart enough to keep my distance instead of pressuring you to see me."

Eve got up and walked to the sink. She put her hand on his shoulder. "Nate."

"Hmmm." He turned and looked at her.

"That's a bunch of self-pitying garbage. Didn't I pour my guts out to you a few days ago?" She didn't wait for a response. "Sounds like you walked away from an ugly scene with some baggage. Well, join the club, pal!"

Nate didn't know how to respond, so he followed his instinct. He gripped her arms and kissed her as though he would never stop, as though she had become a lifeline.

When she felt a pull inside, she instinctively tried to retreat.

He drew her back and brushed his fingertips across her mouth. "I haven't shaved, my beard's rough on your skin. But I want to kiss you again."

"That kiss will last me for a long time." She rubbed her hands across his face. "Is someone helping you?"

He nodded. "Yes, someone's helping."

Eve tried to break the physical contact but Nate pulled her closer. He wrapped an arm around her, pressed her to his body, and captured her mouth again. The pull she felt with the first kiss turned into an ache low in her belly and she gave in to her feelings.

His needs deepened with her response and he wanted her with no constraints. His other hand stroked her side and teased the crest of her breast beneath her cotton shirt. He felt her breath catch.

Eve knew she had to stop. With mixed feelings, she pushed her hands against his chest to break away from his embrace.

"I'm not ready for you, Nate. I'm not sure I'll ever be ready for you."

"You're wrong about that."

"You're coming on too strong. I have to go now."

He followed her to the front door and opened it. As he watched her walk away, he asked himself why he wanted her so much … and at this time in his life.

VIII

Within the marshlands of Edisto Island, long-standing live oak trees create havens for long-legged wading birds that flock to them nightly. At dawn, egrets and herons take flight as they search for the day's first meal. Nate watched the exodus and wondered how Eve had captured this scene on her canvas. Then he cursed himself for thinking about her again.

Later that day, Nate forced himself to keep his next appointment with Joe Reynolds. The waiting area looked the same, unoccupied. The door to Joe's inner office stood ajar, so Nate poked his head through the opening and saw Joe at his desk with the phone against his ear. He motioned Nate to come in and pointed toward the sitting area. Joe ended the conversation and got up from his desk.

"Hello, Nate."

"Hello, Joe."

Joe walked to the small refrigerator and took out two bottles of water. He put one on the table next to Nate then closed the office door.

"How was your week?"

"Nothing to rave about. I woke up with a bad headache about three this morning. I took aspirin but couldn't get back to sleep, so I read for a while then drove out to Edisto and ran a few miles."

"Any flashbacks?"

"I had a strange flashback last Saturday." Nate described the incident with the photo of his mother. He briefly mentioned Eve, saying that she had witnessed the occurrence. He enumerated the headaches, insomnia, and one episode of his recurring nightmare.

There was silence while Joe finished making some notes. "Tell me about Eve."

"What about her?"

"You didn't mention her last week. Is she an old friend?"

"No, she isn't. She's a new friend." Nate clammed up. Joe waited.

Nate circled the plastic bottle and watched the water move inside. "I think I'm in love with her, and the timing sucks!"

"Why?"

Nate glared at Joe. "Because my heads screwed up and she doesn't want anything to do with me." Nate paused and lowered his voice. "It's not just me—men in general. She was hurt and scared by someone and she hasn't gotten over it."

"Let's go back to you."

"Yeah, let's do that. Until I'm over this crap, I should stay away from her."

"Why?"

"If you search those damn notes of yours, maybe you'll remember what I told you. I couldn't keep a hard-on with a woman."

"Every person is different, Nate. So is your reaction to them."

"Yeah? A woman like Eve doesn't need a fucked-up soldier with a limp dick chasing after her. She's written off men and I should do the same thing with women—especially her."

Nate got up and paced. Joe remained silent. "I don't deserve her, but God knows I want her." He sat back down and watched the water circle inside the bottle. "I have to put her out of my mind."

The silence became overwhelming. "You know what, Joe? That's not going to happen." He stood again. "It's time to get in the game before I go nuts standing on the sideline." He laughed. "What the fuck? I'm already crazy. What do I have to lose?" Nate capped the half-full bottle and lobbed into a wastebasket. "I'm done for today. Unless you've got something important to tell me, I'm out of here."

Joe remained seated and looked up. "Okay, Nate, I'll see you next week."

Late that afternoon, Nate called the gallery. Randall answered the phone and proved, once again, to be an ally. Today was Wednesday, and Eve had devoted her time to planning a new display of her work. He promised Nate to keep her focused on the project until closing and that he wouldn't mention the call.

Nate walked into the Charleston Place flower shop where an attractive, mature woman greeted him.

"I'd like flowers for a lady I'm taking to dinner."

The woman noted the bare ring finger. "Is she a special woman?"

"Very."

"Your lover?"

"Hopefully."

"No red roses yet." She smiled. "I have something in the back." Nate looked at the arrangements in the refrigerated cases. The variety of flowers boggled him. Why didn't she just point to something?

She returned a few minutes later with a small but attractive bouquet of white roses with red tips that bled into the petals. "Do you like these?"

Nate nodded. "They're nice flowers."

"White symbolizes purity while red symbolizes love … the lustful kind." She smiled at him and added, "This bouquet tells her your intentions are honorable, but you don't promise to keep them that way forever."

"I'm saying that with these flowers?"

"Trust me … women know."

"They're perfect. How much do I owe you?"

Shortly before 6:00 PM, Eve looked up from her notepad and saw Nate enter the gallery. He wore a dark tailored suit that accentuated his broad shoulders and long, lean frame. The collar of his white dress shirt created a stark contrast against the suit, his tan skin, and his dark hair. He carried a small cluster of roses. "Someone has a special night planned. Who's the lucky lady?" The grinning Tweetie Bird and a scowling Sylvester on his red tie made her smile.

Nate looked down at the characters. "I thought of Boots when I tied it." He handed the roses to her. "Do you have a Flintstone jelly jar for these?"

She reached for the roses with surprise. "These are for me?"

"They are."

She studied the flowers. Then she looked up at him. "I think I can do better than Fred and Wilma." Randall entered from the back office and commented on the flowers. "You look like you're all dressed up with no place to go, Nate."

"I have reservations at the Charleston Grill." He looked at his watch. "We have time for drinks and dancing before dinner."

"We didn't have plans for tonight."

"We do now."

Eve looked at Randall, who was smiling at her and making a shooing gesture. "Go out and have a nice evening. You're certainly entitled to one." He turned to Nate. "Will you take good care of the princess?"

"Promise."

"I can't go like this. I've been in this dress all day long."

Nate scrutinized her thoroughly. Her knee-length dress was a soft floral print with a scooped neckline and a gathered skirt. She wore high heels made with skinny straps that eventually wrapped around a pair of shapely ankles. "You look incredible to me. Stop making excuses."

She looked at Randall then back at Nate and finally gave in. "I'm starting to feel outnumbered. Give me five minutes." She walked to the back office.

When she returned, Nate took her hand and told her she was beautiful. Then he sniffed at her neck and added that he liked her perfume. They said good night to Randall and walked toward the gallery door. Nate looked down at her dainty high heels and thought of the uneven sidewalks along the way. "Do you want to walk or take your car? You decide."

"Let's take my car and I can drop you off on my way home after dinner." Nate didn't intend to let her drive home by herself after dinner, but he remained silent.

They had dinner at the Charleston Grill, a fine restaurant inside the Charleston Place Hotel. A trio of musicians played quiet music as background for dining or dancing. Nate held true to his word—he danced with Eve before dinner and again afterward. Throughout the evening, they talked about growing up in the Low Country. Both of them had gravitated to the water and spent a great deal of their youth swimming and sailing. Eve told him she had made her first sketches of shorebirds, live oaks, and tugboats when she was eight years old. She asked Nate about his military career and he sidestepped the subject by describing a storm he experienced while aboard ship in the Pacific Ocean. When she admitted being unfamiliar with that part of the world, he described the differences between the two vast bodies of water. The conversation flowed easily and sporadically. Neither of them had to fill every moment by talking. Eve was mellow when the valet brought her car to the door.

Nate tipped the valet, took the keys, and walked Eve to the passenger side. When she protested, Nate opened the car door. "I'm driving you home. When we get there, I'll take a cab back to town—before or after you offer me coffee." Eve wanted to argue but thought about the wine she drank throughout the evening. It was also a very dark night because of a new moon. She would let Nate drive her home, serve him coffee, and call him a cab.

When they arrived on Sullivan's Island, Eve unlocked the front door and they entered a large foyer flanked by two large rooms. The ceilings were ten feet high and both rooms had several tall windows with wide sills. The dining room held a large hardwood cabinet with all sorts of dishes and glassware. Eight straight-backed antique chairs surrounded a long wooden table. The living room ran the length of the house and featured a massive stone hearth and fireplace;

there was a baby grand piano in one corner. The rooms reminded him of scenes pictured on the covers of his mother's *Southern Living* magazines. Nate remembered how Eve spoke about her sister's music—artistic talent ran deep in the O'Connor family. Eve pointed to an entertainment center and suggested he pick out the music while she made coffee.

Nate removed his coat and tie, draped them on the back of a chair, and flipped through Eve's CD collection. Her taste in music was broad and overlapped his. He selected Nora Jones, a female vocalist known for her sultry voice and bluesy arrangements. The sound filled the living room when Eve brought the coffee and sat beside him on the sofa.

Halfway through the CD, Nate put his empty mug on a table and did the same with hers. A song filled the room with a slow, sensual beat and a sexy voice. Nate reached out to Eve and drew her toward him. He held her and enjoyed their closeness. She put her head against his chest and was soothed by the steady rhythm of his heartbeat. His body warmed her and his arms made her feel safe.

With one hand, he gently stroked her arm and then her leg. His fingertips caused small quivers up and down her body. His mouth teased her lips, then her cheeks and eyes and forehead, then her lips again. She drifted into a sensual calmness, almost like floating. Her pulse rate quickened when his fingers stroked against the side of her breast. Then she felt the tugging in her groin as his thumb rubbed against a hardened nipple. Her body responded to his touch in wonderful ways—warm, moist, and wanting.

His hand stroked up and down her thigh while his mouth started a gentle assault on her neck and her throat. Her breathing deepened and her body ached, a sensation she hadn't experienced in a very long time. His hand slid between her thighs and felt the warm, wet swatch of silk. He let a quiet groan escape from deep inside his throat. He slipped his hand beneath the silk and let his fingertips roam. Then they centered on her and stroked. A small moan started in her throat and grew louder. She shuddered and clung tightly to him as tremors took over her body. He held her tightly while she drew in a deep breath and arched her back. A moment later, her body went limp. Her orgasm had primed his body, strained it. He wanted release so he pulled her from the sofa. He tangled his fingers in her hair and devoured her mouth. "Your bed ... I want you in your bed." They stood at the bottom of the staircase where she hesitated before moving to the first step.

He stopped her from taking the next. "Be sure, Eve. As much as I want you, a single night won't cut it. Tell me you're ready for this and won't have doubts tomorrow."

She turned to him. With her hands on either side of his face, she kissed him. Then she whispered to him. "It's been a long time, so be patient with me. I want to enjoy all of it."

He scooped her up. "Let's try this for starters." Then he slowly climbed the stairs.

During the ascent, she pressed her mouth against his shoulder to suppress a giggle. "I feel like Scarlet O'Hara."

"Is that good or bad?"

"Oh, it's good."

When they reached the top, she pointed to her bedroom.

He put her back on her feet and kissed her as he unzipped the dress and eased it from her shoulders. The dress puddled around her feet and she stood in front of him wearing a pale blue bra, matching silk panties, and lace-topped stockings. Eve reached for a button on his shirt but he stopped her. "Please. Let me finish." He lowered her to the bed, sat on the edge, and started with her stockings. Soon, Nate was awed by the nude female form covering the mattress next to him. He tossed half his clothes aside and slowly stroked the length of her body. Then he stood and unfastened his trousers. He didn't have a little blue pill and prayed he wouldn't need one—he couldn't imagine getting any harder. Then he wondered about Eve. "Do I need a condom?"

She shook her. "I use a contraceptive. Who wants all those periods?" Eve let her eyes roam as he finished undressing. "You have an incredible body, Nate, scars and all."

"Hmmm. Try to ignore the scars." He lowered himself next to her and used his fingertips to put her mind and body into another trance. His mouth moved to her breasts; his teeth and tongue tantalized both nipples into hard peaks. When his hand slid between her legs, he found her hot and wet … again. Then his mouth followed his hand. Moments later, he felt her back arch as she came to another peak. Her body quivered as she reached down and gripped his shoulder.

"I want you inside me."

He moved above her and she opened for him. When he entered, he waited for her body to adjust. Then he began a slow, steady rhythm. Her hands explored his back, his shoulders, and his arms. She matched his rhythm with her hips as their pace quickened. The movement of his chest as it brushed against her nipples caused new sensations to build up inside her. Her hands moved down his back and gripped his hips. She concentrated on his groin pressing her into the mattress and moving in unison with hers. Nate drove into her, faster and harder as the pressure inside both of them built. Her breathing became labored and her nails dug into his flesh. When she arched and cried out, Nate reared backward. He felt her spasms and heard a deep groan rumble from his throat as he thrust into her and emptied himself inside.

After a silent prayer of thanks to the god of virility, Nate shook his head and opened his eyes. She smiled up at him. If Sylvester had ever caught Tweetie, the expression would have been similar. Nate eased himself out of her and carefully rolled to the side. He gathered her into his arms and they lay motionless, wordless, waiting for their heartbeats to slow down.

Moments later, Eve spoke. "I told you I wasn't frigid."

"Good Lord, you're amazing."

Eve planted a kiss on his lips. "So are you."

They slept soundly through the night. Early the next morning, Nate woke up feeling well rested and very aroused. They made love again, this time more slowly. There was no sense of urgency to explore and discover. Instead of tasting, they savored. Instead of touching, they caressed. Their bodies knew how to mesh and their rhythms matched naturally. They peaked and fell together.

He thought his body was spent from the two episodes of lovemaking, but soaping Eve's body in the shower gave him another mild ache. When he began lathering her for a third time, Eve pushed him out of the shower and reached for her conditioner. Nate grabbed a towel from the bar and began drying himself while he enjoyed the profile of his lover rinsing her hair under the shower spray. In an effort to suppress his arousal, he closed his eyes and briskly toweled the excess moisture from his hair. As he wandered toward the bedroom, the hair on his neck prickled and he sensed some else in the room. He yanked the towel from his head.

Katie O'Connor stood just inside her sister's bedroom scrutinizing the naked man in front of her. *Lordy, Lordy, look what followed my big sister home.* "Hi there, I'm Katie."

Nate remembered the face in Eve's sketchbook and connected it with the young woman standing in the doorway. He wrapped the towel around his waist. "Sorry, I wasn't expecting company."

"No need to apologize for a body like that."

Before he could respond, Eve walked out of the bath, pulling on her robe. "I must be hearing things. I swore I heard …" She trailed off when she spotted her sister. "Katie!" The two women rushed toward each other and shared a genuine embrace. They hugged for several seconds.

Katie looked at Nate, and then back at her sister. "So, what did you use? Reese's Pieces?"

Eve laughed at the inside joke. "That's not ET."

"No, he isn't!"

Eve laughed again. "Katie, meet Nate Dunlevy." He nodded at Katie as he stood in his towel with his arms crossed. Eve went on. "I didn't expect you until tonight. What are you doing here? I had planned to pick you up at the airport."

"I got the red-eye last night and thought I'd surprise you. Looks like I did a good job, huh?"

Nate grunted and tried to remember where he left his clothes. Katie saw the look on his face. "Your pants are on the floor over there, big guy." She nodded toward the other side of the bed.

Nate strode past the two women. He grabbed his pants and sat on the bed. "Why'd you call me that? Did Devon set up you?"

"Call you what and who's Devon?"

"You called me 'big guy.' Devon's my brother and it's a nickname he's used since we were in high school."

"Well, Nate, for some reason it just popped into my mind. I'm sure your brother had his reason. I just hope it wasn't the same as mine."

Nate shook his head and started to pull on his pants. Eve's sister was a live wire. He thought of his brother. They would probably get along well together.

"Listen, I'll make coffee while the two of you … whatever. I'll see you downstairs." Katie turned and left the room.

Nate stood and fastened his trousers as Eve walked over and put her arms around his waist. "I wanted you to meet Katie, but I hadn't planned on this. Sorry." Nate returned her embrace and kissed her on the forehead. "She knows me much better than I'll ever know her." They both finished dressing.

As she made the coffee, Katie wondered about the man who had spent the night, a rare occurrence and the first since Wade Simmons practically destroyed her sister's interest in the opposite sex. She hoped this one was very special. If not, she'd do whatever she could to send him packing.

When Nate entered the kitchen, Bootsie greeted him by entwining herself between his legs. The feline's tail arched and her hindquarters quivered as she went through the feline marking ritual with Nate. He reached down, picked up the cat, and scratched behind its ears. The cat purred loudly. "Eve will be down soon. She's doing something with those little jars on her vanity." While holding the cat in one arm, he poured coffee into a mug and drank. Katie watched him drink it black. The cat changed positions and Nate gently put it on the floor.

To Katie, the bonding between Nate and Bootsie was a good sign. "I'm sorry if I embarrassed you. I didn't see a car in the driveway or I would have been a bit more cautious before I walked into Eve's room. You didn't hear the cab or the front door because you were in the shower."

"I hate surprises. But the apology's accepted."

"Good, then you won't mind my next question. Are you in professional sports or did that build come from honest, hard labor?"

Nate understood the question game. Lord knows he and Devon put every one of Olivia's boyfriends through the same routine from the day their father allowed her to double date. Katie wanted to know his background and would waste no time getting it. "Military ... twelve years."

"That'll explain it." She thought about the improbability of her sister getting involved with a career soldier.

"I'm not like Wade Simmons and I won't hurt your sister."

Katie decided Nate had brains to go with the body. He knew she had disguised her question as a compliment. And her sister trusted him enough to talk about Wade Simmons. Until now, she and Randall were the only people who knew about him.

Eve came into the kitchen, accepted the mug Nate handed her, and gave him a big smile. Katie saw her sister looking happy ... even content. Nate Dunlevy deserved a chance.

"Katie, I had planned to pick up groceries before I went to the airport. I still need to shop and I'm giving Nate a ride to his house in Charleston. Then I'll be home."

That answered another question. Nate lived in Charleston. "Don't rush on my account. I spent the night on a plane, so I'm ready to crash."

Nate went to the living room, picked up his suit coat from a chair, and returned to the kitchen. After saying good-bye to Katie, they drove from Sullivan's Island back to Charleston. Eve chattered about her plans with Katie during the next few days and stopped the engine when she arrived in front of Nate's home.

"I don't suppose I could convince you to join me for another cup of coffee?"

Eve shook her head. "I have things I must do, and I want to get back to the house soon. Nate, last night ... the whole night ... dinner, dancing, lovemaking ... it was wonderful. Thank you for pulling me out of an abyss."

"Someday I'll tell you what last night meant to me, but sitting here on Tradd Street doesn't cut it for me. Enjoy a few days with your sister, but I want to stop by on Sunday. The three of us can do something together if you want."

Eve agreed. By Sunday, she'd be ready for whatever happened next with Nate Dunlevy.

IX

The setting sun cast a golden glow on the marshes between Charleston and Beaufort. A lone armadillo scurried across the road seeking safety within the dense forest that still thrived along sections of the highway. The high tide caused the water level to rise within a foot of the road, and several small fish jumped in the streams that skirted the causeway. Nate enjoyed the view and smiled to himself as he drove his silver Porsche toward Beaufort. He parked his car in front of the family home on Craven, where his father waited. Then the two men walked down the quiet, tree-lined street to the Beaufort Inn, a restored Victorian B & B that featured one of the best restaurants in the historic district.

Nate's mind drifted to Eve several times during dinner. He told John about the latest renovations to his house. "Eve suggested office built-ins that match the kitchen. I met with the cabinet guy and we came up with a good design."

"Sounds like you and Eve have become friends."

"I convinced her to have dinner with me two nights ago."

"I'm glad the two of you are seeing each other."

Nate waited for the server to pour their coffee and walk away from the table before he continued. "I think we're beyond that. I'm in love with her. She just doesn't know it yet."

During their walk home, Nate's cell phone rang. He looked at the LCD display. "This can't be good." John remained silent as Nate dialed. A voice on the other end answered, "Dispatch."

"It's Dunlevy, and I'm on a cell." This let dispatch know their conversation could be intercepted.

"Commander, we've received a request from a person named Eve O'Connor. She's asked that you call her at this number." He recited the number and Nate memorized it.

"I've got it."

Nate punched in the number and knew she wasn't calling from home or the gallery. A sinking feeling settled in his gut when a disembodied voice announced *Medical University of South Carolina. If you know your party's extension, please dial it …* Nate didn't wait for the recording to continue. He punched in the extension dispatch had given him.

"Hello?"

"Eve, this is Nate. Are you okay?"

She struggled to keep her voice level. "Actually, Nate, I've had better days." After a short pause, she continued. "I'm sorry to call you at this number, but I think I need help. I tried your father. He's not home."

"He's standing right next to me. You sound hoarse, Eve. Are you sick?" John raised an eyebrow but remained silent.

"Oh, that's good … that he's with you, I mean. I need some legal advice." There was silence.

Nate wanted to crawl through the phone to see if she was okay, but he kept his voice calm. "Eve, why are you calling me from the hospital? Were you in an accident?"

"No, not an accident." After a pause she added, "It was intentional." Nate heard her voice hitch and felt the blood drain from his head. "He came for me, Nate … he came and he hurt me … he hurt Katie, too." She stopped talking as she fought for control.

"Who hurt you, Eve? Was it Wade Simmons?"

"Yes."

"Damn it!" Nate closed his eyes and pushed two fingers against his lids, hoping the scene he imagined would go away. Then he refocused on the call. "Eve, where are you at right now?"

Eve regained her composure. "We're in the ER. They've treated us and we can go soon. The police will take us home."

"Listen, Eve, don't go anywhere, do you hear me? I want you to stay where you are until Dad and I get there. Understand?" Nate had visions of Eve and her sister going back to their home while Wade Simmons still prowled the area. He hoped the police had apprehended the bastard, but he would not take that chance.

He heard Eve speaking to someone else nearby. Then she said, "There's a place where we can wait." She listened to someone and added, "We'll be in room 107. It's very close to the ER. Ask for directions at the registration desk when you get here."

"We'll be there as soon as possible. I'm in Beaufort, so it'll take us about an hour, okay?"

"Okay." Her voice trembled slightly. "Thank you for coming." The phone disconnected.

Nate combusted. "Goddamn it to fucking hell!" He looked over at John. "I knew I should have tracked down that son of a bitch and threatened to kill him with my bare hands!"

Nate started walking fast and John matched his pace. "What happened?"

"She's been hurt. The bastard came after her."

"You'll fill me in on the way to Charleston."

When they arrived at his home, John called a neighbor to take care of Rufus and grabbed his briefcase from his desk. Seventy-two minutes after Eve's call, Nate parked his father's SUV near the MUSC Emergency Entrance. A volunteer at the information desk showed them how to find room 107.

Nate pushed through the door of a small, private waiting room. He saw Eve and her sister sitting on a brown vinyl sofa and looking down at magazines. His heart rate slowed for the first time since he got the call. Then Eve looked up at him and her battered face made him think of murder. A mass of bruises covered her cheekbones. Her lips had been split open and were puffy. The flesh around one eye was dark and swollen. Her neck revealed the handprints of the man who had choked her. Nate tore his eyes from Eve and looked at Katie. A sling supported one arm, a large bruise colored her cheekbone, and a bandage covered her left eyebrow.

The two women remained seated and silent as the men entered the room. John sat down in a chair near Katie while Nate crouched directly in front of Eve and focused on her at eye level.

"I want to kill him." Nate softly placed his hand on hers. "We'll take you home, and then you'll tell us exactly what happened. Okay?" Eve only nodded. She didn't trust herself to speak, fearing that she would break down.

Katie got up from her seat slowly. "The police left about twenty minutes ago. They're still looking for Wade Simmons." She looked at Nate. "Eve's going to need help. He also did a number on her ribs."

Nate stayed in front of Eve. "Shouldn't you spend the night in the hospital?" Eve shook her head. "No, take me home. Please." Nate helped her get up from the sofa.

Seconds later, a woman entered the room. "Ah, I see your friends have arrived." After scrutinizing the two men, she said, "I'm Maura Brodie, a victim's advocate for the police department. I have a law degree and help crime victims ... especially women and children."

John introduced himself and Nate. "Eve has asked me for legal advice, but I hope you'll stay involved with the case."

Maura nodded. "For as long as I'm needed." She gave John her card and one for the detective in charge. Then she turned to Eve. "I'll stop by your house tomorrow, unless you need me tonight."

Eve shook her head and steadied herself with Nate's arm. She looked down at the scrubs she wore. "I'll return these tomorrow. Thank you for helping us."

Nate asked, "What happened to your clothes?"

She shrugged, moving her battered body as little as possible. "The police wanted evidence." Nate let it drop. He'd learn what happened soon.

John asked Maura, "Can I get a copy of their medical charts and the police report?"

"I'll have the medical information waiting for you at the desk. Eve and Katie will have to stop there to sign discharge papers. There will be instructions and phone numbers for follow-up appointments. You'll have to contact Detective Ferrigna for the police report."

Katie looked at Maura and then John. "When we left with the police, the kitchen had broken glass and ..." She trailed off and then looked at Maura. "Is it okay to clean everything up?" Maura told them the police had all the evidence they needed from the scene.

The trip back to Sullivan's Island was a quiet one. When they arrived, Eve let Nate help her from the car and into the house. She moved slowly and deliberately. After they entered the foyer, she turned to him. "I'm going upstairs to shower and change. I'll be down later."

Nate gripped her arm as firmly as he could without hurting her. "I'm concerned you'll do more harm to yourself in the shower. The pain meds they gave you are making you unsteady."

"Katie will help me. I need to clean up. We'll be down when I'm done." She headed for the stairs, gripped the banister, and slowly ascended to the upper floor.

Nate glanced at the sling on Katie's arm. "Can you handle this?"

Katie stopped and looked down at her arm. "It's sore, but it works, and my head's clear. I'll call you if I need help."

He dropped the argument. "I want to check the house." He quickly went through Eve's room checking closets, window locks and the French door that opened to a veranda. Then he left the two women alone and did a similar search in Katie's, a room that mirrored Eve's suite. A small room separated theirs and had ceiling-high bookcases and overstuffed chairs. He checked the lock on the French door and quickly moved to the two bedrooms on the front of the house. Then he climbed another staircase to Eve's studio on the third floor. After checking the window locks, he searched the widow's walk that surrounded the roofline. He used the vantage point to scan the full panorama around Eve's home and surrounding water. He came inside and locked the door.

Nate heard the shower in Eve's room as he came down from her studio. He stood outside her door in silence and thought of the night they spent together. Then he went downstairs and completed his security check.

Nate met his father in the kitchen. "I've cleaned up a broken vase and flowers," John said. "There's blood here, and someone must have been sick."

Nate struggled to control the rage boiling inside and felt the bile rise to his throat as he helped John scrub the floor. He straightened overturned chairs and discovered Bootsie hunkered down on one that was still tucked beneath the table. The cat hopped down, rubbed vigorously against Nate's leg, and yowled loudly.

When they finished cleaning the kitchen, John sat down and picked up the medical reports. Nate went upstairs and met Katie coming out of Eve's bathroom. "We'll both be down shortly, Nate." Eve wasn't ready for a confrontation. "Could you make us drinks? I'd like vodka with orange juice. Make it strong, please. Eve wants ice water."

Nate glanced at the closed door to Eve's bath and decided not to invade her privacy. "Is she okay?"

"She's upset … just give us a few more minutes."

Nate returned to the kitchen to make drinks for Eve and Katie as well as a pot of coffee. He poured two mugs, joined his father at the table, and picked up the discharge instructions the nurse had given them. Most of it was boilerplate stuff, so he scanned the handwritten instructions at the bottom of the form. He stopped when he came to the line that read, *Take second Levonelle tablet before 6:00 AM.* He thought about the scrubs and the shower. Then he prayed he was wrong. "Dad, I think she was raped."

John looked up from the report but said nothing.

Nate's pulse raced. "This mentions Levonelle. That's the morning-after pill."

John put a hand on his son's arm and spoke firmly. "I'm afraid you're right, Nate. Now don't add to her trauma."

"I'll kill him, Dad. I'll kill him slowly and painfully."

Seconds later, Eve and Katie entered the kitchen. The bruising on Eve's face had worsened. Before either man could say anything, Katie said, "Let's sit on the porch. The furniture's more comfortable and the lighting's not so harsh." Eve didn't say a word as she walked across the room.

Nate closed his eyes and fought for control. Then he picked up the two drinks and carried them to the porch. John followed with two mugs of coffee.

Eve saw the look on Nate's face and her hand trembled as she took the glass from him. *He knows what happened to me.* Tears began to well up, but she wiped them away.

Nate didn't miss the struggle and he clamped down hard on the fury churning inside. They sat on the porch for a few moments of strained silence.

Eve thought she would explode. She roiled with anger, shame, and guilt. Then she prayed she would wake up from this horrendous nightmare. She felt something brush her hand. Before Nate could rest his hand on hers, she snatched it away and winced at the pain the sudden movement caused. Nate shook his head and apologized, but he wouldn't avoid the question any longer. "Eve, please tell us what happened here tonight?"

Eve stared at him. "I don't know if I can." She waited, then looked at her sister. "Katie?"

Katie took a sip of her drink and waited for several seconds before she began. "I went for a run on the beach and got back an hour later. As I came around the pool, I heard a man shouting. I ran into the kitchen and saw Eve on the floor … and he was on top of her." Katie focused on the floor as she continued. "She struggled to get away, but he sat across her legs and she couldn't move her arms … they were caught in her sleeves … her smock was pinned beneath her … he was hurting her." She looked at John. "Eve saw me and told me to run, but I lunged at him and hit him with my fists. I didn't faze him, and he punched me in the face." Katie pointed at her bruised cheekbone. "It must have stunned me for a moment. Eve struggled, but she could hardly move. He grabbed my arm, twisted it, and then shoved me. My head hit the counter—it must have hit hard, because everything got fuzzy." She shook her head. "I don't know for how long." Katie paused. Her hand shook as she took a sip of her drink. "I heard Eve screaming, and when my focus came back, he was raping her."

Eve leaned forward, put her face into her hands, and forced back her tears.

Nate wanted desperately to hold her, but he worried this would only hurt her.

Katie started to cry. "He didn't see me crawl around the cabinet. I got to the phone and dialed 911, and I left the phone on the floor. I thought about the knife drawer when I saw the vase of flowers on the counter. I stood up, grabbed it, and ran over to them. I used it to hit him on the head. Then I backed up before he could grab me. I screamed that the police were on the way and he heard a voice coming through the phone. He got up, pulled up his pants, and took off through the front door." Katie suppressed a sob. "I'm so sorry, Eve. I didn't know how to stop him sooner."

John took her hand. "You did everything you could, Katie, and made him go away."

When Eve looked up, her cheeks were wet with tears. "It sounds like it happened to someone else. But it didn't. It happened to me."

The room remained quiet for several seconds. Then Eve explained. "I couldn't fight him off ... that was the worst part. I wanted to hit, scratch, bite, and kick ... anything. But my clothes trapped my arms and his body weight crushed my legs."

Nate looked at the abraded skin on her wrists. "How did he get in and overpower you?"

"He marched right in ... came through the porch. I had just come down from my studio. I heard the screen door open and close and assumed Katie had come back from her run. I went to the kitchen to pour lemonade for us. I had planned to swim when Katie got back, so I wore a painter's smock over my bathing suit. The smock had long sleeves with two buttons at the wrist. Suddenly, he was choking me from behind. He yanked the back of my smock to pull it off, but the tight sleeves caught at my wrists. He grabbed my hair and hit me in the face several times. I guess I faded in and out. The next thing I remember, I was lying on the floor and he was standing next to me. He kicked me in the side several times and called me every filthy name imaginable. I rolled onto my knees and struggled to free my arms. I remember being sick. He pushed me back to the floor, straddled me, and started choking me again. I smelled alcohol on his breath, but he wasn't drunk—he was insane." Eve stopped. "I can't talk about it anymore. Please don't ask me anything else."

The room got quiet again. A few minutes later, the phone rang and John went to answer it. Katie followed him through the kitchen and went into the powder room. Nate kept his eyes focused on Eve. "I want to walk out that door, find Wade Simmons, and kill him."

Eve shrugged. "It won't change what happened." She took a sip of water, handed him her glass, leaned toward a sofa pillow, and rested her head. "I took a tranquilizer just before I came downstairs. It must be kicking in because I feel groggy. I'll just lie here for a little bit."

Nate lifted her legs onto the couch then reached for a throw blanket and covered her. He needed physical contact with her, so he leaned down and gently fingered the ends of her hair.

When John and Katie returned to the porch several minutes later, Eve lay motionless except for the light rhythm of her breathing. Katie curled up in a chair with another drink and Nate asked his father about the call. "That was Maura Brodie. We discussed what happened. She'll bring counseling referrals tomorrow. We have meetings with the case detective and the district attorney's office in the morning. There's no news on Wade Simmons, and the police suspect he's out of the state by now."

Nate stood in frustration. "I don't care where the police *think* he is. I'm staying here until Simmons is in custody. It makes no sense for you to drive back to Beaufort tonight, Dad. Why don't you stay at my place?"

Katie slowly got up from her chair. "You can both use the guest rooms. It's the least I can offer in return for your help tonight. Right now, my body needs a soft bed."

Nate looked down at Eve. She was asleep. After checking her pulse, he carefully lifted her, cradled her in his arms, and followed Katie upstairs. Katie had pulled back the linens on Eve's bed. Nate gently put her down and covered her. She barely stirred.

When Nate returned to the kitchen, his father had finished making notes for his meetings the next morning. "Dad, I need to run home and get my laptop and a few other things. Will you stay here until I get back?"

"Sure, Nate, then I'll head out and grab a few hours of sleep at your place."

Nate headed toward the front door. "I should be back in an hour. Lock up behind me."

Nate arrived at his home and drafted an e-mail message that included an attached file of facts he had learned about Wade Simmons. The message stated he wanted to find the man without relying on the police and without their knowledge. He encrypted the message, flagged it as high priority, and sent it to two recipients. One was his brother. The other was Thomas Jenkins, also known as Tee-Jay to the majority of his clients. DMG, Inc. kept this man on a sizeable retainer. His most sought-after talent was his ability to hack unseen into a vast array of computer networks. He carefully screened his clients before he agreed to work for them. A handful of people working under the auspices of the CIA and Homeland Security used his skills, but they would never admit it.

By tomorrow, Nate would know more about Wade Simmons, including credit card numbers, bank account numbers, and aliases. He would have similar information on members of the Simmons family without a court order and without asking the police.

Thirty minutes later, he tossed a small suitcase and a laptop into his car and headed back to Sullivan's Island.

X

Like many other mornings, boats slowly glided past the weathered wooden pier that juts out from the O'Connor property. Shrimp trawlers returned from the sea, decks laden with early-morning catches, gulls trailing behind screeching loudly, diving for the chum washed from the boat. Eve always enjoyed the morning view from her bedroom veranda. But today she stood with her arms gripped tightly across her body and tears streaming down her face. She saw the flash of a silver mullet jump two feet out of the water to avoid being eaten by a larger fish. Eve felt like a hapless mullet that had already been swallowed.

Bath-robed Katie walked into the kitchen and found Nate engrossed at a laptop computer. He wore jeans and a T-shirt that were equally faded. A day-old beard darkened his jawline, and he unconsciously raked his fingers through disheveled hair. When he looked up, the bruise on Katie's cheekbone caused him to grimace as he imagined how Eve's face would look this morning. He banged his toe when he hopped up from the table and muttered an obscenity. "I didn't hear anyone moving around upstairs. I planned to see if you or Eve needed anything." He glanced at the sling on her arm. "How are you feeling?"

"I'm sore, but I'll be okay." Katie looked at the tense, weary man. "Did you get any rest?"

"Yeah, I nodded off for about three hours. It was enough. Dad said he'd stop by after his meetings this morning." Nate nodded toward a counter stool. "Sit down and let me get you something."

Without arguing, she sat on a stool. "How long were you a SEAL?"

"What brought that up?"

"Your shirt—it has a logo, the seal and bayonet."

He looked down at his shirt. "Oh, right. I have a bunch of these. They don't seem to wear out. I served with them for eight years. Before that, four years in the Marine Corps."

Katie watched as Nate bent down and stuck his head in the refrigerator. "Eggs are good … right? They're easy to eat, good for you, light on the stomach. The coffee's fresh."

He put a carton of eggs on the counter and leaned down to get a skillet. Frying pan in hand, he stood and turned as Eve slowly walked into the kitchen. She wore a plain, loose-fitting cotton dress that hung almost to the floor. The daylight made the bruising on her face and neck look much worse than it had during the night. Nate clamped down on his rage.

Eve stood at the counter near Katie. After waking in a very bad mood, she had taken her pain meds. They hadn't kicked in yet and her body ached all over. While she was in her bathroom, she looked inside the little envelope for the second dose of Levonelle and found it empty. The nurse at the hospital had told her to take the contraceptive as an added precaution against pregnancy. Had she lost the other pill or taken it during the night? Nate put two mugs of coffee, spoons, milk, and sugar in front of them. "How are you feeling?"

"Not so hot. Did I image things, or were you hovering around me during the night?"

"I put ice packs against your face and your side a few times." He had discovered the ugly bruises on her right side while she slept. "You woke up early this morning and I gave you some meds. Then you went right back to sleep."

Eve had a vague recollection of Nate helping her to and from the bathroom, bringing her water, and handing her pills after she had eased her sore body onto the mattress. "How did I get into bed last night?"

"I carried you there."

Her disposition rejected the idea of tenderness from any man, including him. She said with cynicism, "You missed your calling—you should have been a nurse instead of a soldier."

Her tone surprised Katie, but she stayed quiet.

Nate kept his voice level. "A soldier's been known to play medic when one of his buddies is hurt." Nate turned his back to her and began breaking eggs into a bowl.

Watching him beat the eggs made her mood even worse. "It looks as though soldiers do just about anything they want. I see you've taken over my household."

Nate's eyes iced when he turned back to her. He strained to keep his voice low and calm. "If I had done everything I wanted to do, Simmons wouldn't have gotten to you." His control slipped, and his voice grew louder. "I wanted to help, to make sure something like this didn't happen!" The moment he said it, Nate regretted it. Eve didn't need his guilt dumped on her. The apology was on his tongue, but she cut him off.

"Oh! Here we go—now this is all about you. Why do men assume that everything that happens to a woman, good or bad, revolves around them? That attitude must come from those goddamn sex organs hanging between your legs."

Nate had stirred the pot and triggered her anger. Eve walked around the counter, and stood bare-toed with him. She poked her finger against his chest and shouted, "I'm the stupid one who dated the jerk. I'm the dumb ass who got into bed with the bastard. I'm the nitwit who didn't tell the police about him, and I'm the idiot who got raped." Eve looked down at the carton of eggs then grabbed one and hurled it across the room. Pain shot through her body as the egg smacked against the wall. He watched the innards ooze down and handed her another one. Despite the pain, she yanked her arm back and readied to throw again. Then she stopped and crushed the egg in her hand.

She fought back tears. Nate moved to put his arms around her, but she raised her other hand. "Don't touch me … please don't touch me." She stared at the raw egg dripping between her fingers.

No one said a word while Eve rinsed her hand and walked out of the kitchen. Nate wondered what he should do next. A minute later, he asked Katie to check on her.

"She's probably taking another shower. It's therapy. She wants to wash him off her. The nurse said it may be a compulsion for a few days." Katie paused. "She's hurting real bad, Nate, inside and out. Her anger is misdirected. She is upset with herself—and with you. At some point, Wade Simmons should face her wrath. If it helps, I think you're handling this whole thing incredibly well."

Nate shook his head. "She wouldn't agree with you, but thanks. I'm doing the best I can. Right now, I just want to get food into her. She shouldn't be taking those pills on an empty stomach."

Katie got up from the counter. "I'll go see how she's feeling. Then I want eggs while we still have some left. She has a good arm." Katie's smile coerced a reluctant one out of Nate. She went upstairs to help her sister.

If a dark mood permeated the O'Connor house, the weather did not mirror the gloom. The afternoon brought a glorious, southern autumn day, with temperatures hovering around eighty degrees. After convincing Eve to stretch out on the porch sofa, Nate cleaned up the breakfast dishes. Katie announced the weather was beckoning her to catch some rays by the pool, and she went upstairs to change out of her robe.

Nate was engrossed with his laptop when Katie marched into the kitchen wearing a few colorful triangles of fabric connected by fancy cord. Her sling was gone. Nate felt awkward when he glimpsed at her—the same way he felt when noticing Olivia. A brother never wants to see a sister the way other men do. Katie had a well-toned, curvaceous body and her skimpy bikini covered very little of it. Nate glanced back at the computer. "Shouldn't you be wearing your sling?"

She moved to the refrigerator and fixed herself a cold drink with her good arm. "I'm just going to sun and dip into the water if I get too hot. I'll be careful with my shoulder."

Nate got up from the table, glanced into the porch, and saw Eve dozing on the sofa. "Dad should be back soon. Then I'll grab a shower and shave."

"Go do it now. I'll stay with Eve until you're done."

"I'll wait." The breeze stirring through the porch felt good, so he sat in a chair near Eve.

Katie walked into the porch. "What are you doing on the computer?"

"I'm looking for Wade Simmons and waiting for him to make a mistake."

Eve was not asleep on the sofa. She opened her eyes and looked at him. "You don't have to make this your personal vendetta. I'm sure the police can handle it without your involvement."

Nate shook his head, stood up, and walked back to the kitchen.

John returned to the house along with Maura Brodie and they discussed their meetings with the police and the district attorney. Wade Simmons was still at large, and the police felt certain he was out of state. The district attorney's office was prepared to prosecute charges of rape and two counts of aggravated assault when Wade Simmons was found and brought to justice in South Carolina.

Maura gave Eve the names of two rape counselors. She strongly encouraged Eve to make an appointment soon. Then she took Katie aside and asked her about Eve's frame of mind. Katie described the past day. Maura told her Eve's reactions were good … part of the healing process. She acknowledged Nate had become the "whipping boy" and she hoped he could deal with it.

Late that afternoon, Randall called Eve about a painting he had sold that day. Nate tried to make an excuse for Eve, but she overheard the conversation and asked for the phone. Although he knew nothing about her trauma, Randall heard the strain in her voice. "Princess, what's the matter? Has Nate done something to hurt you? Just say yes and the cops are on their way. I'll be right behind them."

Nate had no compunction about standing within earshot during the conversation. "No, Nate hasn't done anything to hurt me." She gave him an uneasy look and started to tell Randall about Wade Simmons. Then she choked up. Nate took the phone from her. "Hang on a minute, Randall." He tried to comfort her, but she moved away. "Should I tell him?" Eve nodded and left the room. Nate told him about the harm Wade Simmons had done to Eve and Katie. Randall felt devastated.

An hour later, the doorbell rang. Nate opened the front door and found Randall holding a large box of food. As Nate followed him to the kitchen, Randall announced that he was in charge of dinner that night. "I have chicken and pasta Alfredo from Magnolias—it's one of Eve's favorites and easy to eat. Where is she?" Nate took the box of food, put it on the kitchen counter, pointed him to the porch, and followed. Randall looked at Eve's face and turned to him. "I don't care how you do it; just promise me that he'll be severely punished." Nate nodded. Randall moved to sit next to Eve and wrapped his arms around her. "We'll get over this, princess. Trust me on that." He saw tears forming in her eyes and snuggled her against him. "You go ahead and have a good cry." Nate suddenly felt like an intruder and left the room.

That evening, Nate watched Eve push the food around her plate. She ate some, but not much. After dinner, Nate and Katie cleaned up, and Randall spent more time comforting Eve before he went home.

In the blackness between midnight and dawn, an explosion shook Nate from a sound sleep. He woke sweat soaked and head pounding. When his mind cleared, he fumbled through the guest vanity for aspirin and couldn't find any. After tugging on his jeans, he groped his way down the oak staircase. He remembered a bottle of aspirin in the cabinet next to the refrigerator—he'd seen it there today. A soft light illuminated the kitchen throughout the night. Now it blinded him and forced him to squint hard. He made his way to the cabinet and grabbed the aspirin inside. Then he stood in front of the sink and tossed back four tablets and a glass of tap water.

Eve sat quietly in her dark office and watched him go through the ritual. She had seen him do it before … in his own kitchen. She felt torn. Should she be quiet and linger in her own torment? Should she reach out and help him with his? A second later, he took the choice away from her. After sensing her presence, he turned to meet her gaze. He stood still and stared. He had nothing left inside. Neither moved nor spoke, but both wanted, both craved, just a word or a touch. But neither moved nor spoke. Then Nate left the room.

The next day, Eve sat at the kitchen table and Nate put a bowl of soup in front of her.

Eve tried to make her voice sound civil. "Thank you, but I'm just not very hungry."

"That's too bad. You're losing weight and you need to eat." Eve glared at him then picked up a spoon.

The phone rang and Katie answered. She handed the phone to Nate. "Devon McLean is calling for you."

"Dev, what's up?"

"We found your boy."

Nate listened to information his brother had regarding the whereabouts of Wade Simmons. "I've been watching his credit and ATM cards, but nothing has showed up yet."

"An hour ago, he checked into the Marriott Peachtree Plaza as Russell Simmons."

"Are you sure it's not his father?"

"Not unless the man is in two places at once. I made some calls. The description fits Wade Simmons."

"Do you have his room number?" He committed it to memory and told Devon he'd explain the situation another time. Then he thanked him, hung up, and turned to his father. "Can you take over here?" When John nodded, Nate packed up the laptop and headed for the stairs.

John stood in the guest room and watched Nate take his Mark 23 pistol from the dresser drawer. Katie and Eve stood outside the doorway. John said firmly, "I see that look on your face, Nate. I don't want you running off half-cocked. I've no desire to defend my son in a criminal case. Let's call the police."

Nate moved toward a closet and struggled to control the volume of his voice. "I'm not going anywhere half-cocked, but I'm going to find this mother fucker. I'll be sure the police arrest him, and you can put the sick bastard behind bars. Then I'll use whatever connections I have to pick his cell mate—a big, burly guy who's hung like a horse and horny as hell!"

Nate picked up the laptop and a jacket that he would wear to cover the handgun tucked in a shoulder holster. He walked toward the bedroom door. "Dad, let me know right now if you can stay here with Eve and Katie for the next day or two. I need to make some phone calls if you can't."

Eve shouted. "When did I become an infant who needs a babysitter? You tell me what to eat, when to sleep. Now you decide who is going to stay in my home. I don't need you running my life."

Her words stung, but Nate pushed them aside. "We did things your way the last time. Now we're going to do things my way. I guess you'll just have to live with that. But don't worry. When Simmons is put away, you can shove me entirely out of your life."

John touched Nate's arm. "I can stay, son, but I expect you to call me from Atlanta." He handed Nate the keys to the SUV as Nate walked to the doorway.

Eve grabbed his arm as he attempted to move past her. "You don't have to do this. The police will find Wade Simmons."

"You just keep thinking that, Eve." Nate went downstairs and slammed the front door behind him.

XI

The Ravenel Bridge connects motorists from Sullivan's Island and Mount Pleasant to downtown Charleston. The new six-lane roadway replaced the old Cooper River Bridges, two miles of truss structures that were built in 1929 and 1966. Few people guided their vehicles across the very narrow and very high roadways without cringing. Large openings along the sides of the old steel structures gave travelers a frightening view of the flowing river 150 feet below. Nate simmered as he sped his father's car across the new Ravenel Bridge. Then the last remnants of the old bridges came into view. Eve had crossed the outdated and dangerous spans for years, and the thought put a shudder up his spine.

When he arrived at his home, Nate changed into a suit and sorted through various IDs. He picked the identity of Matthew Andrews. He tossed extra clothes, his digital camera, and a few other items into an overnight bag and grabbed the laptop. His car was still in Beaufort, but it didn't matter. He wanted a nontraceable rental car for his trip to Atlanta. Matthew Andrews rented one from a local agency, and then Nate called John to let him know where to pick up his SUV.

Before he got to Georgia, Nate stopped at a mall and bought a prepaid cell phone that he would throw away at the end of his trip. Before he reached Atlanta, Nate stopped at a pawnshop and bought a buck knife. Then he went to a discount store and bought a package of handkerchiefs.

That night, Nate checked into Marriott Peachtree Plaza as Matthew Andrews, using a debit card and Maryland driver's license. He told the desk clerk he was meeting Russell Simmons and asked if the person had arrived. The clerk acknowledged Russell Simmons was in house and asked if he wanted to leave a message. Matthew Andrews declined. He would meet Mr. Simmons the following morning.

Nate got to his room and looked at his watch. It was 9:00 PM. He called room service and ordered a medium-rare filet with steak fries and a salad. When his dinner arrived, he ate most of it quickly and realized he hadn't eaten much at all that day. Then he took his purchases and dinner plate into the bathroom. He mixed ketchup with the remaining beef juice and decided it looked enough like blood. The mixture would look more realistic when it dried. He put on latex gloves he had packed, splattered the mixture onto a fresh handkerchief, and wrapped it around the buck knife. He wrapped these items securely inside the plastic store bag. After washing his hands, he removed the gloves and put them in his pocket. Then he focused his mind on a next few hours—nothing else mattered but the next few hours.

Shortly after midnight, Nate reached for the disposable phone. He dialed the main number for the Marriott and asked for Russell Simmons. After several rings, a bleary voice answered. Nate spoke in a friendly, enthusiastic, and slightly slurred voice. "Shelly, baby, I thought we were getting together tonight. Where are those hot buns of yours?"

He got the response he expected. "Huh?"

Nate slurred his speech a little more and continued. "Who's this? I've room 323, right?"

This time, he got the response he wanted. With equally slurred speech, the other man replied, "No, you idiot. You called 423."

Nate hung up. That confirmed Simmons had not changed rooms during the last day. Clearly, the man was not a pro at avoiding pursuit. Tee-Jay had alerted him that Simmons had sold his Jaguar for cash when he got to Georgia. Nate left his room to find Simmons's current mode of transportation.

When he got to the lobby, he used a remote house phone and entered the number for valet parking. The attendant answered. "This is Russell Simmons from room 423. I'll need my car tonight." The attendant asked him to wait for a moment. A few seconds later, the attendant told him his car would be available at the main entrance within the next five minutes. Nate walked through a side exit and stood out of the valet's sight. He held a quiet imaginary conversation on his phone. A few minutes later, he walked up to the main entrance and saw an older model Grand Marquis parked in front of the valet stand. He nodded to the attendant and walked into the hotel. Again, he used the house phone to call the valet. "This is Russell Simmons. I won't need my car tonight after all. I'll be sure to add a valet tip to my bill. Good night." He waited a few seconds and watched the Marquis move away from the entrance before he headed to the elevator.

Nate showered, shaved, and put on jeans, a dark shirt, and black rubber-soled shoes. He set his watch alarm for 4:00 AM and stretched out on top of the bed. His training had taught him to sleep when he could. He forced his body and mind to unwind. Three hours later, Nate woke and went to his suitcase for his digital camera and other items that he concealed in his clothing. He put on a dark windbreaker, put the store bag containing the buck knife in his pocket, and left his room. Using a rear door, he entered the parking garage and began his search for a brown Marquis with a "Tag Applied For" sign. He spotted it six minutes later.

Nate went to the driver's side windshield and used his digital camera to snap a picture of the vehicle identification number. Then he moved to the passenger side and pulled out a slim-jim he had tucked into the waistband beneath his shirt. He used it to pop the lock on the door. Once inside, he reached over and hit the trunk release button. Inside the trunk, he quickly disconnected the wiring to the taillights on the left and placed the buck knife wrapped in the stained handkerchief into the recess of the light assembly. With a clean handkerchief, he wiped his prints off anything he had touched and used it to close the trunk. He walked back to the passenger-side door, listened, and waited. He didn't hear any sound in the garage. He opened the door, got in the car, and closed the door. Nate stayed low and pulled a set of lock picks from his back pocket.

While he worked the lock on the glove compartment, he heard footsteps echo inside the concrete garage. He stopped all movement and focused on slowing his heart rate and breathing. He remained motionless as the footsteps came closer. Nate closed his eyes and followed the echo of the footsteps with his ears. They were still coming in his direction. Nate's mind left the brown Marquis. He was in Eve's kitchen ... she was pinned down on the floor ... her arms were trapped near her sides ... she screamed out in pain. Nate felt the nausea rising in his stomach, and it brought him back for a split second. Nate fought hard to recall his current situation and to push Eve from his mind. The footsteps had stopped, but he waited for another minute, listening with his eyes open this time. He went back to work on the lock of the glove compartment and two minutes later it sprung open.

After putting on a latex glove, Nate sorted through papers and removed the temporary car registration; then he closed the compartment and relocked it. He wiped the car for prints, but not the steering wheel—he had avoided touching it and didn't want to remove any of Wade Simmons's prints. He noted the odometer reading and looked around the car for any other important details. Using the handkerchief, he opened the door, hit the lock button, got out, and closed it. He waited, listened, and walked to the rear exit.

A few blocks away, Nate found an all-night convenience store. There he poured a large cup of coffee, paid the clerk, and left. He tore up the Marquis's temporary registration and tossed it and the empty store bag into a nearby trash can. Nate found a place near the hotel where he could keep an eye on the valet activity without being seen. He would wait before walking through the hotel lobby and back to his room.

At 7:30 AM, Nate strode into the Marriott. No one at the valet stand or front desk looked familiar from the previous night. He nodded at a desk clerk as he reached for his room key and headed to the elevators. In his room, Nate downloaded the image with the vehicle ID number onto his hard drive. After enlarging it, he could easily read the Marquis' VIN. He logged into the Georgia DMV and flagged the Marquis as having been stolen two days earlier. Then Nate changed into his business suit, packed his things, rumpled the bed linen, and checked out using the express service on the television. He retrieved his rental car from the valet and parked it near the hotel entrance. Using his disposable phone, he dialed the Marriott and asked for room 423. When a man answered he began, "Mr. Simmons, this is Detective Ferrigna from Charleston, South Carolina. We'd like to ask you a few more questions about your son." He heard the abrupt click.

Nate guessed fifteen minutes would pass before Wade Simmons vacated the Marriott. The man moved slowly—it took him seventeen. The Marquis had been parked in front of the valet before he appeared. He didn't tip anyone, just got into his car and sped off. Nate followed from a safe distance. He hit a preset number on his phone and waited for the Atlanta police dispatch to answer. "Hello, I'd like to report a reckless driver—he may be drunk. He's in a brown Mercury Marquis with a temporary license plate traveling south on Peachtree. I think he's taking the on-ramp for I-75 south." He paused then responded to the other party, "Just doing my civic duty."

Nate followed the brown Marquis onto Interstate 75. After traveling a few miles north, Nate peered in his rearview mirror and saw a police cruiser approaching from behind. The cruiser passed him and moved behind the brown Marquis. The traffic was stop and go due to the morning rush hour, and the Marquis did not have any brake lights on the left side. The police cruiser turned on its cherry top and Nate thought of the impending stop—the police would find a reason to detain him. When Simmons saw the police lights behind him, he cursed and moved into the right lane but did not pull off to the side of the road.

Instead, he signaled his intention to exit at the next off ramp, not realizing Nate had set him up.

The ramp exited into an industrial area. Nate drove past the Marquis and police cruiser, pulling into a parking lot in the next block. He got out of the car with his phone and a map and appeared to be calling for directions. He watched the Marquis while the police officer went through the steps—license, registration. Several minutes went by, and Simmons remained in the vehicle while the police officer used his radio to call for backup. Two more officers arrived in a patrol car and instructed Simmons to get out of the Marquis. Wade started to lose his composure as an officer patted him down. Then they escorted him to the rear of the patrol car while they thoroughly searched the Marquis, including the trunk and tail light assembly. The first police cruiser remained with the vehicle while the patrol car pulled away with Wade Simmons secured in the rear.

Nate looked forward to his next phone call. His father answered. "The Atlanta Police Department detained Wade Simmons for questioning. Can you get him behind bars?" Nate listened to the response and asked his father to call him that night. Then he hung up. John would contact Dan Ferrigna and ensure the Atlanta police knew about the arrest warrant for Wade Simmons in the state of South Carolina. Wade Simmons would be remanded to the Charleston Police Department and kept in custody until his arraignment. Nate got back in his car and headed for Charleston. Five hours later, he neared the city, stopped at a deserted construction site, and tossed the disposable phone into a Dumpster.

At ten o'clock that night, Nate answered his kitchen phone, expecting his father on the other end. Instead, he heard his brother's voice. "Nate, I ran a sheet on Wade Simmons today. It appears the Atlanta police picked him up on a minor traffic violation then came across something suspicious in his car—one that had been reported stolen two days ago." He paused. "So, how was your day?"

"Uneventful."

Devon chuckled briefly, and then his tone became serious. "He's also wanted in South Carolina for aggravated assault and rape. So, what's with this Simmons guy? Please don't tell me he's hurt someone we know."

Silence hung in the air for several seconds before Nate responded. "You don't know how much I want to, Dev." After another long pause, he continued, "Simmons is the man Eve dated before I met her. The assault charges involve Eve and her sister. Last Friday, Wade Simmons beat and raped Eve."

"Oh no!" Devon paused. "I was afraid to ask. Was she badly injured?"

"She's bruised everywhere. He did a number on her face and her ribs and choked her. You can still see his handprints on her neck."

"Any broken bones?"

"No, thank God. Eve looks delicate, but she's sturdier than I thought." A few seconds of silence passed. "She's become important to me, Dev."

"If that means what I think it does, I'm surprised Wade Simmons is still breathing. How are you handling all this?"

"I told Dad I wouldn't do anything that could put me in prison."

"Why aren't you with her?"

"Christ, Dev, I don't know what to do for her. I make her miserable."

"Nate, she's mad at the world right now. A big, strong guy like you makes for an easy target. Don't forget, it's not over for her. She'll have to relive the whole thing in court."

"Damn it, I don't want her dragged through that."

"I'm sure you did your homework. His daddy has money, and the family has political clout in South Carolina. They'll get an excellent criminal defense attorney involved. Before it's over, they'll try to convince the judge and jury that Simmons is the victim."

Nate's guts churned while he envisioned a slick, high-powered lawyer badgering Eve on the witness stand.

"You okay, Nate?"

"I'll manage."

"I'm so sorry about what happened. You know I want the bastard to pay, so keep me in the loop on this. I'll help anyway I can."

"We'll talk again after his arraignment. Thanks for the call."

Nate hit the flash button on the phone, then called Eve's house. He masked the disappointment in his voice when Katie answered. "Hi, Katie, this is Nate. How's everyone doing tonight?"

Katie told him about Wade Simmons's arrest. "I don't know what you did, but thank you."

He told her he had nothing to do with his arrest, which was technically true. She did not believe him, but they dropped the subject. Then he heard her say, "It's Nate. Do you want to talk to him?" There was a long pause.

"Hello."

Nate felt useless, awkward, and inept. "Hi, Eve. How are you feeling tonight?"

"Better, thank you. You know about Wade Simmons?"

Nate thought she sounded stiff, almost brittle, like something you could break into pieces. "I heard the police have him in custody. That's good."

"It is … yes. We have to see what happens next. John explained depositions and hearings to me. I appreciate how much he's taught me."

"Dad will do his very best for you, Eve."

"Yes … I know. He's right here. I'll put him on. Good night."

Before he could add anything, he heard his father's voice. "Hello, Nate."

"Can you tell me what happens next?"

"He's in custody and his arraignment will occur in two days. I hope the district attorney can prevent bail and we can keep him locked up until the hearing, which should take place within four weeks."

"If he makes bail, we'll have to make plans for Eve and Katie. I'm going to stay off the radar screen for now."

"I agree. I'll let you know what happens at the arraignment."

"Dad, please tell Eve to call me if there's anything I can do for her."

"I will. Take care of yourself, and I'll be in touch with you soon. Good night, son."

XII

Nate engrossed himself in the renovation of his home. Long, grueling hours of manual labor helped him punish an unknown demon that tormented him. He forced himself to eat and tossed aspirin like candy to ward off severe headaches. After another failed attempt to sleep, Nate got out of bed and remembered Wade Simmons would be arraigned today. There was no reason for him to attend. His father would contact him when it was over.

With a quick glance at his calendar, Nate realized he had an appointment with Joe Reynolds that morning. One side of his brain told him to cancel, while the other made him go. The psychiatrist looked up when Nate entered his office. For the first time, he saw a hostile man. Nate surprised Joe when he started their discussion with a revelation. "Last week, I made love to Eve." He waited for Joe's response, but didn't get one. "That's good news, right?"

Joe sensed a dangerous edge to Nate's mood. "What went wrong? Did you have a serious fight?"

He shook his head. "God, I wish it were that simple." Then he relayed Wade Simmons's crimes.

Joe listened in horror and expressed his sincere sorrow for both women. "How are you coping with all of this?"

"I want to kill the bastard, slowly and painfully."

"So would I. How does hanging him by his balls sound to you?"

"That's one of many images I've had in mind."

"How is Eve doing? Right now?"

"I don't know. I haven't spoken to her in two days, and the last conversation we had was very brief."

"Why?"

"I just knew you'd ask that!" Nate responded angrily. Then he got up and started to pace. He thrust his hands deep inside his trouser pockets as though they would reach out of their own accord and snap the closest object into pieces.

"Christ, Joe, I just wanted to her to be safe. I sure screwed that up royally. Then I made love to her ... just two nights before he attacked her ... before he raped her." He struggled for control. "Now she won't let me near her. Her gay friend can hold her and comfort her, but I can't even put my arms around her. I tried my best to help her. I worried about her losing weight and made her eat. I stayed at her house until he was found. I tried talking to her a few nights ago and she wants nothing to do with me." He stopped pacing and stood still for a full minute. Then he turned to Joe. "Listen to me! I'm a flaming asshole, aren't I?" He sat down and put his head in his hands. "I thought I had problems the first day I walked through your door. But this past week has been the most emasculating experience of my life."

Joe nodded. "You want to be in control, but your life has spun way out of orbit. You couldn't get a handle on yours, so you took charge of Eve's. Try to imagine how she felt."

"I'm a bully."

"You're not a bully, Nate. Bullies like to intimidate rather than protect; they use fear to gain power. You never said that you frightened Eve. If I had to label you, Nate, I'd say you're altruistic. Simmons is the bully, an amoral one despite his religious rhetoric."

Nate thought about what Joe said and felt certain that Eve wasn't afraid of him. But he sure took charge of her life after Wade Simmons stripped her of control and violated her body. Nate thought about her words: *You tell me what to eat, when to sleep, who should stay at my house.* While his good intentions helped him feel useful and even preoccupied him, Eve was fighting to rebuild her entire being. The more he dominated, the more she had to fight.

Joe remained silent as he watched Nate recall his words and actions. A sense of calm emerged in his client, which relieved him immensely. The man who had walked through the door of his office teetered on the verge of something very scary.

Nate and Joe agreed to end their session for the day. They would gain nothing by discussing insomnia, flashbacks, and other symptoms considering the events of the past week. Joe chose not to mention Nate's success in bed. Why bring attention to a problem that might have solved itself? They agreed to meet again next week.

On his way home, he received a call from Tee-Jay. Nate wasn't the only one delving into the Sovereign Church of God. The religious organization had captured the interest of the FBI. Nate called a former SEAL who now worked for the Bureau. He learned that the church was affiliated with a paramilitary group called the Sovereign Soldiers for a Better America. The FBI began to suspect them of several crimes, including the rape of a prominent senator's niece.

Maura Brody and John Dunlevy attended Wade Simmons's arraignment; Eve and Katie did not. The prosecutor presented the state's evidence and the judge agreed the case would go forward.

Harold Spencer, Simmons's attorney, requested bail for his client. The prosecutor argued heatedly against bail because the defendant proved to be a flight risk and posed an ongoing threat to the victims. The defense attorney capitulated. He had already planned the outcome of a trial—if it ever got that far.

After the arraignment, Harold Spencer approached the prosecutor and offered a guilty plea on one count of aggravated assault. His offer was promptly declined. He told the prosecutor that the evidence and the history between his client and the plaintiffs would give a judge reason to accept a plea. When that happened, Simmons would receive a fine and be sentenced to time served. Otherwise, he could easily convince a jury to acquit his client.

When John left the courthouse, he decided his son had exiled himself from Sullivan's Island long enough. He was glad when he saw the message from Nate and returned the call. "We just got through with the arraignment. The court charged Wade Simmons on all counts and denied him bail. I thought you'd be glad to hear the news."

"I am, Dad. Have you told Eve and Katie yet?"

"Maura Brodie called them as we left the courthouse. Their home is our next stop. I thought you might want to come."

"I'll meet you there."

Late that afternoon, they sat on the back porch and discussed the details of the arraignment. Randall was there when Nate arrived. Eve's bruises had started to fade, but she looked thin, almost frail.

John gave the group a brief synopsis of the arraignment and the discussion between the prosecutor and the defense attorney. When he finished, Katie looked dumbfounded. "Please be honest with us. How can Simmons's lawyer suggest he's guilty on one count of assault? Think of all the evidence to the contrary."

John deferred to Maura. "You should explain it."

Maura nodded. "No one is going to like listening to this, but we should get the facts on the table." She looked at each of them. "Simmons's attorney is Harold Spencer, and he's very good at what he does. He will go on the offense immediately. First, he will try to get the charge of aggravated assault involving Katie dismissed because Simmons was only protecting himself from her. Her testimony clearly states she attacked him with her fists before he touched her."

Katie jumped up from her seat and shouted, "He was beating the hell out of my sister when I did that."

John reached out for Katie's hand and held it in a calming way. "We know, sweetheart. Let Maura finish, then we'll sort through all of it."

Maura continued, "I want to explain how Spencer will chip away at each charge. He'll try to convince the judge that Simmons had not harmed Eve when Katie attacked him." Maura held up a hand to avert a second protest. "Then he will claim Wade Simmons did not rape Eve. He'll tell the court they were having consensual sex, and he'll use their history to reinforce his case." Maura waited for the backlash.

Katie wanted to go ballistic, but Eve cut her off. "Wade Simmons and I never had sex—not on the day he raped me, not during the one night I let him touch me that way. In both instances, I was nothing more to him than a vessel for his sperm. He told me that to my face."

Nate stood up and paced the room. "Wade Simmons belongs to a church with extreme views toward women." He recited the biblical passage Wade Simmons used when he assaulted Eve earlier that year. "His church teaches that women are inherently evil. Painful childbirth is punishment for original sin. Women who enjoy sex or have it out of wedlock are whores and married women must submit to their husbands." He paused. "We can use this sickness to our advantage."

Katie had listened to him carefully. "How do you know so much about him and his beliefs?"

He sat down and made eye contact with Eve. "I began investigating Wade Simmons and his church the week before he hurt you. I unfolded a few layers and avoided probes that could draw attention. At the time, I didn't think he was an imminent threat to you." Nate looked down at the floor and shook his head. When he looked up, his face portrayed his emotions ... those of guilt and defeat. "I was very wrong about that, and I can't describe how sorry I am that I misjudged him."

Eve didn't respond, but Katie did. "You and Eve have to start blaming the right person for what happened ... his name is Wade Simmons."

Randall agreed, then added, "Nate said something important a minute ago … about using his sickness to our advantage. Maybe his extreme religious beliefs could hang him in court." He directed his question to John and Maura. "Could the prosecutor get him all worked up and then get him to admit to the crimes because he doesn't think he did anything wrong?"

Maura told him that the chances of the defense attorney allowing his client to take the stand were almost zero. "Harold Spencer will pick at Eve the way a buzzard works a carcass, but he won't expose his client to cross-examination."

Katie shook her head. "Now there's a cheerful thought."

Nate told Randall he had the right idea. "Simmons is a zealot and we should let him preach."

John looked at his son. "Are you suggesting we arrange for him to be out on bail?"

"No, we let him stay where he is." He knew the senator had put incredible pressure on the FBI. They might orchestrate his arrest for information he could draw out of Wade Simmons.

Everyone looked puzzled, except John, who looked concerned. "I think I know where you're going with this and I don't like it." Katie asked for an explanation. "Nate wants to go inside and set up Wade Simmons. Let him expound on his beliefs and brag about his conquests." He frowned at his son. "Are you proposing a wire?"

"It's the only way to remove any doubt. He can tell his entire story in his own words."

Randall spoke. "I don't know how you make a living, Nate. Your idea sounds brilliant, but scary. You're talking about jail time … right?"

Eve erupted, "No! You won't go into a cage to protect me."

"You just don't get it. I'll do almost anything to keep you from being dragged through the muck and reliving what happened."

She shouted, "I'd rather see Wade Simmons walk away a free man!"

Nate shouted back, "Either way, I'll end up in a goddamn cage. It's only a matter of how long I'll be there."

Everyone remained silent as he got up and started to pace again. Then he spoke in a quieter tone. "I'm done talking about it." A few seconds later, he turned to Eve. "I want a few minutes alone with you … please." Eve wasn't sure how to respond. Nate took her hand and gently pulled her from her seat. "We'll use the little room upstairs."

Her feelings were in turmoil, but she allowed him to lead her from the room. When they reached the small library, he pointed toward a comfortable chair and asked her to sit down. Then he shut the door and looked around. By now, Nate had regained his composure. When he spoke, his tone was remarkably soft and even. "I like this room, Eve. It feels warm and safe, like a cocoon. Do you spend much time in here?"

Eve had prepared herself for a second round and even imagined heaving a crystal candlestick against the wall. His demeanor had disarmed her, and she struggled with her warring emotions. To prove she had control, she tried to match his casual tone. "I do in the winter, when the weather gets too cold to enjoy the porch."

Nate nodded. "That makes sense. I've made progress with my place since you last saw it. The office built-ins are installed—you had a very good idea about the cabinetry. You offered to help me pick a paint color. Remember?"

"I remember." She shook her head. "That seems like a lifetime ago."

"It was less than two weeks ago, Eve. We became friends. You opened up to me. A few days later, you got a private viewing of a problem that's been plaguing me. You asked if I had someone to help me."

She nodded.

"I'm asking you the same question. Who have you seen?"

"No one ... not yet ... I'm not ready." Her eyes met his and he saw resentment. "Why do you care so damn much?"

He felt anger, but pushed it back and kept his voice calm. "I'm tired of watching you punish yourself, and I'm tired of you punishing me. I made mistakes, took charge, domineered—whatever. I'm sorry if I made things worse for you, but I honestly don't know if I could have acted differently." He crouched before her as he had done that night in room 107. "I'm asking you to get professional help. I want a chance for us to be together, but you have to take the next step."

He stood, leaned down, and kissed her forehead. "Promise me you'll think about that."

Then he left.

XIII

Edward "Buck" Walters entered the Charleston County Correctional Facility for assaulting and raping his girlfriend. He would remain there until his arraignment. Earlier the same day, a bunk opened up in the cell housing Wade Simmons. Wade observed his new cellmate, long and lean, midthirties, scruffy-looking hair and beard stubble. He probably lived with white trash. Despite his first impression, Wade warmed up to Buck. They agreed on important things: get what you can out of life, nice guys finish last, women want men to be the boss—the list went on.

That night Nate stared at the ceiling from his upper bunk. He could kill Wade Simmons right now and make it look like death by natural cause. Wade was a young man, just thirty-two years old, but he didn't resemble to the sketch in Eve's book. He had been handsome before he gained excess weight and became bloated by alcohol.

Nate closed his eyes and prayed the nightmares would stay away. Then he opened his eyes and looked around. A caged life was a nightmare. He hadn't spoken with Eve since the day of Wade Simmons's arraignment. Last night, his father told him Eve and Katie had flown to Ireland to spend time with their parents. Should he call her when he got out? What would she think about his days in a jail cell with Wade Simmons? Would she hate him for not killing him? He stared at the ceiling and eventually drifted into a restless sleep.

The next morning a very large guard banged his nightstick on the bars of the cell. He had ebony skin, a shaved head, over two hundred pounds of solid muscle, and a cruel expression. The guard bellowed, "Walters, you come with me—now!" Buck and Wade exchanged looks as Buck reluctantly got off his bunk and moved to the entrance of the cell. The guard forced him to walk in front, shoving the hard stick into his lower back, prodding him to move more quickly. He escorted Buck to a small cinder-block room with a steel door, no windows, and a single drab, dented metal table. No one could see or hear what happened inside the four walls. When the guard slammed the door, it locked automatically. He slapped the club against the palm of his hand and shouted, "Strip!"

Buck lowered his eyes and began unfastening his orange prison jumpsuit. Then he looked up at the guard. "You're overacting, Isaac."

The men smiled and grasped hands. Isaac put his club on the table, reached into his pockets, and removed several items. "I hope you enjoyed your communal shower this morning. It will have to last until we get you out of here."

"I'll make the sacrifice. That's a scary place." Isaac handed him a small recorder and cut several strips of strong adhesive tape. Nate lowered his jumpsuit and strapped the device to the inside of his thigh just beneath his crotch. When the recorder was securely in place, he pulled up his prison suit and attached a small voice activated microphone inside the seam of his waistband.

"I have some new information, Nate. Reverend Manfred Dodd has a brother with a military background. After an unimpressive career, the United States Army discharged Everet Dodd. His record shows allegations of misconduct involving a female subordinate but charges were never filed against him. Around the time Manfred started his ministry, Everet left the country to work as a mercenary. He's back now and the two brothers have attracted a larger following. Manfred runs the church; Everet runs the SSBA. His base of operation is still a mystery and we don't want to play our hand until we can tie them to these crimes."

"I'll see what I can coax out of Simmons."

Isaac reached into his back pocket, pulled out a battered copy of the Old Testament, and handed it to Nate. "I hope this helps prime the pump." Isaac picked up the club and moved toward the door.

Nate stopped him before he could open it. "Wait, Isaac. Hit me in the face. Hard."

Isaac shook his head. "I wish you were a bastard, so I could enjoy this." He made a fist and pulled back his arm. A second later, bone collided with bone. Nate shook his head to clear his vision. The two men clasped hands and returned to their roles of prisoner and guard.

When Buck returned to the cell, he stretched out on his bunk and closed his eyes. The guard closed the cell door with a loud clank and banged the stick on the bars. "I'll be watching you, Walters." Then he strode away.

Wade saw the bruise forming around Buck's right eye. "What'd you do to deserve that?"

"He got enthusiastic with a strip search and I called him a faggot." Nate pulled a book from inside his jumpsuit. "You've never been here before, have you?"

Wade shook his head.

"It's called *you're in jail and you're fucked*. Someone brought me this because I asked for it. The guards wouldn't just give it to me; they had to bully me first. Understand?"

Wade nodded and looked at the book in Buck's hand. "So, you're into the scriptures." Buck nodded, opened the book to a dog-eared page, and began reading silently.

Forty-eight hours later, the same guard came to take Buck to his scheduled arraignment. As he left the cell, Buck handed Wade Simmons the copy of the Old Testament. "You can have this."

He took the book. "I hope we meet outside of this place."

Buck nodded. "Count on it."

The guard escorted him to a van waiting outside the prison and entered the vehicle with him. When it drove away, Buck Walters disappeared.

Nate didn't expect to see his brother inside the van. The two men grasped hands. "I thought you were stalking the streets of Washington, Dev. What are you doing here?"

Devon shrugged. "I answered all the questions about the Secret Service proposal; now we're in a holding pattern. Since I had the time and the inclination, I told Isaac to expect me."

Isaac smiled broadly, his white teeth shining in contrast with his dark skin. "It feels good to work with members of my old SEAL team again."

While another agent sped the van west on I-26, Nate took off the prison suit and tugged at the tape holding the recorder to his body. He winced when some of the adhesive clung to hair on his testicles. After a quick, painful yank, Nate handed the device to Isaac and put on civilian clothes. When Isaac began playing the recording, Nate asked him to forward the disk about halfway. After listening at several intervals, Nate held up his hand and they heard Wade Simmons say …

First, I pinned her arms with her shirt so she couldn't fight me. But she bit me, so I beat the hell out of her. Then the sister showed up and I had to knock her around too. I started on the whore and planned to do the sister next. She had a set of tits I wanted to hold good and tight while I did her from behind. The blond bitch I was raping squirmed and screamed like a cat with its tail caught in a ringer. I lost track of the sister and she called 911 then busted a vase over my head.

Isaac shook his head and stopped the machine.

Devon frowned at his brother. "And the man's still breathing? How'd you get the black eye?"

"I made Isaac hit me and became Simmons's jailhouse mentor. It got him talking. So did the bible." He turned to Isaac. "Simmons told me about Colonel Everet Dodd, the brother of Reverend Manfred Dodd."

"The man promoted himself several times since the army dumped him."

"Well, the Dodd brothers run a religious camp on the Georgia side of the Blue Ridge Mountains. They conduct programs several times a year and Simmons went for alcohol rehab. Unlike Simmons, most who attend are younger men in their late teens or early twenties. Their fathers pay tuition for a 'six week lesson in manhood' … a ten-thousand-dollar donation to the Sovereign Church of God. The reverend gives rousing speeches about elite soldiers training to fight for God's noble cause—the purity of the white race. Then the colonel takes over and they're bullied, broken down, and brainwashed. Those who excel become members of the SSBA. Simmons wasn't soldier material, but they made him a deacon for the church and his main role is fundraising. Those who become soldiers meet on weekends and run training maneuvers. They roam the Blue Ridge, look for hikers, and practice scare tactics."

Isaac nodded. "Rangers have reports of beatings in some remote areas of the Blue Ridge. It's not far from the area where two men raped the senator's niece. She and a friend hiked into the mountains just across the North Carolina border. We just got a missing-person case in that area as well. We'll compare notes when we get to Columbia."

Knowing the former SEALs could augment the skills of the FBI agents, Isaac requested approval to keep them involved with the case. Nate called the admiral and asked him to use his pull. Despite the territorial attitude of the FBI's upper echelon, they wanted the case closed. Later that day, Isaac had assembled a team in Columbia, South Carolina. The SEALs were part of it.

Special Agent Dan Walker summarized the information they had collected. "The victims are minorities, gays, and women. Usually, they're just assaulted and told to stay away from the mountains. The recent rape case involved two research students—the senator's niece and her Hispanic friend, a student from Argentina. They were apprehended by five men dressed like soldiers. Two were ordered to rape her. The man who gave the order said she'd thank him for the 'white meat'.

Then he stood by and watched. Before her companion could intervene, the other two men beat him severely. We suspect that other rapes occurred, but the victims are too frightened to report them. The men are described as fierce soldiers who dress in fatigues, wear face paint, and carry automatic weapons. The hikers think they've stumbled upon a secret encampment and the United States Government has the right to incarcerate them."

Devon shook his head. "Don't tell me nature lovers and leisure hikers actually believe our military does that stuff?"

Isaac interjected, "To some people, these men come across as actual soldiers."

Dan Walker continued, "Two days ago, a woman and her male companion hiked into the mountains near the North Carolina border. She was white and he was mixed race. They beat him until he passed out. When he woke up, she was missing. He's convinced they took her. We think they did, too. Her name is Diana Weaver and here's a picture of her." The team saw a pretty, smiling woman in her early twenties.

"How big an area are we talking about?" Devon asked.

"Big!" said Isaac as he pointed to a map on the wall. "Everything from the Pisgah to the Nantahala ranges. It's steep, heavily wooded, and sparsely populated territory within North Carolina. That's why it's taken us awhile to find a pattern."

Dan Walker added that the information Nate got from Simmons helped them zero in on a location. "We presumed their base was in Georgia near the borders of the Carolinas. After running a search of the property records, a large hunting preserve adjacent to the Buzzard Roost Heritage Preserve caught our interest. After digging through hidden layers, we traced the ownership to the Sovereign Church of God. Diana Weaver disappeared from the Nantahala range. Although that's in North Carolina, it's not very far from there."

Devon muttered, "Buzzard Roost ... a great place to find scavengers." He turned to Isaac. "Why aren't we paying this place a visit?"

"Because we need probable cause to invite ourselves through their front gate. Some people call it the Constitution."

"Bullshit!" He imagined Diana Weaver's nightmare and was disturbed by Isaac's glib answer. He glanced at Nate. "If the FBI can't act on it, we can get in there at night."

Isaac worked for the FBI and had to go by the book or the courts would throw out any case he could put together. They both understood that. Devon thought of the woman; he wanted to find her and make her safe.

So did Nate. "If she's there, Isaac, the girl is going through hell. We need to get her out."

"I agree, but I won't knock on their door and give them a reason to kill her. We don't want a hostage situation or a media circus. God forbid … let's not repeat Ruby Ridge."

Dan Walker spoke up. "We have a plan to infiltrate the camp. The lodge receives bottled water from a company every week and tomorrow is the next scheduled delivery. An agent can take over that run."

Nate responded. "Great. We need surveillance inside that compound. Max is on his way and he's an expert in that area. Let's come up with a story that puts two people on that truck."

XIV

The Low Country terrain is so flat that few areas have elevations more than twenty feet above sea level. Travel west from the coastline for three hundred miles and the terrain changes drastically. That's where the Blue Ridge Range climbs up to six thousand feet. North and South Carolina, as well as Georgia, converge in these mountains, where the terrain is steep, rocky, and heavily forested.

They watched from high-powered binoculars as Agent Charlie Potts and Max Gibb drove a bottled water truck to the gate of a private hunting preserve. Charlie used an intercom and announced their arrival. Moments later, a pickup truck arrived and a man dressed in hunting clothes emerged carrying a rifle.

"Where's Glenn?" he asked.

The agent shook his head. "He's having a bad time of it. His pretty, young wife took off two days ago and went home to her momma. Glenn went after her. He's in Mississippi. I'm Jimbo and this here is Toby. We're covering his route. What's your name, pal?"

"I'm not your pal. You can deliver the water, but Toby here stays put."

The agent shook his head. "Sorry, no can do. I'm driving because I know the route, but I ruined my back hauling these jugs a year ago. Toby does the heavy work. He may become your regular if Glenn doesn't come back. Can you show him where to put the bottles?" Toby looked dumb and innocent as he gave the man a shrug.

The gate opened for the truck. "Follow the fork to the left. I'll call ahead and tell them to look for you. They'll show you what to do when you get to the main building."

Charlie saluted the man. "Have yourself a good day now!"

One half-mile down the left fork, they came to a clearing and a group of buildings made from logs. A man and a woman waited for them in front of the largest building. Without speaking a word, Toby jumped from the truck and pulled out a handcart and several heavy bottles of water. The woman pointed toward the building and told him he'd find a water cooler and a storage room inside. Jimbo addressed the couple and began telling Glenn's sad story of the runaway wife.

Toby returned with empty jugs and stopped in front of the building with his hand truck. He propped his foot on the stoop and retied a loose shoelace on his work boot. The couples' attention went back to Jimbo, who was admiring their two hunting dogs.

"You've got a real nice pair of hounds here, Hank; I keep some smoked pig ears in the truck." He chuckled. "We like to reward the ones who don't bite us. Mind if I give them one?"

Toby scanned the area as he returned to the truck with his empty bottles; he spotted an outbuilding that contained toilets and showers. After storing his hand truck, he politely asked the couple if he could use the bathroom before leaving. When he finished in the latrine, he stopped at the dogs' shelter and stooped down to watch them gnaw on their treats. Then he walked to the truck, nodded bashfully to the couple, and climbed inside. Jimbo started the truck and drove back toward the gate. They waved to its keeper and headed to the main highway.

From his surveillance point on the ridge Nate murmured, "That went smoothly."

Moments later, Isaac spoke. "We've got a signal. Turn on your earpieces. McLean, let's open up that monitor and see what the cameras show us."

They saw a split-screen image from two separate cameras. A device planted beneath the front step of the main building scanned much of the compound. A second video device hidden at the latrine surveyed the main building. The equipment rotated by remote control. Max had planted listening devices behind the water cooler inside the main building, near the latrine, and on the doghouse in the center of the compound. The audio signal was excellent, and the group listened to a conversation going on between the man and woman at the compound.

You didn't have to flirt with that new driver, Ellie-Jean!

I wasn't flirtin', Hank. I wanted to hear about Glenn and his wife. It gets boring around here, and news is news!

Don't tell me what you were or were not doing. If you're so bored, I can fix that right quick. Now get our lunch on the table and do it before I get back.

They listened to a door slam and then watched Hank get into a pickup and drive into the woods beyond the compound.

Moments later, the gatekeeper arrived at the main building and went inside.

*Bobby Lee, you take your hands off me right now. If Hank catches you touchin'
me, he'll kill both of us and you know it!*

*He won't catch us and you won't tell him. I'm entitled to grab a feel every now and
then. You love it, so don't go telling me otherwise.*

Just go over there and wash up. Here come the others.

Up on the ridge, Devon muttered to Nate, "He's a poacher."

While listening to the lunch conversation, it became clear that four men were
caretakers. Hank was the boss and his wife served as a housekeeper. The men discussed how many men they expected tomorrow morning. Cabins, rifle ranges,
and obstacles courses had to be ready for the weekenders.

Lunch ended and the men left the main building. One turned toward Hank.

When do I get that girl again, Hank?

Shut the fuck up, Dwayne!

*Earl had her this morning. I know you're going to get rid of her before the week-
enders get here. I want another turn with her.*

*If you shut up, you can take her back to the mountains tomorrow morning. Get up
at five and she's all yours. Wipe that stupid smile off your face.*

Three men got into the truck and drove into the woods beyond the
compound.

The team on the ridge watched Ellie-Jean and Hank carry a plate of food
toward one of the cabins. Hank made Ellie wait outside while he put a hood over
his head and went inside. A moment later, he came to the door and removed his
hood.

I took off her gag and she's blindfolded now.

Ellie went into the cabin with the food. The devices Max planted could not
pick up any sound from inside the cabin after they closed the door. Twenty minutes later, Hank and Ellie came out.

*When are you going to let that poor girl go, Hank? Her family has to be crazy with
worry over her whereabouts.*

*They weren't so worried when she went trudging through the mountains with a
mongrel, were they? They were just crazy.*

Maybe he was just a friend.

Ouch! Let go of my hair, Hank. You're hurtin' me. Please, Hank.

*Listen to me and listen hard, Ellie-Jean. You gettin' on my nerves and you know
what happens when you get on my nerves. Men have needs, Ellie-Jean. Bobby can find
women who satisfy his. But Dwayne and Earl couldn't attract a housecat in heat—
that doesn't mean they don't have needs!*

Why don't they just pay for a woman?

They watched Hank slap her sharply across her face and heard flesh meet flesh.

Because men like us don't pay for women! Have you got that clear in your stupid little brain?

During the next several hours, Devon and Nate moved along the perimeter of the compound, marking a trail and using fresh meat to make better friends with the two hunting dogs that roamed the preserve. The dogs were on the opposite side of an eight-foot chain-link fence topped with razor wire. Devon used a bolt cutter to create breaks at the base of the fence in three different spots. He stuffed fallen branches into the fence not far from the breaks to mark their location. From the ridge, Isaac and the others kept surveillance on the compound.

Several hours after darkness fell, Devon, Nate, and two FBI sharpshooters moved down from the ridge and belly crawled through a hole in the fence. The sliver of a moon was a blessing. The woods were dark as pitch, but their night-vision goggles lit their path. When they got to the compound, the darkness would work to their advantage. The group traveled through the woods for almost a mile, then Nate and Devon split off and the sharpshooters moved into positions that would cover them at the compound. The two dogs had picked up their scent and met them halfway through the woods. They gave both dogs a snack of raw meat laced with tranquilizers. They wouldn't chance barking when they reached the cabin where Diana Weaver was held captive. Forty minutes after breaching the fence, they moved to the edge of the clearing. They removed their night-vision equipment and waited for their eyes to adjust.

After circling the compound, they approached Diana's cabin from the side. Their worst fear was doing something that would cause her to scream out. Devon slowly moved a tiny infrared camera under the door and rotated the device to learn the layout of the room. He focused on the cot, which bore the still body of a woman. Diana lay on her side with her back to him. He studied the slow and regular breathing and saw her cuffed ankles. He could not see her hands but guessed her body hid cuffed wrists. A hood and a rag hung on a chair near the bed, and he did not see a gag tied around her head. He signaled to Nate, who pulled lock picks from his pocket and began working on the padlock that secured the door. They knew ways to get through the door quicker, but not quieter. His fingers moved cautiously—time was to their advantage; noise was not. A full minute ticked by as Nate worked the padlock while Devon kept watch on the sleeping body and the compound. Nate looked up as he gently slid the lock from the door latch and put it in his pocket. He and Devon exchanged silent signals.

They moved through the door quickly and watched Diana's body tense when she heard them. Both men wore camouflage with darkened faces. She would view them as abductors.

Before she could scream out, Devon's hand clamped over her mouth. He whispered, "Be quiet, Diana, the FBI sent us." He waited for his comment to register. "We won't harm you." The men waited a few more seconds. The traumatized woman would need time for her brain to function.

Nate asked, "Can you move when we free you?" She nodded. "We're going to cut the cuffs on your hands and feet. Promise not the make any noise?" She nodded again. "Your friend Alex reported you missing." He worked carefully to remove the cuffs from her raw, abraded skin.

Devon kept his hand firmly over her mouth. Then he asked, "Promise to be quiet?" She nodded as tears started rolling down her cheeks. Nate removed the restraints while Devon slowly lifted his hand from her mouth and whispered. "This will be over soon, darling. The bastards who did this are going to pay."

She wore light khaki cargo pants and a white sweater. Nate pulled a dark jumpsuit from his gear and helped her slip into it. He used a tin of smudge and darkened her face for additional camouflage. Then he found her socks and boots under the cot, and the two men quickly put them on her feet. Devon went to the door while Nate helped her stand and regain her balance. Considering her captivity, her steadiness impressed him. "Can you move quickly, or should I carry you?"

She whispered, "I'll try to keep up. Just take me out of here—please!" She started to choke up.

Nate nodded. "Okay." He held a finger to his lips and then he put an arm around her waist. Keeping held her close to him, he moved behind Devon at the door and handed him the padlock.

Devon had lowered his night-vision goggles and cracked the door. Then Max's voice came through their earpieces. *We have a light and movement in Building D—that's two buildings to your right. Do you copy?*

"We copy."

Stay put and I'll update you in a minute. Do you copy?

"Roger."

Diana started to talk and Nate gently put his hand over her mouth as Devon signaled her to remain quiet. They waited and heard Max's voice.

There's movement outside Building D, one tango, moving in your direction.

Nate whispered to Diana and moved her away from the door to the far side of the room while Devon removed a knife from its sheath at his side. No one said another word. Seconds ticked by before they heard back from Max.

Tango changed direction. I repeat. Tango moved toward Building F. Away from your location. Hold position but be ready to move.

Nate and Diana moved directly behind Devon at the door and waited in silence.

Tango just entered building F. There's no other movement. It's your call.

Building F was the latrine. They needed thirty seconds to reach the safety of the dense woods, and they had to get there quietly.

Nate whispered to Diana and lowered his night-vision gear as Devon cracked the door and quickly scanned the compound. When Devon gave him the signal, Nate firmed up his grip around Diana's waist and propelled her swiftly out the door and across the clearing toward the woods. She stumbled on a tree root, but Nate's arm kept her from going down. He didn't turn around or look back. When they reached the woods, he slowed the pace to lessen the noise they would make in the underbrush. For the next twenty minutes, he led Diana toward the perimeter fence of the compound without stopping or saying a word.

Nate spotted motion on his left and quickly pulled Diana to the ground, sheltering her body with his. For several minutes, they stayed down low on the damp leaves without moving or speaking. Nate watched for other motion in the woods surrounding them; then he heard Max's voice.

McLean has your position, and he's approaching from your left. Do you copy?

Nate expelled a slow breath. "Copy that." He remained on the ground with Diana and focused his goggles to the left. Devon emerged from a dense patch of underbrush just twenty yards away. Nate got up from the ground and kept watch while Devon reached down for Diana. The two men helped her climb a steep slope and travel through a dense section of the forest. They reached the perimeter fence, and Devon belly crawled through the opening. Nate told Diana to lie flat on her stomach with her arms in front and her head to the side. He pushed hard against the broken links and Devon reached for her hands and quickly dragged her through the fence opening. While he was helping her to her feet, Nate crawled through the fence, and soon after, they stopped to let her rest.

She was winded when they sat down on a fallen tree trunk. Devon handed her a piece of hard candy from his pocket. She took it gratefully. Then he transmitted their status to Max. "We're about ten minutes from rendezvous point. Phase 2 is in Isaac's hands. Roaming tango is secured in the woods behind building F."

Diana had caught her breath and now she fought back tears. Nate got to his feet and held his hand out for her. "We're about five hundred yards from a logging road. An agent from the FBI will meet us there. You can watch what happens next from a monitor."

Diana swallowed hard and smiled weakly as she reached up to take his hand. "Good, let's keep going. I want to see Phase 2."

An hour later, the FBI team quietly infiltrated the compound. The squad rousted three men and one woman from their beds. Bobby Lee was dragged from the woods behind Building F wearing nothing but his pants around his ankles. Diana watched the monitor as they searched the group, handcuffed them, and loaded them into a van.

Diana approached Nate and Devon. "I don't know what to say."

Nate took her hand between his. "Just heal from this and let someone help."

Devon added, "You survived, Diana. It will get easier with time."

Diana saw empathy in their eyes. She turned and wiped away tears as she walked to the vehicle where a female agent waited for her.

XV

Nate and Devon walked into the room of a one-story motel near Clayton, Georgia. The motel was the type used by desperate travelers for a single night or one that locals would rent by the hour. They didn't care. After washing away grime in a shower that was too small, too low, and too short on hot water, each man crashed face down on the two beds that crowded the room.

Four hours later, Nate groped around for his ringing phone.

"Where are you?" Isaac asked.

Nate watched Devon roll in his direction on the other bed. "Where are we?"

Devon looked around the room. "Some motel near Clayton. Hang on." He fumbled around the nightstand between the beds. "It's *A Little Motel.*"

"I know it is. What's it called?"

"*A Little Motel.*" Devon held up a well-handled flyer that advertised a restaurant and a strip joint. At the top, in bold print, it read *A Little Motel* and listed a phone number.

Nate shook his head. "Get this Isaac. We're at *A Little Motel.*"

Isaac surprised him by asking for the room number.

Again, Nate turned to Devon who held a key with a plastic tag.

"Five."

"I'll be there in twenty minutes."

Nate rolled onto his back and stared up at the ceiling. "Christ, Dev, I'm tired right down to the bone."

Devon yawned and stretched as he rolled to a sitting position, "You must be getting old."

Nate laid on the bed in silence. Then he asked, "Why'd Max blow out of here so fast?"

"When he dropped us off, he told me he'd catch some sleep in his car on the way back to Washington. He's in love and wants to get home."

Nate murmured, "God help another doomed man."

Both men were up and wearing faded jeans and sweatshirts when Isaac pounded on their door. He briefed them on the latest events. The IRS was having a field day with Reverend Dodd's finances, his connection with the SSBA, and the flow of money between the two organizations. FBI agents had assumed the roles of the caretakers at the compound. Throughout the morning, several men were taken into custody and questioned. Some were detained.

Devon asked, "Were any of them connected to the senator's niece?"

Isaac nodded, "One was identified as the man who beat the companion. To cop a plea, he rolled on the others, including the man who ordered the assault and rape ... the colonel himself. But the others never appeared at the camp. Overall, it was a small turnout for the weekenders."

Then Isaac told them about his conversation with Ellie-Jean. "She became very cooperative when we charged her as an accessory to kidnapping and rape. She described the camps ... she called them retreats. They're intended to give young men spiritual and corporal guidance. Caucasian males with similar religious convictions are recruited. Those with drug, alcohol, and behavioral problems are accepted if their families belong to the church."

"That coincides with what Simmons told me."

"Ellie-Jean told me about a particular young man whose father sent him there because of gay tendencies ... he wanted to attend an art college. Everet Dodd took a *special* interest by inflicting beatings and constant abuse. After three weeks, the boy tried to hang himself."

"What happened?"

"I spoke to him an hour ago. He lives with a friend now. After he healed from the physical abuse, Manfred Dodd sent him home. He told the boy's parents their son couldn't be saved by his church and suggested an inpatient psychiatric facility."

"For the parents ... I agree. It's time to stop these men before they kill someone."

"First, we have to find them. On a different subject, thank you both for helping us with Diana Weaver. I'll give Charleston's district attorney the evidence against Simmons before his hearing. Since it came from this investigation, Nate, you'll be a very credible witness."

"Thanks, Isaac. I'll call you when I get back." Then he looked at Devon. "How are we getting back?"

Isaac smiled. "There's a minor detail the two of you can handle for me. The van from the Charleston County Correctional Facility is outside and has to be returned. Charlie's waiting in a car to take me back to Columbia. I'll be working on this case from there before I go back to Washington. Can you drive the van back to Charleston?"

They looked at each other and shrugged. Then Devon said, "Not our favorite ride, but okay." Isaac handed him the keys. "We'll see each other soon, my friends."

Nate and Devon watched the nondescript sedan pull out of the motel lot. Then they loaded their gear into the van and headed east.

Shortly after they left the motel, Devon glanced over at his brother. His head leaned against the backrest with his eyes closed. A ten-day growth of beard covered Nate's face and the bruise from Isaac's fist still circled his eye.

Devon rubbed his own three-day beard. "You've had a miserable week, big guy. I didn't mean that remark about getting old, you know?"

"Hmmm ... doesn't matter."

"I don't think I could have done it, Nate."

"Done what, Dev?"

"Sat in a cell with Simmons and listened to what he did. I don't know where you get the restraint. Holding back like that takes its toll."

"I had no choice. If I touched the bastard, I'd be the one going to prison."

Devon spotted a sign for a small restaurant two miles ahead. "You want to stop, get coffee, something to eat?"

"Yeah. I would."

A middle-aged waitress greeted them when they walked into the small eatery. It had four stools at a counter and six tables off to the side. The place wasn't fancy, but the aroma of coffee permeated the air and fresh-looking pies sat on tall chrome stands with plastic domes. They asked for two cups of coffee as they moved to a table in the corner of the room. Since it was between breakfast and lunch, there were no other customers. By habit, both men chose seats with their backs to the wall and a full view of their territory.

The waitress came over with their coffee. "I'm Maggie. The cook won't be back for another half-hour, but I can fix you sandwiches if you're hungry."

Devon responded, "Hi, Maggie. How's the ham?"

"Real good. It's country style."

"I'll have ham and cheese on rye with mustard."

Nate picked up his coffee. "You can double that."

While waiting for their sandwiches, they heard tires spit gravel as a pickup truck with a crew cab pulled into the parking lot. Nate and Devon watched through the window as four large, overweight men in hunting gear got out of the truck. Two of them showed great interest in the South Carolina van parked in front, while two others took a leak at the edge of the parking lot. The men moved around the van, murmuring to each other for several minutes.

"All four together wouldn't make the sharpest pencil in the cup," Devon commented.

"Is it hunting season?" Nate asked.

"Small game only."

"Who would wander around the woods while guys like that carry loaded guns?"

Dev shrugged. "Ask the vice president."

Nate laughed aloud.

They watched as the hunters came through the door and looked at them. One said, "You two belong to that van outside?"

Devon remembered the printing on the side of the van: *Charleston County Department of Corrections*. He responded, "Why? You lookin' for your momma?"

Nate rolled his eyes and Devon muttered his regret. They looked at each other and drew the same conclusion … both of them looked like felons on the run.

Dev murmured to Nate, "You carrying?"

"He shook his head. You?"

"Who'd have thought?"

Nate spoke to the hunters. "Just passing through."

Another hunter replied, "Looks like you're running from the law."

Devon responded, "Sure, pal, that's why we're driving around in a paddy wagon." The absurdity was lost on the group. Nate rolled his eyes again.

The hunter looked at his friends. "I'll bet there's a good size reward for these two!"

Nate started to reply, but stopped in mid-sentence when one of the men pulled out a hunting knife. The other three followed his lead. Devon jumped up and grabbed his chair. Nate sprang to his feet as Devon raised the chair and struck Nate in the head. Blood dripped from the gash as he flipped over the table in front of them. Devon crashed the chair across the edge of the table and it broke apart. He tossed one of the wooden legs to Nate and gripped the second leg in his right hand. The four hunters moved toward them and Maggie ran to the kitchen.

Even with their knives, the four hunters were no match for the two men who had been highly trained in hand-to-hand combat. When the first man lunged, Devon planted his left foot and kicked high with his right, landing a solid blow to the man's chest. The impact shoved the hunter into a nearby table and he lost the grip on his knife. Meanwhile, Nate shoved an attacker back with his stick and pounded his fist into the face of another. Then he cracked the stunned man over the head with the stick and saw him topple. Nate and Devon moved away from the debris and the two fallen hunters keeping their backs to the wall and their sticks poised. The remaining two assailants rushed at them with their knives. The two Navy SEALs responded in unison. They each planted their left foot and kicked out with their right, landing a boot solidly in their opponent's groin. When the men doubled over, they cracked them on the head with the chair legs. The altercation was over in a few short minutes.

Nate grabbed a paper napkin from its holder and used it to wipe blood from his eye. He looked down at the remnants of the wooden chair. "Christ, Dev, you almost put my eye out with that thing."

Devon looked down at the mangled piece of furniture. "Sorry about that, big guy." He saw Nate gripping his side with his other hand. "What happened to your side there?"

"I'm okay; it's just a bad scratch." Nate looked at the blood on Devon's arm. "It looks like someone got a piece of you."

Devon glanced at his torn sleeve. "Damn it. I've had this sweatshirt for fifteen years and it's one of my favorites." He heard distant sirens and saw Nate's phone on the floor. He reached down then handed it to him. "We'd better call Isaac."

Nate made the call while Devon walked to the kitchen. Maggie was gone, but he saw their two sandwiches on a cutting board. He tossed money on the butcher block, then carried the food to the counter and overheard Nate. "Isaac, we've got ourselves a little problem just outside Clayton, Georgia."

XVI

Joe Reynolds heard Nate enter the waiting room and closed the case folder he had been studying. Nate appeared in the open doorway carrying a delicatessen bag. He held it up. "Thought we'd try something different. I got some coffee."

"Sounds good. Come in, Nate."

"I hope you got my message last week, Joe. Sorry I had to cancel on such short notice, but it was unavoidable."

"No problem. Your message said something very important had come up."

Nate handed Joe a cup of coffee and leaned on the corner of the desk. Joe looked closely at Nate's face. He had stitches above his left brow.

"Should I bother to ask?"

"I was hit by a hard object."

"Can you talk about the reason you had to cancel last week?"

Nate shook his head. "I'm involved in an ongoing case. I know we have doctor-patient privilege, but the less said the better. I can tell you that I spent time in the field and didn't suffer any major setbacks."

"Were you out of the country?"

"No. I was pretty close to home."

The two men sat in their same chairs. Joe sipped his hot coffee. "This is good. Thanks." Nate nodded and Joe looked down at his notes. "I'd like to veer off a little today. Do you mind if we discuss your mother's death?"

He shrugged. "I'm not sure what there is to discuss. The doctors diagnosed her with ovarian cancer; she died six months later. I loved her very much and still miss her in my life."

Joe picked up the hint of emotion in Nate's voice. He waited for a moment. "How did you react when she died?"

"We grieved but had to keep living. A week after she died, Dad went back to work and Olivia and I went to school."

"I'm hearing an adult describe the experience. How did the fifteen-year-old boy to cope with his mother's death?"

Nate better understood the question. "I remember waking up in the middle of the night crying. I guess it was harder for Olivia. She acted out in school, got snotty with her teacher. Out of sympathy, the teacher let her get away with it, and it got worse. Her best friend told her mother, and my Dad got a phone call. He took her to a grief counselor. He wanted me to go too."

"Did you?"

Nate smiled. "Joe, I was a fifteen-year-old sophomore in high school. Have you ever tried to tell a teenager anything?"

"You can't. They already have all the answers."

"That's exactly right. If I got into fights or bucked authority figures, my father wouldn't have given me a choice. He'd have hauled my ass into an office similar to yours. But I didn't. I minded my own business and kept my grades up. I skipped basketball tryouts that year. I told my father my grades were more important. He had his hands full with my sister, and he was dealing with his own grief, so he didn't press the point."

"Were you a loner at that age?"

"No. I never thought of myself that way. I played sports, had friends, hung out." He thought. "I guess I became withdrawn after Mom died. If you're asking me to narrow in on a behavioral change, that's as close as I could come. My friends became awkward around me; they weren't sure what to say. A few girls told me they were sorry, but the opposite sex scared me back then. I just didn't talk about it until I met Devon."

Joe smiled. "At fifteen, I'd look at a girl and think of nothing but breasts. Then I worried about burning in hell for eternity."

"Catholic school?"

"You got it—impure thoughts, sin, guilt, the whole nine yards. Elvis was the Antichrist. If we were lucky enough to avoid hell, we would still spend years trying to dodge the flames in purgatory. Although the doctrine is less severe now, there's twelve years of it stuffed into the recesses of my brain."

"My mother was raised Catholic, but she never forced religion on us. My parents taught us strong morals and didn't hesitant to reprimand us when they found ours lacking. We were held accountable for our actions but never threatened with reprisals from God."

"Doesn't sound like you're waiting for a lightning bolt to strike you down for the things you've done as a solider."

"No. I'm not. As far as damnation is concerned, I've been to hell and back more than once. I don't plan to live there in this life or any other."

Joe made notes while Nate drank his coffee. "When did you meet Devon?"

Nate thought for a moment. "Devon came to our school the winter after Mom died. I met him at a basketball game. I heard that he had moved to Beaufort to live with relatives after his parents died in a car accident. That night at the game, I sat next to him in the bleachers. I introduced myself and just said it. I told him I was sorry about his parents. We became tight after that, talked about our families. One day, Devon told me his sister, Kelly, died along with his parents. I felt like someone had bricked me. Even the rumor mill had missed that."

"Sounds like you were good for each other."

"We were. He hung out at my house a lot. Dad and Liv both liked him. He moved in with us by the end of the school year."

"How did that come about?"

"His uncle was an alcoholic and an abuser. He went crazy one night and beat the living hell out of Devon. My father intervened and became his legal guardian."

"The more I learn about your father, the more I respect him."

"He's always been an anchor for me. Where are we going with all this, Joe?"

"I think we've eliminated religious beliefs as a factor contributing to your disorder."

"You'll get no argument from me."

"I did learn quite a bit about how you deal with emotional stress. You internalize it. There's nothing wrong with that—many people do. When your mother died, you withdrew. Your friends couldn't relate to your pain and you didn't want to make things worse for your father or your sister, so you clammed up until Devon showed up. When you reached out to help him, you helped yourself heal in the process."

Nate thought about the analysis. "You're saying that I should open up more. It's not in my nature to do that, especially about the last fifteen years of my life."

"You don't have to focus on the gore, Nate. Just try trusting people to understand what's going on inside you."

"I'll think about it."

The following Saturday, Nate met Devon at the Charleston Airport and they headed south. An hour later, the Porsche rounded the corner of Craven Street.

Eve and John sat on the front porch when Nate's car pulled up in front of his father's house.

She looked at John. "Did you know about this?"

"No, sweetheart, I didn't. But I'm always glad to see them." Rufus pulled himself up from his afternoon nap and stood wagging his tail while Nate and Devon got out of the car.

Eve remained seated on the porch while John greeted his sons. He stepped back and looked at them closely. Nate had stitches above his eyebrow and Devon's arm had a fresh-looking cut just below his bicep. "The two of you found trouble somewhere. What happened to your head, Nate?"

Nate's eyes met Eve's as he answered. "Dev hit me with a chair."

"That's the truth," Devon laughed. "I swear it was an accident."

John smiled. "What makes me think there's more to this story? Stay for dinner. We're having pot roast at seven and there's plenty."

Devon replied, "We missed your birthday last week, so we thought we'd surprise you and take you to dinner. But who can say no to a Dunlevy pot roast?" He approached Eve when she stood up to greet him. He wrapped his arms around her and whispered, "I'm so sorry about what happened." When he stepped back, Eve saw emotion in his eyes … it was more than just sympathy. He turned to his father and gave his shoulder a quick squeeze. "I could use a beer. How about you?" John nodded and the two of them walked into the house.

Nate approached Eve. He lifted her hand and held it. "I'm very glad to see you, but I had no idea you'd be here. I thought you and Katie were in Ireland."

Eve gave him a cautious smile and pulled her hand from his. "We got back three days ago." She wrapped her arms around her body as though trying to hold something tightly inside. "I've had some difficult moments thinking about you, Nate."

He braced himself for another round of rejection. Then she said, "I owe you an apology and gratitude that's long overdue."

Anxiety drained from his body. "You don't owe me anything, Eve." He needed to touch her and allowed his fingers to stoke her cheek lightly. To his relief, she didn't flinch. He studied her face and smiled. "Your bruises are gone." He fought the need to embrace her. "Where's Katie?"

"She's in Jacksonville. A friend invited her to a symphony." Eve laughed quietly and shook her head. "She was hesitant to go. I told her it was time for a separation or we'd soon be joined at the hip."

Nate smiled, "She was there for you and helped."

"Yes, I know. The trip to Ireland was good for both of us … me especially. My mother cuts right to the bone and puts life into perspective. I'm done being a victim, Nate."

They stood in silence for several seconds before he reached for her hand. "Will you take a ride with me before dinner? We won't go far, I promise."

Nate headed south on the Sea Island Parkway. When they reached Hunting Island State Park, Nate pulled the Porsche off the highway and followed a dirt road into a forested area. He turned to Eve.

"Let's walk."

They followed a path through the trees and came to a beach where the St. Helena Sound and Atlantic Ocean meet. Nate guided Eve to a large, twisted oak branch that hung over the sand and they leaned against it.

"I came here all the time when I was young." He pointed toward a distant trawler; it dragged its long nets as it harvested shrimp from the cooling waters. "I dreamed of owning my own shrimp boat—just me and Lieutenant Dan plying the local waters, riding out hurricanes, pulling in huge catches of fresh shrimp."

Eve smiled as she watched the trawler and thought of a young man's innocent dreams.

"Then I started coming here with Susie McNeil and stopped thinking about shrimp." He grinned. "We came here a lot and taught each other about sex."

"What was she like?"

"She was pretty and sweet and funny, and she had a heart of gold. Her hair was dark and curly and she had freckles across her nose."

"Did you love her?"

Nate thought for a moment. "I did."

"What happened to you and Susie?"

"I went into the Marine Corps and she went to USC. We wrote and saw each other when we could, but we grew apart. Last I heard she married a prominent realtor on Hilton Head Island."

"Do you regret losing her?"

He shook his head slowly. "She was very special to me at that age, but I can't see myself with her now."

"Were you ever in love with anyone else?"

"Isn't it my turn to ask questions?"

Eve shrugged. "What do you want to know?"

"For starters …" He turned toward her, put his hand behind her neck, and moved his mouth over hers. The kiss was warm and gentle, he let it linger and hoped he hadn't imagined her response. He stopped when he saw tears well up in her eyes.

"I'm sorry, Eve."

She quickly brushed away the tears. "It's not what you're thinking, Nate. I care about you, but that scares me. Maybe that's why I treated you so badly when you just tried to help. It's no excuse, and I'm sorry."

"I said it before—no apology is necessary. But if I accept, can we put it behind us?"

Eve nodded. "I've been to a few sessions with a counselor. I know that Wade Simmons is the only person responsible for what happened to me. I've even stopped blaming myself."

"That's important, Eve. We can't pretend it never happened. I have nasty stuff churning inside me, too. We'll deal with it. I'm willing to go slowly, but I won't stand still anymore. I'm in love with you."

She shook her head and held up both hands. "I'm not ready to accept those feelings, Nate. I don't know if I can reciprocate them."

"I'm not asking for guarantees."

"I can't think about the future until this ordeal is behind me. Right now, I'm too angry to give you what you need … what you deserve from me."

Nate drew her into his arms and held her. "We'll get through this together." He felt her shiver. "We should head back."

XVII

When they returned to the house on Craven, the table was set and the pot roast rested on the cutting board. Eve apologized for not being there to help, but Devon stopped her. "I've put dishes and things on that table for many years. I do a darn good job of it!"

The men worked easily together in the kitchen. John sliced the roast, Nate made the gravy, and Devon arranged the beef, potatoes, carrots, and onions on a large serving platter. Rufus had positioned himself silently next to Devon, his tongue lolling and his eyes pleading.

Eve watched their progress. "The three of you know what you're doing."

Nate looked up at her. "When Mom got sick, we learned to cook or we got hungry; cooking was better."

John interjected, "It was part of my survival tactic; everyone took turns with meals, cleaning, and laundry."

"Yeah, when they took me in, it was a real hardship," Devon kidded.

Within minutes, they sat at the dining room table with a wholesome meal and a decanter of red wine. Eve looked at the stitches in Nate's forehead. Remembering Devon's words, she asked, "How do you hit someone with a chair by accident?"

Her question earned a chuckle from John. "Just spend more time around them."

Nate and Devon grinned at each other.

"Tell them what happened at that diner, Dev. You provoked the fight."

"I guess I did." After sipping some wine, he began, "We left Clayton, Georgia in this van ..." His abbreviated story made the four hunters sound like dim-witted cousins of the Three Stooges. Nate admired his brother's ability to describe the episode as a comic book adventure.

Eve was amused when she asked, "Did they arrest you?"

"Briefly."

She thought for a moment. "Why were you in a van from the Correctional Facility?"

Nate replied, "We had a job. I'll explain it after dinner. Enough about Dev and me." He poured her some more wine. "Tell us about your trip. Why did your parents move to Ireland?"

"My mother inherited a small house there."

"Are they retired?"

"Yes and no. Dad uses the Internet to manage their investments and they travel throughout the United Kingdom. Mom writes travelogues that include short stories."

"Are they happy living there?"

She nodded. "I've never seen them happier."

Devon asked, "What kind of stories does she write?"

"Mostly fiction based on Celtic history or folklore. Did you know, Devon, that you've got both Celtic and Norse blood?"

"If you say so, darling, but how do you know?"

"You have subtle red tones in your hair. I'll bet your beard is redder when it grows."

"It is. What does that tell you?"

"Most people think red hair is an Irish characteristic, but the trait came from the Norse. They invaded Ireland in the eighth century, stayed around, and interbred with a lot of Celts."

Nate glanced at Devon. "That explains your barbaric nature."

"Maybe so. That part about breeding explains a lot, too."

Eve smiled and tapped Nate's hand. "Don't be too smug there, Braveheart. The Dunlevy's were Scots ... they have their own brutal history."

"How do you know so much about our ancestry?"

"My mother showed me her research and I've read Edward Rutherford's *Princes of Ireland*. Did you know ancient Celtic warriors went into battle wearing nothing more than body paint?"

Nate raised his eyebrows. "That sounds pretty damn risky to me. I'm surprised the bloodline survived the practice."

Devon stabbed a potato. "Sounds like those who kept their parts had their work cut out. Still do."

Eve laughed aloud and Nate enjoyed the sound of it.

Suddenly, her expression sobered and her eyes welled up. Devon reached out and covered her hand with his. "Did I say something to upset you?"

She shook her head and quickly wiped a tear. "No, Devon. You made me laugh. It felt good." She couldn't dismiss their concern. "My parents wanted to come back when I told them what happened to me. The thought of them sitting in a courtroom and listening to the details horrifies me. I told them they'd upset me more by being here and made them promise not to come for the hearing. But if it goes to trial, they'll come."

When dinner was over, Nate told Eve he wanted to answer her question about the Charleston County van. He held a chair for her at the kitchen table and asked his father to join them. Devon poured the coffee as Nate began, "The week before last, I spent three days in the Charleston County Correctional Facility."

Eve remembered his threats to kill Wade Simmons. "Why? Were you arrested for a crime?"

"No ... technically I wasn't arrested. The FBI set up my stint there." He paused. "What I'm going to tell you cannot be repeated. Okay?"

She nodded and waited for him to go on.

"I'm involved with a case ... one that involves a group of racists, including Wade Simmons. The FBI wired me to collect information." He saw her confusion. "Eve, I spent three days in a cell with him."

Her eyes grew wide. "With Wade Simmons?"

He nodded.

Her voice shook. "I'm having a very difficult time with this."

"I know, sweetheart, but hear me out. The information I got helped the FBI. Last week they raided a compound and arrested several people for crimes against women, minorities, and gay men."

"What kind of crimes?"

"Assault, rape, sodomy, even kidnapping."

Eve looked incredulous. "You're serious, aren't you?" She looked at Devon. "Were you involved, too?"

Devon nodded. "The information Nate got from Simmons helped the FBI find a young woman who'd been missing for days. She was held at their compound. We got her out and four men were arrested for kidnapping and rape. Later that day, the FBI detained others for questioning. Some are still in custody."

She looked dumbstruck and Nate reached for her hand. "Eve, listen to this next part very carefully." He waited for her to focus on him. "Wade Simmons told me what triggered his attack on you." Eve's mind spun in several directions as she waited for him to continue. "The night we had dinner, we were seen together by a friend of his. Simmons just heard that you were with another man; he didn't know it was me." He paused. "When my arrest was processed, I was Buck Walters, an ignorant man charged with beating and raping his girlfriend. Wade Simmons told me about hurting you and Katie. He described raping you. I recorded everything he said to me."

Her cup slipped, coffee spilled over the rim, and her hand shook when she put the cup down.

John rested his hand on hers. "Eve, this is very solid evidence. The FBI conducted an official investigation of an organization; he was a member. No one coerced a confession from him. If the FBI submits this evidence and Nate testifies, Harold Spencer will have a very difficult time getting an acquittal. The case may not even go to trial."

Eve heard only half his words.

Nate felt anxiety build as he struggled to control where his mind took him. He pictured the small cell and the smug look on Wade Simmons's face. He suppressed the overwhelming urge to kill him and choked down the bile rising in his throat.

Devon saw the sweat beading on his brother's forehead. Before he could intervene, Eve exclaimed, "How could you do it?"

Nate shook his head to clear his mind. "Do what? Let the bastard live?"

"How did you sit in a jail cell and listen to him describe what he did to me?"

Nate reared up from his chair so quickly it toppled backward against the wall and he rushed through the back door.

John found him bent near a large shrub, his arms bracing against his knees, his stomach emptying itself. "Are you okay, son?"

He nodded and took the handkerchief his father offered. After a final bout of heaving, he used the garden hose to clean his mouth and the yard. "I worked hard not to do that when he described what he did to her. Guess I just postponed it."

From the doorway, Eve watched Nate then she covered her face with her hands. Devon wrapped his arms around her and drew her against him. "Come on now, darling, what just happened out there isn't your fault." Eve pushed her face into his shoulder and tried to suppress a sob. He led her from the door and kept his arm around her while he poured brandy and handed it to her. "Sip on this. He'll hate that he made you cry."

"It *is* my fault. I've treated him badly ever since that night." She looked up at Devon. "I imagined Wade Simmons bragging to Nate and just lost it. Do you understand?"

"I do. It's hard on both of you. Nate's been dealing with all sorts of crap lately. He's trying to handle it all, and he's doing a better job than I would. I'd probably be on trial for murder right now."

"Devon, you saw something happen to him that I missed. But I've seen it other times. What's wrong?" Before he could respond, Nate came back inside. Eve turned to him and fought back new tears. "I'm so sorry, Nate, about my reaction ... what I said ... how I said it."

He muttered an obscenity. "Come here, Eve." Without waiting for her to move, he crossed the floor and pulled her into his arms. He felt her sob against his chest and silently cursed himself again. John came inside and walked down the hall to his office. Devon followed.

Nate held Eve closely and rocked their bodies slowly. He waited until she calmed. "We're going to have a long talk ... just us two ... tonight. We need to clear the air before the hearing. Okay?"

Eve nodded. "I want to hear the recording. I want to hear him say what he did to me."

Nate had anticipated this. She watched him shake his head. "I don't have the recording, Eve. It belongs to the FBI." He had lied. Nate would never give up a copy of that testimony, but he didn't want Eve to hear it tonight, and neither did he.

Devon stood in front of John's desk and flipped through a file. He saw a photo of Eve taken at MUSC and felt repulsed. "The bastard did a number on her." John nodded. Then Devon came across a picture of Katie showing her injuries.

John glanced at the photo. "I know exactly how Nate felt when he lost his dinner tonight." John took the file and stored it in his briefcase along with the notes he had just written on a legal pad.

Nate spotted Devon coming out of his father's office. "I'm driving back to Charleston with Eve tonight. Can you take the Porsche?"

"Sure."

XVIII

During the drive back to Charleston, Nate spotted movement near the road ahead and braked hard. A white-tailed doe bounded across the highway a hundred yards in front of their car. He kept his speed slow and checked his rearview mirror for headlights. It was rutting season, and when a doe is spotted, a buck is probably nearby. A second later, a large buck lunged from the woods and stood on the side of the road. Anticipating the animal's next move, Nate brought the car to a stop.

He spoke aloud as though the deer could hear him. "That's a handsome rack. Hope you survive hunting season." The stag took one magnificent lunge to cross the paved road and another to disappear into the woods.

"Do you hunt, Nate?"

"Not animals."

Eve thought about his remark as he pressed down on the accelerator. He glanced at her. "I don't hunt or kill for pleasure; it's not a thrill for me."

After a moment, Eve interrupted their silence. "Last year, I did a painting for a client who has a lovely home overlooking a marsh. She asked me to put deer in the landscape and showed me old photos of them wandering through her yard. Although she cherished the animals, others considered them a nuisance. Hunting was prohibited on the resort island, so wildlife management experts were hired to reduce the herd."

"How?"

She shuddered. "Marksmen set up blinds and baited the deer. When enough gathered, they shot them."

"That's slaughter." Images of mass graves flashed through his mind and Nate forced his mind to focus on the road and Eve's voice.

"Here's the irony, Nate. We stood in this woman's yard while landscapers worked next door. They used gasoline-powered mowers and blowers and whackers and trimmers. I couldn't hear myself think. The deer would have pruned those shrubs quietly and for free."

He reached out and took her hand, but couldn't find any words.

When they entered Eve's home on Sullivan's Island, the phone rang. "That's probably Katie. She insisted on calling me tonight. If I don't pick up, she'll worry." Eve answered the phone and Nate listened. He could tell that Katie questioned Eve about her well-being and about his presence. They went back and forth for a few minutes. Then Eve ended the call.

"Katie says hello."

Eve walked to the refrigerator. "Would you like something to drink?"

He peered over her shoulder. "I'll have a beer." She handed him a bottle and got a soft drink for herself.

"Katie's spending the night in Jacksonville. I planned to be alone tonight ... the first time since the attack." After a pause, she added, "I can verbalize that I was attacked. I guess that's a good sign." When Nate took a glass from a cabinet and handed it to her, she remembered the time he had spent in her home.

They walked into the living room and sat on the sofa. "Eve, I need to tell you more about me ... I'm afraid you won't like most of what you hear."

She held up a hand to interrupt him. "Earlier tonight, I never meant to judge you."

"Don't be too quick with your absolution."

She stopped him again. "If your work puts you in jail, then I don't like your job."

"Actually, jail isn't so bad compared to some places I've been." Eve waited for him to continue. "I became a soldier because I felt it was an important duty. I've killed people who were threats to our country. And I've seen others die: innocent men, young soldiers, women, and children. After twelve years, I wanted a break from war and the Middle East. I told the admiral I wouldn't re-enlist."

"What did you do?"

"My experience, rank, and degree caught the CIA's interest, so I interviewed with them. But I hate politics, platitudes, and deal making. I can't see myself in Washington DC with a long-term career there."

"I thought you and Devon enlisted after high school. When did you attend college?"

"Dad made us attend USC, Beaufort and get associate degrees before we joined the Corps. Although we argued at the time, he stood firm. After our first tour of duty, Dev and I got undergraduate degrees while we served, otherwise, we wouldn't have earned our rank."

"Your father gives very good advice."

"Yes, he does. Devon earned his MBA last year. I speak Spanish and we both know a little Arabic. My graduate degree is in National Security. But neither one of us knows how to lead a quiet civilian life."

"What do you do?"

"Before my enlistment was up, the admiral suggested an opportunity. Officially, I'm no longer active duty. What the record doesn't show is reserve status. Although I'm involved in my own business, the government *employs* me to solve problems."

"I don't understand this business you're describing."

"Dev, Max, and I started a company called DMG, Inc. Our partner, Max, was also a SEAL and has degrees in electrical engineering and computer sciences. The three of us blended our skills to consult on security matters; many of our clients are wealthy people in private industry. But the government hires us for special projects. We go to places where we aren't welcome and they pretend we aren't there."

"You're spies?"

"Not always." He hesitated. "Sometimes, we're paid to kill people."

"Oh."

"During our last *project,* I was injured and I'm still healing … mentally. I get flashbacks like the one you saw in my kitchen several weeks ago."

"What happened, Nate?"

"I shot a young boy."

"How young?"

"Not even twelve years old by my guess. We destroyed a terrorist camp. It housed several trainers who brainwashed naïve young men to commit suicide for a cause that no sane person understands. While we drove through the desert, this child appeared from the brush and ran toward our vehicles. I could tell he had explosives stuffed under his shirt. He reached for the cord and I shot him in the head as he pulled it. I saw his expression through my scope as I squeezed the trigger. He feared his death but felt powerless to stop it. His face still haunts me."

"What happened after you shot him?"

"He blew up in front of me. The explosion knocked me out and Devon pulled me away from the rubble. I spent time in a field hospital and Bethesda. The docs gave me a clean bill of health ... physically. The mental symptoms started later. Right now, I'm seeing a doctor in Charleston. I've got post-traumatic stress disorder."

"You're very lucky to be sitting here, Nate. I feel awful about that child and all the other victims of this horrible war, but you didn't pull that cord."

"Our timing has not been good, Eve."

They sat in silence for a long time. Nate put his beer on the table and turned to Eve. "I lied to you earlier."

"What about?"

"The recording, the one from Wade Simmons. I'd never give up a copy until we're over this. I just didn't want us to deal with it tonight."

She remembered listening to him heave up his dinner in the backyard. "It's okay."

Eve put her glass on the coffee table, leaned back against the sofa, and closed her eyes. "You've given me a lot of information, Nate, more than I could imagine."

"Are you ready to throw my ass out of here?"

"No, but my brain is in overload." She opened her eyes and looked over at him. He had also leaned back and closed his eyes. And his face reflected the stress bottled up inside him. He needed someone to understand him and accept him. So far, she'd been too self-absorbed.

Eve took his hand. "Let's get some sleep ... we're both exhausted." At the top of the staircase, she turned to him. "I'm not ready to share my bed."

"I'm not ready for it either. If I climb in with you, I'll want to touch you. The thought of hurting you terrifies me. I'm well acquainted with the guest room." He gave her a chaste good-night kiss and walked down the hall.

The next morning Nate yanked back the shower curtain and saw her standing in the doorway. She quickly scanned his body. "You've lost weight, and there's a fresh scar on your side."

He shook the water from his eyes and reached for a towel. "The O'Connor's must have a voyeuristic streak."

She smiled. "It was a test."

He looked down at his body. "Did I pass or fail?"

"Oh, you passed just fine. But it was my test." She saw the puzzled look on his face as he began toweling himself dry. "I came upstairs and saw your door open. Then I heard the shower. It made me wonder how I'd react when I saw your body. I passed too. It doesn't frighten me. It stirs other feelings, though, good ones."

Nate wrapped the towel around his waist. He reached for Eve and pulled her gently toward him. They were separated by his loosely wrapped towel and her snug jeans. He kissed her lightly on the lips and felt her respond before he eased his hold on her. "Are we ready for finals?"

Eve shook her head. "Not just yet. I need to take this one step at a time."

He lifted her chin so their eyes met. "Take as many steps and as much time as you need. I'm not going anywhere." Then he sniffed the air. "Do I smell bacon?"

She nodded. "There's fresh coffee, and I'm making a Sunday brunch. I came upstairs to tell you." She kissed him softly on the mouth. "I've got to turn the bacon." She kissed him on the mouth again. "You're a good man."

XIX

Tall steeples spear the skyline and pealing bells announce services throughout Charleston. The architecture reflects the city's long-standing reputation for religious diversity and tolerance dating back to the 1600s. Historic buildings represent the various congregations who worship within ... cathedral, church, temple, or mosque. In Iraq, several innocent civilians and two United States soldiers had died when a religious sect triggered a bomb outside a mosque. Sweat beaded on Nate's forehead as he stared into the face of terrified young boy. Then he turned off the news channel covering the carnage and forced the scene from his mind.

While Eve cracked eggs into a bowl, Nate poured a second cup of coffee and offered to help. She refused. "It's my turn to do something nice for you. Just sit and relax."

Nate tried to focus on something other than the news from Iraq. When his cell phone rang, he looked at the display and welcomed the distraction. "What's up, Dev?"

"Am I interrupting?"

"Eve's fixing breakfast and I'm trying to stay out of her way. Where are you?" He listened to Devon then saw Eve signaling him. "Hang on. Eve's trying to tell me something."

"Tell him to stop by for brunch. I have more than the two of us will eat."

Nate spoke into the phone. "Eve wants to feed you. I told her she'd be sorry." He laughed as he disconnected the call. He moved behind Eve and wrapped his arm around her waist. "I've got to warn you about my brother. If you start feeding him, he won't go away." As he nuzzled her neck, Bootsie jumped from a chair beneath the kitchen table and twined herself through their legs. "It looks like we've got two beggars on our hands today." Eve smiled and beat the eggs.

During breakfast, Eve watched Nate consume almost as much as Devon. Their appetites were contagious, and even she ate more than usual. Afterward, Nate and Eve cleaned up while Devon made a pitcher of Bloody Marys.

They had moved to the back porch with their drinks when the front door opened and slammed shut. Katie's voice echoed throughout the house. "All men are pigs!"

Katie walked to the back porch and saw Devon. "Oops, I didn't know we had company."

Devon wasn't prepared for the woman who entered the room. Her thick, wavy auburn hair fell to the top of her shoulders. A jade leather skirt stopped midway down slim, firm thighs, revealing an extraordinary pair of legs. The colorful knit top clung seductively to her body and scooped low enough to show a hint of healthy cleavage.

"Katie, this is Devon McLean, Nate's brother."

"Hi."

Devon nodded and returned the brief greeting.

Katie looked at Nate and Eve sitting together on the sofa. Bootsie had curled up in Nate's lap and was purring loudly as Nate gently scratched behind the feline's ear. "You're the exception to the pig rule, Nate. What happened to your head?"

Before he could respond, Devon said, "I hit him with a chair." He stared at her and watched the gold flecks in her green eyes flash with her temperament.

"Why'd you do that?"

"Because I'm a man, so I must be a pig."

Nate told her not to worry about his head and just tell them what had her so fired up.

She sat in a chair next to her sister and put her head in her hands. Eve leaned forward on the sofa. "Are you okay?"

"I will be. I just need to get this off my chest." She looked up and saw Devon divert his eyes. "That's a figure of speech, so stop gawking at mine."

"If you don't want it noticed, you shouldn't display it so nicely."

"Do you have a problem with my shirt?"

"I've no problem with that shirt at all, darling." His grin added to the fury building inside her.

"I'm not your darling, buckaroo." She turned to Nate. "Are those Bloody Marys?"

"They are. I'll get you one, and then you'll tell us why you're so upset." He got a glass and ice from the kitchen then poured her a drink.

Katie took a sip and nodded. "That's a good Bloody Mary."

"Devon made them."

She turned to him. "Well, we know you're good for something."

Devon replied. "I guess raw beauty has its price. A good disposition paid for yours."

His words provoked her. "Have you ever woken up with someone and found out it was a huge mistake, one that would haunt you?"

"I've gone to bed with women that looked like goddesses. The next morning they were just women—few of them were goddesses. Are you having next-day regrets over some coyote ugly stranger who bounced you around the mattress last night?"

"Listen up, hotshot. He wasn't ugly and I don't sleep with strangers."

She turned to her sister. "You remember Rob Thornton."

Eve nodded. "You were close to him in college, but broke up before you graduated."

"Different story, different lifetime, but he's the one. He lives in Boston now. The Jacksonville Symphony performed *Peer Gynt* this weekend and they invited him as a guest percussionist."

"I'm glad his career is going so well."

"At the time, so was I. *Gynt* was one of our favorites. He sent me a box seat ticket. We've exchanged e-mails about our careers, but I haven't seen him in two years. Yesterday, I thought we'd renewed our relationship. Picture us sightseeing along the river, me watching him perform with the symphony, then having late-night cocktails and dinner together." She shook her head. "I enjoyed being with him and I invited him to my room. God was I stupid!"

Devon didn't hold back. "You look more like a siren than a schoolmarm. But I guess the man was an animal and dragged you into bed. Or did he club you first?"

Nate glanced at his brother. "Enough."

Devon nodded. "That was out of line."

The apology came too late. His words caused Katie's temper to boil. "I got there all by myself, Alley Oop! And, yes, we made love! Don't tell me about cavemen. I'm looking at one, aren't I?"

The animosity that flowed between their siblings surprised both Eve and Nate.

Eve reached for her sister's hand. "What went wrong?"

Katie shook her head and looked down at the floor. "We ordered room service this morning. Rob insisted on paying. When the waiter arrived, he was in the bathroom shaving. He asked me to get money from his wallet. As soon as I opened it, I found the picture of a young woman and a cute little boy. I paid the waiter and left the wallet open on the table. At first, I tried to fool myself and deny the obvious, but Rob doesn't have a sister. My gut told me the truth."

Devon muttered, "Bastard!"

"You figured it out, didn't you? Do you believe he had his own condoms? He came out of the bath and saw the photo. Then he put on this shocked look. He must have thought I was an idiot ... *he wanted me to find it*! When he admitted it was his wife and six-month-old son, I threw a plate of Eggs Benedict at him, told him to get dressed, and get out." She looked at her sister. "I swear I didn't know he had a wife, much less a son."

Eve tried to soothe her. "I know you, Katie. You'd never do anything that would hurt someone's family. I pity his wife."

Devon added, "I pity his kid."

"Oh God, I'm pond scum!" Her eyes filled up as she got up from her chair. Nate grabbed her hand before she could walk away. "Don't blame yourself. He lied, and it sounds like he makes a habit of doing it."

"I know, but I should have known not to trust him. When am I going to learn?"

Katie left the room and Eve turned to Nate. "He hurt her. Katie doesn't treat sex casually. Before they split up, he asked her to marry him so she wouldn't accept the grant from UCLA. She knew they weren't ready for marriage; otherwise, Katie would be the unsuspecting wife."

Devon regretted his remarks. "She was smart not to let the asshole run her life years ago. Tell her that I'm sorry about the cracks I made. I'll bet the wife knows; they usually do." He walked to the sink, where he washed his glass.

Eve and Nate followed him to the kitchen. "Are you headed back to Charleston, Dev?"

"That's my plan. Do you need your car?"

"Not right now. Before you leave, remove these stitches for me. I tried to do it myself, but I kept blinking and almost poked my eye out. I don't want to show up in court looking as though I just walked away from a barroom brawl."

"It wasn't a barroom and barely a brawl. But the next time I feel the need to bust up furniture, I'll tell you to duck." Devon turned to Eve. "Have you got tweezers?"

"You're serious, aren't you?"

Both men nodded and Nate asked, "Do you have those small scissors, the kind ladies use to trim around their nails?"

"I do. What else to you need?"

Devon replied, "Do you have bourbon or rubbing alcohol?"

"I've got both."

"We'll use both."

When Eve left the room, he asked, "How's she doing?"

"Better."

"Did you tell her about our work?"

"Yes."

"The flashbacks?"

"Yes."

Devon shrugged. "You're still here."

Eve showed up with a cuticle scissors, tweezers, rubbing alcohol, and a bottle of Jack Daniels. Nate held the tools over the sink and splashed alcohol on them. Devon looked at the black label on the bourbon. "Good stuff."

Eve asked, "Is that for Nate?"

"Hell no. This is for me." He opened the bottle, poured a shot into a glass and tossed it back. Then he turned and winked at Eve. "See my hands? Steady as a rock." She looked down at his shaky hands and laughed.

Tired of waiting, Nate leaned against the counter. "Just take out the stitches, Dev."

Still smiling, Devon turned to his brother. "Turn toward the light and tilt your head down a little. That's good. Now close your eyes so you don't blink."

Eve watched as he quickly and expertly extracted the four stitches just above Nate's left eyebrow. "Those little dots where the stitches were should disappear by tomorrow. The doc did a decent job. You can hardly see the gash."

Eve commented, "I can tell you've done this before."

"Many times, darling, many times. We usually take out our own, but sometimes there are areas you just can't reach, so we've come to rely on each other. I had to draw the line once—a good friend came to me after he'd had a vasectomy. Who could blame him for never wanting to see the urologist again? He told me the doc pulled three feet of thread beneath each testicle for a few tiny stitches." Both men shuddered.

Nate reached for the bourbon, poured a shot, downed it, and handed the bottle to Devon.

After toasting his friend, Devon gave the bottle back to Eve. "I like your choice of bourbon. Now it's time for this pig to vacate the premises."

She apologized for her sister and told him Katie wasn't her usual self. They walked toward the front door and heard the piano. The melody was beautiful but heart wrenching.

Nate commented, "That's from an opera, one my mother liked. Do you know what it is?"

"I don't know the name of the song but it's from *The Pearl Fishers*, by Georges Bizet. He also composed the opera *Carmen*. Katie can answer your question."

"Don't interrupt her." They listened quietly for a minute, and then Devon left.

Nate and Eve sat in the room he called "the cocoon." It was the small library near her bedroom. He pushed the play button and Wade Simmons' voice filled the room. Eve listened to him describe how much he despised her. Then he expressed his need to punish her when he learned she was seeing another man. Nate paused the recording.

"Are you sure you want to continue this?"

She nodded. "So far it's helping me. I'm beginning to understand how unstable he is."

As they listened, Eve remained surprisingly calm when Simmons described how he overpowered and beat her. She didn't flinch when she heard him describe raping her, but she got angry when Simmons mentioned Katie.

When Nate turned off the recorder, she said, "That is a very sick man."

"Your reaction is not what I expected. I thought it would be more upsetting for you."

"I know what he did to me. I've relived it in my mind too many times. It's like watching a horror movie so often you become immune to what you see. When he described me in that detached way, I realized he didn't view me as a person. He beat and raped an object—a possession that he didn't want anyone else to have. His plan to rape Katie angered me more than anything."

"I'm holding back a lot of rage, Eve."

"I can hardly imagine you being locked up with him. The two of you are so different. You've killed people out of duty but not hatred. Wade Simmons is full of loathing ... toward others and himself." She had dreaded having her personal life dissected by a ruthless lawyer in a room full of strangers. "I'm very grateful for this evidence. Can we tell Katie about this?"

"We can't tell her about the FBI investigation."

Later that evening, Katie looked at him in awe. "How'd you do it, Nate?"

"I can't tell you that."

She looked at her sister. "How'd he do it, Eve?"

"I honestly don't know."

"Your brother was here. Did he help? He looks like a man who could force a confession out of anyone. Did the two of you double-team Simmons?"

"Your imagination is in overdrive, Katie. No one forced Wade Simmons to say anything, and I can't tell you anything else. Hopefully, we'll avoid a trial. You'll have to accept that for now."

Katie nodded. "I need a good night's sleep. Knowing what you just told me will help a lot. I can start putting my stupidity behind me. Guess we all have regrets from time to time. Don't we?"

Eve agreed. "We also have to forgive ourselves and move on. Good night, Katie."

They stayed on the porch and listened to the outgoing tide ripple against the wooden pilings beyond the house. Eve leaned her head against Nate's arm. "There's something soothing about the sound of moving water. The rhythm of peepers after a heavy rain or the lonely call of a whippoorwill on summer nights makes me feel the same way. It's a cycle and no matter how crazy things get in this world, there's a cycle in nature that seldom changes."

Nate closed his eyes and tilted his head so his cheek rested on her head. Then he drifted off to sleep.

Wade Simmons was laughing when Buck Walters vulgarly described his girl-friend. *She's got tits the size of grapefruits, an ass like a Volkswagen, and a brain the size of a B.B. She likes me to knock her around before she gets down on her knees in front of me. And those crocodile tears are a real turn on.* He saw his cellmate's admiration. It sickened him but he kept a sneer on his face. Then Wade described Eve. *The woman I did is gorgeous, but she's an ice queen and a whore. I made her pay dearly for her sins. First ...*

Someone shook him and called his name.

"Nate!"

He opened his eyes and tried to focus on Eve's face ... was it bloodied and bruised?

"Wake up. You're having a nightmare."

He looked around the room, and then scrubbed his hands across his face. "Yeah ... I hope I didn't frighten you."

"I've no idea what you dreamt, but it wasn't pleasant, so I don't want to know about it."

"What time is it?"

"It's two in the morning ... we fell asleep on the porch. Just come upstairs and try not to wake Katie."

He was relieved his nightmare had been a silent one. He never wanted Eve to think him capable of the words or actions that came from the fictitious Buck or Wade Simmons.

When they reached the top of the stairs, Eve took Nate's hand and led him into her bedroom. After closing the door, she took off her clothes then slipped under the covers. Nate undressed and climbed into bed with her. She lay on her side facing away from the center. Nate pressed his body against her back and wrapped an arm around her waist. The length of their bodies curved and nestled together like spoons in a drawer.

Eve focused on the warmth radiating from him and the rhythm of his breathing. She let herself relax. "Are you okay with this, Nate?"

"Hmmm. Couldn't be better. Go to sleep, now."

Just before daybreak, she felt his hardness pressed against her. She turned beneath the covers and gently rolled him onto his back. When he felt her hand grip him, his brain went from half asleep to full alert. She took her time with him—touching, tasting, caressing, and nibbling. He fought the urge to reciprocate. When his restraint had reached its limit, he reached for her. But she moved to straddle him and braced one hand against his shoulder, signaling him to be still. She used her other hand to lower her body onto him. Then she pressed both hands against his chest and started a slow, steady rhythm.

He groaned quietly and watched her silhouetted in the moonlight that shined through the French door. His arms remained flat on the mattress, though he could barely resist wrapping them around her. She rewarded him when she became entranced in their mating. Nate reached for her breasts and felt her pulsate around him. He sat upright and wrapped his arms around her waist. When he captured an erect nipple in his teeth, her breathing quickened. She pushed him back to the mattress. He positioned a hand between his groin and her clitoris to heighten her sensation. The other hand gripped her hip. Her fingernails dug into his shoulders. She threw her head back and quietly let a long, satisfying moan escape her lips. No longer in control of his body, he grabbed both hips. With a few final thrusts, he emptied himself into her.

He stroked the blond hair that lay across his chest. When she lifted her head and smiled, he held her face and kissed her softly.

"I love you, Eve."

"I love you, too."

XX

Early Monday morning, John Dunlevy met with Julia Burke, the young attorney assigned to prosecute Wade Simmons. Despite her age, she had an impressive record in court. Together, they listened to the recording from the FBI. Then they discussed a strategy that would send Wade Simmons to prison for several years. Julia felt strongly that the evidence would convince Simmons's attorney to plea bargain. The district attorney said he wanted a sentence of ten to fifteen years with five years mandatory time. Since Nate had become a key witness, John recused himself as Eve's attorney. But Julia wanted John present during the proceedings and asked him to prepare Eve, Katie, and Nate for their appearances in court. John's next stop was Nate's house.

Devon opened the front door. "Good morning, Dad. I just made coffee."

"I'll have a quick cup then Nate and I should head to Sullivan's Island. I just met with the district attorney, and we need to prepare for the hearing tomorrow."

They walked to the kitchen. "Nate's not here. He spent the weekend at Eve's."

"Hmmm."

Devon laughed as he got coffee mugs from the cabinet.

"What's so funny?"

"You and Nate don't realize it, Dad, but the two of you sound so much alike at times." He poured their coffee. "Anyway, I spoke with Nate a few minutes ago. I have his car and I'm picking him up this afternoon. He needs a haircut before court; I could use one, too. Then we're going to the base in Charleston to work out. I told him to burn some *energy* before he sees Simmons again. I even offered to get in the ring with him."

John choked on his coffee. He remembered that last time the two men climbed into a boxing ring together.

"Don't worry, Dad. We know better."

John finished his coffee, called Eve's house, and said he was on his way there. Devon walked him to the door. "Is there a problem with me being in the courtroom tomorrow? I'd like to be there for support."

"If Eve doesn't object, I'll tell the prosecuting attorney that you'll be sitting with us."

"I'd appreciate that. Just make sure Eve's okay with it."

They sat together on the porch while John explained tomorrow's hearing. "The district attorney has enough evidence to take the case to trial, so there's no need for a grand jury. Due to the nature of this case, the hearing will be private. Only witnesses and people close to the plaintiff and defendant will be allowed in the courtroom."

Katie looked at her sister. "Thank God for the small favors." Eve nodded and they turned their attention back to John.

"During the hearing, the judge will evaluate the evidence. He'll look at the photographs taken by the police and review the medical reports. He'll read the DNA findings that link Wade Simmons to the crimes."

The terror and subsequent humiliation of the night washed over Eve. She remembered the sparse clothes she wore and the blanket the police officer had wrapped around her. When she got to the hospital, they took those things away from her. The thin paper gown the nurse gave her crinkled when she got onto the exam table. The bright flash from the camera caused her to wince when the female officer took pictures of her injuries. During the examination, the doctor's instruments made her feel violated all over again. The blood drained from her head just as it did that night at the hospital.

Nate saw her go pale, reached out, and pushed her head toward her knees. "Keep it down and take deep breaths, Eve. Try to think about something else."

John went to the kitchen for water. When he returned, her color had returned but she took the glass with a shaky hand.

"I'm sorry. I know I can't let that happen in court tomorrow."

Nate rubbed her back. "Don't apologize for your feelings about that night, Eve. Just remember that tomorrow may go easier … like the rerun of a horror movie."

She nodded and smiled weakly. "Keep going, John. Let's hear the rest of it."

John patted her hand then continued. "Harold Spencer will present his case for the defendant and try to dispute all the evidence. Listening to him will be very difficult." He paused. "When Spencer's done, Julia will present her case. Nate, she wants to meet with you before the hearing and prepare you to take the stand. You're listed as a witness, but Spencer hasn't questioned your role yet."

"Why not?"

"His strength is litigation and he performs best in front of a trial jury. That's where he plans to take this case. But, I don't think it will get that far."

Eve asked, "Will I have to testify? Or Katie?"

"You're on the witness list for the prosecution *and* the defense. But Julia wants to avoid having either of you take the stand. She's hoping for a plea."

"What kind of plea?"

"The district attorney wants ten to fifteen years in prison with a five-year mandatory sentence. In today's system, that translates to five years—that's the best we can expect with a plea. Can you live with that?"

"I want to put this behind me."

"It doesn't sound like much of a price to pay, Eve, but five years in prison for someone like Wade Simmons will be staggering. He's yet to spend any time in a real penitentiary."

John gave everyone a moment to think about it. Then he looked at Nate. "It might be wise for you and Eve to distance yourselves until the hearing is over."

Two hours later, Nate left Sullivan's Island with Devon. After a grueling workout, they went back to Nate's house and Devon tried to preoccupy his brother with discussions about their work. Later that night, they walked to Grill 225 and ate dinner at the bar. Devon signaled the bartender for two more beers. He noticed Nate's swollen knuckles. "That boxing bag must have had Wade Simmons's face on it. How are your hands?"

Nate flexed his fingers slowly. "Sore."

The next day, they sat in the courtroom behind a barrier that separated them from the lawyers and the judge's bench. John sat in a row between Eve and Katie. Maura Brody sat on Eve's other side. As planned, Randall, Nate, and Devon sat directly behind them. They all wore conservative suits. Eve and Katie had tied their hair back and had applied makeup lightly.

On the other side of the main aisle sat Wade Simmons's father and his brother. Three women sat behind them. Eve knew one of the women was his mother. She didn't know the others, but guessed one might be his sister-in-law.

A guard escorted Wade Simmons into the courtroom. Before sitting next to his lawyer, he glared at Eve, but paid little attention to those around her.

Everyone stood when the judge entered the room and sat at his bench. The judge reviewed the photographs of the injuries inflicted on both Eve and Katie.

He summarized the police and lab reports. Nate watched his father's hand cover Eve's when she gripped the arm of her chair. Both attorneys acknowledged they had studied the same material before the hearing. Then the judge looked at Harold Spencer. "Are you ready to represent your client?"

Harold Spencer stood up and spun a marvelous story about the romance and sex between Wade Simmons and Eve O'Connor. He was practicing for a trial, where he would totally discredit Eve and plant reasonable doubt in the minds of the jury. That's how he won his cases. He would hold back on his attack against the two women during the hearing. He didn't want to alienate the adjudicator— one he hadn't picked. After this hearing, he'd use his and the Simmons's family connections to shop for his own judge.

First, he described Eve as a tease (which was enough for now—at a trial, he would make her sound like a whore). Then he described her as a woman who enjoyed the game of "slap and tickle" to get her aroused. That explained how her sister found them in the kitchen. He described Katie's attack against Wade Simmons and his need to defend himself. He added that Wade Simmons had used considerable restraint when he dealt with Katie's attack. Unfortunately, she injured herself when she fell against the counter. He concluded that Katie's attack had caused a three-way melee on the kitchen floor and no one could ascertain who had caused whose injuries. He stressed that Wade Simmons had been bitten, scratched, bruised, and required stitches in his head. He presented carefully selected photos of his client as evidence.

When Harold Spencer finished his testimony, the judge called a recess until the afternoon.

During the recess, Julia Burke met with John, Maura, and Nate to review the strategy for the afternoon court session. John had asked Devon to reassure Katie that Spencer's accusations would not stand. Randall suggested Eve walk with him as a way to remain calm.

Katie found Devon waiting for her when she came out of the women's restroom. "Adding to my pleasure today, McLean?"

"If you need to beat on someone, I'm available. But let's keep our little jousting matches away from the others. I want to apologize for the things I said on Sunday. After watching a pro like Spencer twist the truth, you must feel as though there's a bull's-eye painted on your chest."

"You're very perceptive. Or is it primal instinct?"

"I heard the evidence and I know you fought him. You may have saved your sister's life. You were next on his list. So ignore the damn lawyer and give yourself a pat on the back."

"Listening to those lies about my sister and me was very difficult. You have no idea how hard it was not to speak out."

"Maybe not, but I know you'll get satisfaction when you see Simmons take the fall for his actions."

When the hearing resumed, Julia Burke announced a witness for the prosecution and Nate walked toward the bench. A sense of anticipation and apprehension drifted through the courtroom. When he reached the stand, he turned and looked directly at Wade Simmons. His eyes met a stare and a look of puzzlement. Nate looked familiar to Simmons, but he couldn't remember where he had seen his face. He leaned toward Harold Spencer and whispered something to him.

After Nate responded to the clerk's recitation of the oath, Julia Burke asked him to state his full name and his current occupation. Nate spoke calmly and assertively. "Nathaniel J. Dunlevy. I'm co-owner of DMG, Inc., a firm that specializes in security."

"What did you do before starting your business?"

"I was in the military for twelve years."

"What rank did you achieve?"

"Commander."

"What did you do during those years?"

"I fought against terrorism."

Nate's voice triggered Simmons's memory. He thought of a cellmate and a friend … one with knowledge of the scriptures … one with stories about demeaning women … and one with a penetrating stare that gave him a peculiar sense of fear. His eyes grew wide as he said aloud, "That's Buck Walters! He spent three days in a jail cell with me."

The judge banged his gavel and warned Spencer to control his client. Spencer objected to Nate as a witness, stating he had been given no opportunity to prepare a cross-examination. The judge reminded the attorney that full disclosure was not required until the pretrial motions took place. Then the judge turned to Nate. "Commander Dunlevy, tell us why you are sitting here."

"I'm working under contract for the FBI. Wade Simmons is affiliated with a group they are investigating. They legally wired me and put me in a cell with him. I collected information to help their investigation. During that time, Wade

Simmons described assaulting and raping Eve O'Connor. His statements were recorded and turned over to the FBI."

Wade Simmons jumped from his seat. "You fucking bastard!" The judge banged his gavel hard and ordered the bailiff to remove the defendant. Harold Spencer looked at Wade Simmons's father and shook his head. As he was led from the room, Wade Simmons glared at Nate with hatred in his eyes.

When the judge nodded, Julia Burke resumed her case. "Your honor, the FBI provided the relevant segments of Commander Dunlevy's recording to the district attorney's office last Friday. The police lab confirmed the voiceprint of Wade Simmons and validated the integrity of the information. Not that we are questioning the FBI's input on this case, but we wanted to make sure the edited version we received didn't create statements taken out of context. We feel certain the recording accurately reflects the actions of Wade Simmons against Eve Marie O'Connor and Katherine Lynn O'Connor. With your permission, we can play the recording, but I must warn that the defendant's use of foul language is prevalent and his descriptions are graphic."

The judge pointed to Harold Spencer, Julia Burke, and Nate. "You three come into my chambers right now. Counselor, bring that recording. The rest of the court is in recess."

The three women in the Simmons family left the courtroom. Wade Simmons's mother cried quietly on her way to the rear door. Everyone else remained seated and silent.

Twenty minutes later, Nate returned to the courtroom and saw the animosity on the face of Wade Simmons's brother. Minutes passed and no one appeared from the judge's chambers. Katie started to fidget; Eve sat very still. More time passed. John and Maura exchanged a questioning look. Randall leaned toward Nate and whispered that he had come across as a very credible witness. And they waited.

Finally, the two lawyers returned to the courtroom. Harold Spencer motioned for the Simmons men to follow him through a side door, the same door used by the bailiff to escort Wade Simmons to and from the courtroom. When they left, Julia Burke approached Eve. "If Wade Simmons follows his lawyer's advice, he'll be sentenced to eight to twelve years in prison with four years mandatory time. He'll serve his time in a state penitentiary and not a minimum-security country club with barbed-wire fences. Can you live with that?"

"Yes." Eve felt relief flood through her and struggled to control the churning emotions that had been building up inside her. She turned to Nate but couldn't trust her voice. They exchanged a knowing look. He suppressed the urge to take her away from the courtroom and the pain she had relived there.

Julia Burke returned to the judge's chambers and waited for Harold Spencer. After a convincing argument from his father and his lawyer, Wade Simmons accepted the plea. The judge adjourned his court.

XXI

Nate pressed on the accelerator and the silver Porsche screamed across the Ravenel Bridge. Devon looked down at the Charleston Harbor as a large container ship navigated its way toward the bridge. He spotted a pilot boat racing to the entrance of the harbor where two large ships were moored, waiting for a river pilot to guide them along the Cooper River. Neither man said a word until they reached Sullivan's Island.

Devon spoke first. "Do you think Simmons's brother belongs to the SSBA?"

"Don't know, but I'll make some calls."

"Does Sullivan's Island have its own police force?"

"A small one. The station is on the other end of the island … near Fort Moultrie."

When they arrived at the O'Connor home, Nate paced in the driveway while Devon leaned against the car and studied the area around him. "Eve doesn't have many close neighbors, does she?"

"No, and the houses you see are mostly summer places. Eve's parents rebuilt after Hugo, but many others didn't." Before they joined the marines, Hurricane Hugo hit the Low Country. When the category-four hurricane made landfall east of Charleston, the eighteen-foot storm surge devastated parts of the city and the surrounding barrier islands. Nate and Devon had volunteered their time and worked on crews to help clean up the catastrophe.

John Dunlevy's car pulled up to the house with Eve and Katie inside. When it stopped, Nate opened the passenger door and pulled Eve from the vehicle. He led her into the house and upstairs to "the cocoon." After closing the door, he wrapped his arms around her and held her close for several moments. Then he tilted her chin and kissed her softly. "Are you okay?"

She nodded. "I'm so glad it's over."

John went into Eve's office to make a phone call. In the kitchen, Devon loosened the knot in his silk tie and accepted the beer Katie handed to him. "You clean up well for a caveman, McLean." She put the tieback from her hair into her pocket then removed her blazer and draped it over a chair. "I was rude to you earlier. I'd like to call a truce. The way things are going between Nate and Eve, we're likely to see more of each other, so we better learn to get along."

He pointed at her with his beer. "You can start by dropping the caveman reference, it's getting old."

Before she could respond, Nate and Eve walked into the kitchen. Katie wanted to know what happened in the judge's chambers. John joined them as Nate began, "Before the judge listened to the recording, he asked me about my military career. I told him how I had served. When Spencer heard SEAL, he accused me of coercion and suggested that Simmons admitted to crimes he didn't commit. I told the judge the evidence would speak for itself."

Nate paused and looked at Devon. "Except for Julia Burke, they assumed you were FBI and there to testify on our behalf. Anyway, we played the recording. The judge got angrier and Spencer got quieter. We listened to Simmons describe what he did to Eve and his plans for Katie. When the judge stopped the recording, Julia asked him if he heard Simmons say anything under duress. Spencer tried to argue the evidence was inadmissible."

John asked, "On what grounds?"

Nate shrugged. "Who knows? The man appeared to be grasping for straws. The judge looked him square in the eye and told Spencer that wasn't going to happen. He could negotiate with the prosecution or prepare for a very difficult trial. The judge hit a weak spot—Harold Spencer only likes trials when he's likely to get an acquittal. The judge thanked me for my time and asked me to wait in the courtroom. We all know the rest of the story. Now, I'm going to make a few phone calls." He kissed Eve on the forehead and left the room.

Eve and John sat at the kitchen table and discussed the events of the hearing.

Devon approached Katie. "Can we get back to the discussion we started earlier, the one about getting along together?"

"Sure."

Devon gently gripped her arm and led her through the screened porch and out to the pool area. The air had cooled considerably as the sun lowered in the sky. Devon took off his suit coat and offered it to Katie. "Yours is inside. Use mine." She thanked him and draped the coat across her shoulders. He put his hands in his pockets as he surveyed the rear of the house and the enclosed pool area. Colorful flowers bloomed and pool water sparkled. "Nice house." Katie nodded and remained silent.

"I meant what I said earlier, about the remarks I made on Sunday. Your percussionist did a lousy thing to you."

"His name is Rob."

"I don't give a damn what his name is. He's a bastard in my book."

She nodded.

"Do you still have feelings for him?"

"Yes, but they're very different from the ones I had before Sunday morning."

"I don't condone what he did, but I have to admit you make it very difficult for a man to walk away from you. When you stormed in the room that day, I imagined having you … in bed. Your cavemen insult hit closer to home than you think."

She looked at him in surprise. "I thought the sight of me disgusted you."

"Wrong. It sucker punched me. I felt it right here." He pointed to his solar plexus.

"Why did you have such a belligerent attitude toward me?"

"The hostility flowed both ways, darling. It started when you announced all men were pigs. Then you got pissed because I glanced at your chest—after you called attention to it." He saw her temper rising and held up a hand before she could remark. "Just give me a minute, Irish. First, your looks bowled me over—I didn't like the feeling. Next, you came across as a man-hater. I've known a few of them in my life. Then you sounded like a dick-teaser. I've known a few of them, too. I don't much care for either type."

"Dick-teaser! What makes you think I'm a dick-teaser?"

Nate had rejoined John and Eve in the kitchen and they looked out the window when they heard Katie's voice. Nate shook his head. "Looks like they're at it again." They made a half-hearted attempt not to eavesdrop, and then gave in to the temptation.

Devon raised his voice slightly to regain control of the conversation. "I didn't *say* you were a dick-teaser. I said you sounded like one when you invited him into your hotel room and got upset about what happened next." He raised his voice a bit more. "I know differently now, okay? But the thought of you having sweaty jungle sex with a scumbag just pisses me off."

"Listen up, McLean! I didn't know he was a scumbag when we had sweaty jungle sex!"

"That does it." He closed the distance between them, reached behind her head, grabbed a fistful of thick auburn hair, pulled her mouth to his, and kissed her.

When she put her hands against his chest, his other arm wrapped around her waist and trapped her tightly against him. His strength overpowered her. He broke the kiss but the confusion in her eyes urged him to plunder her mouth again. Within seconds, he felt her succumb. Then he loosened his grip and pulled his mouth from hers.

Katie shoved back from his chest. "Why'd you do that?"

He shrugged. "You suggested a truce. Consider that a peace offering."

"I'll remember not to war with you again."

He grinned. "There's little chance of that, Irish. Your sister told me what kind of blood pulses through our veins."

She struggled to erase the image of him as a Celtic warrior, his strong physique adorned with nothing more than body paint, carrying a shield and a broadsword. "Next time you want to make peace or enjoy the spoils of war, ask." Then she handed him his coat and turned. He tossed the jacket over his shoulder and admired her stride as he followed her into the house.

The other three had seated themselves at the kitchen table and pretended they hadn't watched the poolside scene. Katie grabbed her jacket as she walked past the table. "I'm going upstairs to change." She looked at them and added, "Don't misinterpret what just happened out there."

Devon muttered to himself as she left the room.

The group remained silent until Eve looked up at the clock and remembered her promise to call her parents. "It's getting late in Ireland. I should make a call and let them know how things turned out."

John got up from the table. "I've an early appointment tomorrow and need time to prepare for my client."

After Devon said good-bye to their father, Nate walked John to his car. "Thank you for helping Eve through this ordeal. You've been a tremendous help to all of us."

"She's a special lady and I'm glad she's healing." He looked closely at his son. "You're healing, too. I see it in your face."

"I hope so." The two men grasped hands. "Watch your back, Dad. There may be repercussions until the FBI closes this case."

"I will and I trust you to follow your own advice. If anyone has become a target now, it's you. Keep me in the loop."

When Nate returned to the kitchen, he took two beers from the refrigerator and handed one to his brother. After removing and folding his tie, he put it in the pocket of his suit coat. Then he hung the jacket over a chair back and turned up the sleeves of his long-sleeved dress shirt.

Devon opened his beer. "I see your brain working. What's happening?"

Nate shook his head. "Tee-Jay's monitoring the Internet. If any of our names pop, he'll call. He's running a search on the brother, Bradley Simmons, and looking for a secure SSBA Web site, one they use to communicate internally." He paused and took a sip of his beer. "I'm in a quandary, Dev. Should I stay near Eve and Katie or distance myself as much as possible?"

"It's too soon to make that decision. But I'll stay close until we do know more."

"Thanks."

Eve and Katie returned to the kitchen wearing big smiles and flattering outfits. Instead of businesslike suits for court, they wore slacks, sweaters, and clever pieces of jewelry; they did something different with their hair and makeup, too.

Nate complimented them on their appearance and asked, "Are you going somewhere?"

"Mom suggested I treat everyone to a nice dinner. I'm sorry I didn't think of it. I guess I'm still getting my feet back on the ground." Eve gave him a warm hug. "Jack and Marie O'Connor sent that all the way from Ireland. They were relieved and grateful when I told them about the hearing."

He returned her hug.

Katie added, "They want to meet you."

"Hmmm."

They dined at a small Italian restaurant in Charleston. After ordering salads, pasta entrees, and a full-bodied red wine, the two men listened to Eve and Katie talk about their parents.

The restaurant's background music reminded Nate of his own parents. "My mother loved opera, Katie. On Sunday, you played a favorite song of hers, one that Dad still listens to often."

"I needed opera for catharsis that afternoon. Do you know which one you heard?"

"Eve said it was from *The Pearl Fishers*."

"I played *Je crois entendre encore … I still believe to hear*. It's a poignant song. A man still believes he hears the voice of his beautiful enchantress."

Her description caused a lump in Nate's throat and Devon gave him an empathetic look.

Eve sensed the mood swing and changed the subject. "Tell them about your work in California, Katie."

"I'm working toward my doctorate in composition. But to pay the bills, I write music for television, commercials, and movies."

Nate asked, "Are you a songwriter?"

"No. I compose music—just the notes, not the words."

"Do you have a favorite composer?"

"Not just one. A favorite symphony is *Scheherazade* by Rimsky-Korsakov. The composition is very moving and depicts tales from *1001 Arabian Nights*. Now tell me what kind of music you like."

They discussed music throughout dinner and Katie was enthused by their interest and broad taste. Devon saw her in a different light, one he enjoyed.

XXII

When they returned to Sullivan's Island, Nate checked for messages and found one from Isaac. While he returned the call, Katie made coffee and Eve gave Bootsie some of the fettuccini she had brought home. The cat expressed its delight audibly, purring loudly as it licked a creamy sauce from a few strands of pasta. Devon laughed when the cat dragged a long flat piece from the bowl and started gnawing it with side teeth.

Nate ended the call and looked over at Devon. "Things are pretty quiet."

"Glad to hear it, big guy." Eve smiled at the familiar nickname.

"Why do you call him that, Devon?"

"Because I've looked up to him since the day I met him." He added jokingly, "He was three inches taller at the time."

"You caught up to me fast, Dev, but I still have one inch on you."

Katie smiled. "The day we met, you thought Devon had something to do with my untimely arrival because I called you that." Eve laughed when Nate tried to change the subject and Devon wheedled the story out of her and Katie.

When the telling was over, Eve glanced at Nate. "Does that explain it?"

"Oh, you summed it up very nicely." He looked at his brother. "You can stop laughing any time now."

Katie asked them why they had different surnames. Eve knew the painful history of Devon losing his family and tried to divert the conversation. But, he was willing to discuss his past.

"I was fourteen when my parents and older sister were killed in a car accident. It happened fifty miles from my home in Pennsylvania. A trucker fell asleep at the wheel and crossed the double yellow line. A social worker met me at school that day, and I went to a foster home until they could locate relatives."

Both women were stunned by the image of a fourteen-year-old boy in the hands of a social worker and foster home the day he lost his family. Katie asked how long it took to locate John Dunlevy ... assuming a family connection.

"They didn't. We aren't related. I spent four weeks in the foster home. Then I ran away, because I couldn't imagine living there any longer. I made it to a small town and found a little abandoned house." He described pilfering clothing, blankets, and books from boxes people left behind a Goodwill store. "I had nothing else to do, so I read. At night, I foraged Dumpsters for food. One time I found an entire box of unopened cornflakes. You'd be surprised at what people toss, but I never ate anything that looked or smelled as though it had gone bad."

"How long did you live that way?" Eve asked.

"Over a week. I got hungry one morning and took a chance on a grocery store Dumpster. It was the best place to find decent food. A beat cop spotted me and hauled me to the station. Social services got involved again. By then, they had located a distant relative in Beaufort, and I went to live with an aunt and uncle. The woman was a cousin on my mother's side. Other than sending a Christmas card, my parents never associated with them. I found out why."

Devon took a drink. "Do you really want to hear more of this?"

Both women nodded.

He shrugged and went on. "At first, my uncle liked the idea of getting more than one hundred thousand dollars from my parents' life insurance policies to take care of me. And he wanted to make it last. That bastard watched every single morsel I put in my mouth at the dinner table. He'd slap me around if I ate too much or too fast. He'd go out and come home drunk. My aunt took the brunt of his ill temper late at night ... most of his abuse was verbal. I know he had her at night, but I'd never describe the sounds that came from their bedroom as lovemaking. When he started knocking me around, I thought about running away again."

He stood. "I need to hit the head and fix another drink. Take over for me, Nate."

Nate took a sip of his own drink before speaking. "Dev and I met in high school. My Mom had recently died of cancer; he had lost his entire family. Dev made me feel lucky that I still had Dad and Liv. We became very good friends and he spent a lot of time at my house. I knew his uncle hit him, but he made me promise not to tell anyone because social services would send him back to a foster home. At that age, kids do what their friends ask and don't seek advice from adults—even those they trust."

Devon returned to the kitchen, fixed a drink and stood at the counter as Nate continued. "One morning, I went by Dev's place to pick him up for school. No one answered the door, but it wasn't locked. I went up to his room and found him lying on his bed. The night before, his uncle had taken a swing at his aunt and Dev stepped in the middle. So his uncle beat the shit out of him. When he finished using his fists, he took off his belt and added welts on top of the bruises." Nate took a long draw from his glass and shook his head. "I can still remember how you looked that morning."

"I was a scrawny kid at fifteen and my uncle outweighed me by eighty pounds. If I had stayed there, he'd have killed me. I decided to run away as soon as I could get up and walk out of Beaufort County on my own two legs. That day, Nate found me and took me to his home. Then he called his father. I'll never be able to repay John Dunlevy for what he did."

The description of Devon's beating left the two women shaken. Katie asked, "Was foster care that bad? Bad enough to eat out of Dumpsters or put up with your uncle's abuse?"

Devon gave his brother a questioning look and Nate thought before he responded. "I don't think it can hurt, Dev, but it's up to you."

Although he had mixed feelings, Devon decided to answer her question honestly. "The home in Pennsylvania was a farm owned by an older couple. They took in teenage boys who did chores before and after school. They were decent people who gave us a clean place to live and as much food as we wanted. I figured I could handle farm work until I got out of high school. I didn't have much choice, and the animals were cool. Three other boys were living there under the foster care program; two of them were almost three years older, and one was a year younger. I shared a room with the younger boy and he hardly spoke while I lived there. The two older boys were big. Not just because of their age, the farm work had put some muscle on them. When the adults weren't around, they got their kicks ragging on me. I gave them secret names. One had a square-shaped head, so I dubbed him Frankenstein. The other had a gut, so I named him Dough Boy. I never called them that to their face. Michael McLean hadn't raised a stupid son."

He picked up his drink and sat down next to Eve. "I started mucking stalls before school one day. Frankenstein and Dough Boy came into the one I was cleaning and told me they needed my pitchfork. I had a bad feeling when Frankenstein grabbed it from me. When I tried to leave the stall, he wrestled me to the ground. He pushed my face into the dirty straw and told Dough Boy to sit on my head and pin my arms. Then he yanked down my pants and raped me. When he finished, they switched positions and Dough Boy took his turn."

Eve didn't attempt to hold back the tears. Devon took her hand and held it tightly. "I understand what happened to you. Feeling powerless is almost as bad as the physical violation. I tried to fight them with every ounce of strength I had. But it wasn't enough."

She nodded as she wiped tears from her face. She struggled to speak as a fresh wave of tears came. "Can I give you a hug?"

"Sure. Come over here." He drew her into his lap and wrapped his arms around her. She wept openly against his chest as he rocked her. "Let it go, darling. Get it out of your system and put it behind you as much as you can."

Katie brushed tears away from her face as she stood and walked to the powder room. She returned with a box of tissues and set it on the table. She used one to wipe her tears and offered some to her sister. Devon reached for them and said to Eve, "Hey, did your mom ever do this?" He held a tissue over her nose and told her to blow gently.

Eve smiled weakly, took the tissues from his hand, wiped her face, and blew her nose. Then she kissed him on the cheek. "You're a very dear and special man, Devon McLean." He tried to lighten the mood. "All the women tell me that." He smiled at Katie and winked. "Except for your sister."

Eve got up from Devon's lap and said she needed a minute to wash her face. After that, she wanted to hear how John Dunlevy had handled Devon's relatives. Devon tossed the ball back in Nate's court again. "You remember those details better than I."

When Eve came back to the table, Nate recounted the call to his father's office on Parris Island. "I told him I needed him to come home right away. I assured him Olivia and I were okay but that I needed him. He came home quickly and I took him to my room, where he found Dev. We told him what the uncle had done. Dad wanted to take him to the hospital, but he flatly refused to go and said he had to leave. His vehemence surprised Dad, and he asked me to give them time alone. Eventually, Dev told him everything that happened since he had lost his parents. I don't remember all the details, but a doctor friend came to the house and checked you. You had no broken bones, but he told us to call him if we noticed other symptoms."

Devon remembered John making phone calls and checking on him throughout the day. "Dad went to see my uncle that night. They could keep the insurance payout, but he wanted custody of me. If they objected, he vowed to haul them into court on child-abuse charges where they would spend the money on attorney's fees during a lengthy legal battle. My aunt didn't argue, but my uncle took a swing at him. The stupid bastard realized his mistake when he picked himself up off the floor. The next day Dad filed paperwork to become my legal guardian. From that day and until we joined the Corps, I lived in his house and shared a room with Nate."

Later that night, sleep eluded Devon. He looked in the gym bag that had been in Nate's car and found the book he had started reading two days earlier. Then he tried to convince himself that he didn't need the drugstore glasses for reading—they just reduced eyestrain at night. Deep down, he knew he'd inherited Johanna McLean's eyesight. His mother needed reading glasses when she turned thirty-five. The car accident killed her just before she turned forty.

Outside the guest bedroom, the floorboards creaked twice. Without making a sound, he removed the glasses, reached into the nightstand drawer, picked up his handgun, and listened carefully for another sound. He aimed his weapon at the door and waited. Seconds later, Katie stood in the doorway wearing a short nightshirt and robe. She stared at the gun pointed in her direction.

"Damn it, Irish. Don't you know better than to creep into a man's room in the middle of the night?" He put the gun back in the drawer next to the bed.

"I had trouble sleeping, and I wanted tea. I saw the light through the crack in the door and thought you might still be awake."

He noticed her pale complexion. "I'm sorry if the gun frightened you."

"It didn't. A woman shouldn't be shot for walking into her old bedroom. It looks different now, but I grew up in here." She glanced at the book on his lap. "What are you reading?"

"A Vince Flynn novel. Rapp's on the warpath in Washington. It's my kind of catharsis." He put the book and the reading glasses on the night table. "Are you okay?" She nodded unconvincingly. He patted the empty side of the bed next to him. "I'm wearing gym shorts, so climb into bed if you want company."

She hadn't seen him without a shirt until now and she thought of Nate's physique. Although their coloring was different, both he and Devon had incredibly toned male bodies. Then she remembered the gentle man who had rocked her sister in his lap and held the tissues so she could blow her nose. Her mind switched to the image of a young homeless boy who spent months of his life at the mercy of bullies.

Devon watched her expressions change. "It won't happen tonight, Irish, but I promise you won't be thinking about a miserable adolescent boy when I make love to you." He patted the mattress again as she walked across the room and climbed onto the bed.

"You're dreaming, McLean."

"Call it a premonition."

"Do you mind if we change the subject?"

"Say what's on your mind, darling."

"It had to be difficult for you … telling us the part about being raped. You understand how Eve felt that day and that helps her. So thank you."

Devon covered her hand with his. "It's important that she put it behind her. The same goes for you. Getting knocked around and seeing what happened to your sister was hard on you, too."

"What happened to your aunt?"

Devon shook his head. "Dad asked the domestic abuse people to help her, but she'd have nothing to do with them. Shortly after I moved in with the Dunlevys, my relatives sold their home and moved away. Years later, I became curious and used the Internet to track them down. They live in a trailer park in central Florida."

"Do you know what happened to Frankenstein and Dough Boy?"

"No. I don't."

Katie had battled nausea for the last hour and wondered if she had lost the fight. She pulled the covers to her waist, raised her knees, and wrapped her arms around them. Then she lowered her forehead and took a long, deep breath.

"You're not looking too well there, Irish." When she looked up at him, Devon put the palm of his hand on her forehead and then her cheek. "I usually get a better reaction from women who find themselves in my bed." She threw back the covers and made a beeline for the guest bathroom. He found her kneeling in front of the commode, tossing the contents of tonight's dinner. With one hand, he gathered hair and held it back from her face. He gently rubbed her back with the other until her stomach quieted. "Do you think you're done now?"

When she nodded, he let her hair fall to her shoulders and went to the sink. He soaked a cloth in cool water, wrung out the excess, and handed it her. Then he poured water into a cup. "Rinse first, then take a few small sips and see how your stomach handles it." She murmured a weak thank-you as she reached for the cup.

She had the classic symptoms of mild food poisoning, and he thought about their dinners. "You're the only one of us who ate mussels tonight. One or two of them may have been past their prime." When she started to get up, Devon reached down to help. Chills racked her body. "You are one sick puppy, darling.

Let's get you into bed." He led her from the bath. After tucking her under the covers and arranging her pillow, he climbed into bed next to her and engulfed her shivering body with his own. The heat that radiated from him soothed her, and her breathing steadied. Soon they both fell into a sound sleep.

XXIII

When the jet stream dips toward the Tropic of Cancer and a cold front clashes with a warm low-pressure system hovering over the coastline, massive storms called nor'easters are spawned. Katie punched the remote for the weather channel and listened to the forecast. They'd enjoy a typical, sunny day with temperatures pushing eighty degrees, but by nightfall a major front would cover the Low Country and temperatures would fall into the forties. The reporters warned of strong winds, heavy rain, and unusually high tides. She finished a glass of orange juice and headed for the beach.

On her walk to the ocean, Katie thought about waking up with Devon's chest pressed to her back and his arm draped over her waist. The body hair on his strong thighs had brushed the smooth backs of her legs. She had listened to his quiet breathing and enjoyed its steady rhythm. It felt good ... too good. If she didn't distance herself, something would happen that she'd regret.

As quietly as possible, she'd slipped out of bed, but her effort not to wake him had failed. When her feet touched the floor, he asked her how she felt. She told him the sickness had gone and he should go back to sleep. Then she tiptoed back to her room and tried to do the same. But her thoughts kept floating back to the man whose bed she had just shared and she fought the feeling of loneliness that engulfed her. Instead of wallowing in it, Katie donned her running clothes.

The sun had just risen and the run along the edge of the surf invigorated her ... helped clear her mind. Second to music, exercise had always been her way of working through problems. She sprinted down the beach and saw a man walking toward her at a fast pace but didn't think anything of it. Many people used the beach for walking or jogging. She passed him with a smile and a quick wave, but his demeanor made her feel uneasy. Farther down the beach, she slowed her pace, looked over her shoulder, and saw no one in sight. She assumed he took a path off the beach to a side street.

Katie looked at her watch and turned around. With her system low on fuel after the previous night's sick up, she didn't want to wear herself down. She took a slower pace on the way back and let her legs extend in long, graceful strides. Although she saw no one else on the beach, her gut told her someone was watching her—intently. She began to run faster, wanting to get home. Minutes later, she turned onto the path that led to her street and ran headlong into Devon. When he gripped her by the arms, she struggled to catch her breath. "Damn it, why didn't you tell someone you were leaving the house?"

Her eyes flashed as she gasped. "I've never needed permission to run on the beach. So, what's the problem?"

"The way you approached the pathway isn't pleasure running. You ran across soft sand as if a pack of wild hounds was chasing you. Remember, Irish, I watched you hug the toilet last night."

She held up her hands and nodded while she leveled her breathing. "You're right. I ran faster than I intended." They started toward the street that led to the O'Connor house. "There weren't many people on the beach, but I passed one guy who gave me the creeps. He must have taken a path to the road, but I got the sensation of being watched. I guess my imagination's in overdrive."

Nate was relieved when Devon and Katie walked through the back gate. He didn't want to cause unnecessary alarm, but he wanted to exercise caution until he was sure the SSBA would not be a threat to any of them. Katie entered the cabana next to the pool and closed the door.

When his brother walked into the kitchen, Nate handed him a cup of coffee. "Am I paranoid, Dev?"

He shrugged. "I spotted Katie running like crazy from the beach. Someone had spooked her, but she couldn't explain why. Where's Eve?"

"In her studio. She's feeling good today. When we went to bed, we talked and she didn't hold back … thanks to you."

Devon gave his brother a light squeeze on the shoulder. "I'm glad things are working out for the two of you." He picked up the television remote. "Katie said we've got bad weather coming. They're concerned about flooding and beach erosion on the barrier islands." The two men listened to the report about a major storm forming along the coast.

"Eve wants to go to the beach today. If we all go, maybe Katie will spot the person she saw earlier. Regardless, I want to get a better grip on the layout of this island."

Devon agreed as he carried his empty cup to the kitchen sink. He turned on the faucet and glanced out the window. "Good Lord!"

Nate followed his brother's gaze and saw Katie climbing out of the pool wearing her string bikini. "I should have warned you about that."

Devon watched Katie bend over and pick up a long skimmer. Then he shook his head and murmured, "There's no end to the torment."

When Eve walked into the kitchen smiling cheerfully, Nate gathered her in his arms. "The weather's turning bad tonight. Should we invite Devon and Katie to the beach with us?"

The idea brightened her mood even more. "We should indeed. There's a cooler in the garage. If you'll get it, I'll make us a light picnic lunch."

Devon walked out to the pool and took the skimmer from Katie. "Your sister is packing a cooler for the beach. We're invited."

"Sounds great. I just need to put the solar cover on the pool. It'll keep the debris out when the storm comes tonight." Devon put down the skimmer and helped her spread the sheet of special bubble plastic over the water. Katie bent over the edge of the pool and attached a small rope to a cleat recessed into the side. She walked to another spot and repeated the action. Devon watched her scantily clad figure as she moved around the pool. He stopped looking at her and walked to a cleat. "I'll anchor the rest of these while you get ready for the beach."

"I'm set to go." She grabbed a filmy shirt and started to put it on.

He scanned her body and gave her a reproachful look. "As much as I admire your little outfit, that's not my idea of public swimwear."

His disapproval stung, so she snapped. "It's a bikini, McLean. I've spent time on California beaches with less."

"I don't give a damn what you did in California. This is the East Coast."

"I'm sorry you have a hang-up with the female form, but I'm wearing this bikini at the beach."

"I happen to be a huge fan of the female form." Nate and Eve heard their voices from the kitchen. They watched with fascination as Devon picked up the skimmer and used one arm to fling it clear across the pool. "For pity's sake, O'Connor, use your head. Didn't someone give you the creeps when you ran this morning? Any man capable of breathing will look crazed while you strut around in that thing!"

She threw up her hands and shouted. "Fine. You win. I'll change. Let me see if I can dig up granny's bathing suit. It'll cover me to my knees, neck, and elbows!"

He shouted back as she stormed to the house, "That sounds perfect to me."

The conditions on the beach could not have been better—low humidity and seventy-eight degrees at noon. Even in the full sun, breezes from the cooler water kept the air refreshing. They spread out blankets and enjoyed a light lunch. In reaction to Devon's criticism, Katie wore a yellow one-piece suit cut high in the leg, low in the back, and laced daringly up the front. Eve's swimwear was a little more conservative but equally attractive. Both women could compete with models in the *Sports Illustrated* swimsuit issue. In comparison, the men wore gym shorts and shirts that concealed the pistols tucked into holsters at the small of the backs.

Devon propped himself on an elbow and scanned Katie's body. He remembered his observations on the Yucatan beach. She lay flat on her back with her eyes closed and her knees slightly bent. Her position eliminated any doubt he had about her breasts … they were homegrown. He watched a pair of joggers pass by and thought about her sprint on the beach that morning. "How long have you been running, Irish?"

She shielded her eyes with one hand and squinted at him. "For as long as I can remember. I played soccer … even in college. That and music occupied much of my time. I thought about working toward the World Cup team."

"You don't fit my image of a serious female athlete."

"Why? Because I have breasts?"

Nate didn't miss Devon's quiet assessment of Katie's chest. He got comfortable on the blanket and waited to be amused.

Katie had the urge to provoke Devon. "Why do so many men think female athletes have flat chests?"

"You're the one who implied it, Irish, so don't shove your words into my mouth. I'll admit the female athletes I've known weren't built like you, but that's not to say they weren't lovely in their own way."

"So, you're an expert on what, McLean. Female athletes or breasts?"

"I never felt a breast I didn't enjoy, but my remark about you fitting my image of an athlete had more to do with your penchant for music. In my mind's eye, I picture you in a room with candlelight and a piano. You're wearing a sleek black dress with a tasteful show of cleavage and you're sipping champagne. Now I have to imagine you in a locker room wearing a sports bra, waving a T-shirt, and chugging Gatorade."

"I've done both many times."

"I'll just bet you have. You're a real woman of the world—a jockess of all trades." Then he thought, if that were true, why was she so unhappy? He got to his feet and reached for her hand. "Let's walk this off. We'll do some people

watching and see if you spot the guy that made you feel uneasy this morning."
Katie took his hand without an argument and they began walking.

Nate looked over at Eve when they were out of earshot. "How much more
entertainment we can take from those two?"

Eve smiled and shook her head. "I don't understand them. I've grown to love
Devon in the same way I've always loved Katie. I know you feel the same way
about them. They're both wonderful people. Yet when they're together it's like
two opposite forces crashing into each other."

"I see them as opposing magnets, Eve." He laughed. "If those magnets end up
bonding, we may feel the ground shake." Nate reached out and stroked his fingers down her slender leg. "I think Katie fascinates him, but he doesn't know
what to do about her. That's unusual for Dev. He's pretty sure of himself around
women—much more so than I am."

Eve looked at Nate with disbelief. "You don't strike me as an introvert when it
comes to women." Her thoughts shifted back to her sister. "Katie's challenged by
Devon because he won't let her ride roughshod over him. Deep down, she
respects him for it, but she doesn't like giving up control." Nate agreed.

From behind his sunglasses, Devon's eyes scanned the beach. He searched for
anyone who didn't look like a beachgoer.

As they walked along the surf line, Katie admitted he was partly correct about
the musician/athlete anomaly. "When it became obvious that music would be my
career, I made it my top priority. I played soccer for one more season and then
bowed out. But I still enjoy running, and I do it to keep in shape."

"Your effort shows. Now you have to explain why you're so unhappy."

Her face expressed her confusion. "What makes you think I'm unhappy?"

He shrugged. "It's a vibe I pick up from you." He spotted a man standing near
the dunes. "Don't turn your head, Kate. Just shift your eyes to ten o'clock and
you'll see a man near a cluster of palm trees. Does he look familiar?"

She tried to study the man without being obvious. "It could be him. He's
about the right size. He wore a light jacket and ball cap earlier, but the air was
cooler. I can't see his legs from here. The person wore khaki shorts that came to
his knees and work boots with thick white socks. His footwear looked strange on
the beach, but he had a backpack, so I thought of a hiker or a drifter."

"There are two women with the small child ahead of us. When we get close, I
want you to stop and chat … stay near them for a few minutes."

Seconds later, Katie complimented a young mother on her delightful child
while Devon headed toward the dunes. When he returned, he found her digging

in sand with the small boy, answering a barrage of questions from the inquisitive youngster. Devon reached down to help her up. "I see you've made a new friend."

"I have indeed. How about you?" Devon shook his head. The young boy grabbed Devon's wrist with both hands and announced he could climb up his body. Before the mother could intercede, her son's feet reached Devon's waist. Devon gripped the child's arms to prevent a fall. Then he helped the boy somersault safely to the ground. The mother apologized profusely and blamed her husband for roughhousing and teaching their son silly stunts. Devon grinned at her. "That's what Dads are supposed to do. He sounds like a good man." She blushed and agreed with him. When the boy joined his mother, they waved and walked away.

"Do you like kids, McLean?"

"They're cute … but so are puppies."

He spotted Nate and Eve walking near the dunes and the couples met each other along the beach. Devon described the man Katie had seen earlier and the one they had spotted several minutes ago. "I tried to circle around him, but he disappeared before I got there. We can't be certain the two men are the same, but impressions I found in the sand came from heavy shoes."

Eve mentioned that many landscape employees wear work boots and they often wander to the beach during their lunch break. Katie told them to stop worrying about a hiker who gave her a goofy look that morning. The ruins of a looted sand castle still clung to her legs, so she walked toward the surf to rinse off, and Eve went with her. The two men shared their observations of the Sullivan's Island beach area. They discussed the spacing of beach access pathways, the topography of the dunes, the density of the woods, the direction of streets, and proximity of houses.

The wind speed picked up and sand swept across the shoreline while they packed up the remnants of their picnic. As they neared the O'Connor house, Nate's cell phone rang. Devon overheard bits and asked about the call.

"Tee-Jay found the SSBA's private Web site. I've made their hate list. He sent me an encoded link to check out." Nate saw the concern on Eve's face when they entered the house. He gave her a hug. "Why don't you and Katie wash off the salt and sand? By the time you're done, I'll know more."

Eve reluctantly went upstairs followed by Katie.

The two men alternated between quick showers and searching the Web site. By the time Eve and Katie came downstairs, they had a clearer picture of the SSBA's interest in them.

Katie asked, "What's the SSBA and why are you on their hate list?"

Nate explained the connection between Wade Simmons's church and the paramilitary group. He told both women about the ringleaders, Manfred and Everet Dodd. "You won't like this, Katie, but no more running alone on the beach until I know we're safe. Devon has offered to stay here. I hope this will be over soon, but until then, neither of you should go anywhere without one of us."

Eve asked, "Just where do you fall on this hate list?"

Nate clicked and his picture appeared on the computer next to a chart. "There are public figures ahead of me, but I should be flattered. I'm one step above Dan Brown, author of *The Da Vinci Code*."

XXIV

The temperatures began dropping and the wind velocity built. Locals throughout the Low Country prepared for the storm: outdoor furniture was brought inside or tied down securely, bathtubs were filled with emergency water, holders with unlit candles were scattered throughout houses, flashlights were filled with fresh batteries, and nonrefrigerated staples were replenished.

Eve lit the gas fireplace and the chill disappeared from the living room. The two men made a list of clothes and other items they needed from Nate's house. Devon picked up the keys to the Porsche, tossed a sweatshirt over his shoulder, and headed toward the front door. Katie stopped him in the foyer. "Hang on a minute, McLean." She stuffed her arms into a windbreaker. "I want to go with you. We need some groceries." She nodded toward the living room and whispered. "They might enjoy time to themselves."

Devon saw Nate and Eve sitting in front of the fire and called out. "Katie's with me. You can reach us on the cell if anything comes up."

The wind blustered as they walked to the car. A layer of clouds obscured the setting sun, but the rain had not begun. Devon held the door while Katie got into the passenger seat. Then he rounded the car, fired the engine, and shifted into gear. They sailed across the causeway into Mount Pleasant. The waning rush hour traffic came from the opposite direction. After crossing the Ravenel Bridge, they drove through downtown Charleston and parked in front of Nate's house.

Devon suggested Katie scavenge the kitchen for food while he went upstairs to pack the stuff he and Nate needed. He put clothing, weapons, and other equipment into two duffel bags. When he came downstairs, there were sandwiches and beers on the counter. He watched Katie insert a disc into the CD player. "Did you find something that suits your taste?"

"As a matter of fact, I found several. Who can argue with *Clapton Unplugged?*" A softer, gentler version of "Layla" began. "There's a classic for you, McLean, no matter how you wrap it." She walked toward the refrigerator. "I figured you'd be hungry by now, so I used up the lunch meat and cheese. The rolls needed some help, but a minute under the broiler did the trick. Do you like mustard or mayo?"

"Either one or both. I'm not picky." Katie pulled condiments from the fridge and Devon went to a cabinet to get a glass for her beer. "Layla" ended before they sat down to eat, so Devon punched the forward button and Eric Clapton started singing a bluesy song about an old love. The sight of her moving around the kitchen wearing snug jeans, a loose sweater, and sneakers attracted him as much as the little string bikini—maybe more. He waited until she put the mustard and mayonnaise on the counter then he reached for her.

If he just held her, she'd fight his embrace, so he wrapped an arm around her waist and put her hand on his shoulder. Then he took her other hand in his and began slow dancing. Together, their bodies moved around the kitchen to the rhythm of the sensual song. She rested her head against his chest. It felt good there. He led and she followed, feeling safe in his arms and focusing only on the music and the strength of his body. Several minutes later, the song ended. She snapped out of her reverie and pushed back from him. "Why'd you do that?"

"Because I wanted to hold you, and I like that song."

"Is everything that simple for you, McLean?"

"Why does everything have to be complicated?"

"What would happen if I did whatever I wanted?"

"I don't know. Let's find out."

He had challenged her. Her instincts told her to back off, create distance, and avoid the entanglement. But the dare in his eyes moved her to act regardless of the consequences. She put her arms around his neck and poured herself into a kiss that staggered him. After wrapping an arm tightly around her hip, he pressed her against his body. His other hand slipped beneath her sweater and stroked the soft skin beneath. Lips parted, tongues explored, and heartbeats quickened.

He whispered, "I want you right now." He pulled the sweater over her head and felt the first sign of resistance. "You want this as much as I do, Kate. You're lying to yourself if you push me away." The sweater landed on the floor. He covered her mouth before she could object, stroked the side of her breast, and rubbed his thumb over a lace-covered nipple. He deftly released the constraints of her bra and captured her breast with his mouth. She gripped his shoulders, let a soft moan escape, and quietly cursed her carnal demands.

Soon they tugged clothing from themselves and each other until they embraced naked in the middle of the kitchen. He murmured in her ear, "We'll hurt ourselves if we try this on the hard floor." When he hoisted her to his waist, she wrapped her arms and legs around him. He shuddered when she nipped at his neck and earlobe. Then he carried her from the kitchen and climbed the stairs to the second floor.

He fell backward onto the mattress to cushion her. Her grip on him loosened as he maneuvered their bodies to the center of the bed and rolled her onto her back. Using his mouth, his teeth, and his hands, he began an assault on her body. She tried to stay coherent as new sensations ripped through her. The more she struggled to keep control, the faster he took it away. He cuffed her wrists with one hand and used the other to touch her in ways no one ever had. The pressure inside her began as a small ache then deepened. Her brain sent signals of subtle pain mixed with incredible pleasure. She heard herself groan and then cry out as her world exploded. The tingling sensation traveled along her skin from her toes to her throat where it hovered as her whole body pulsated. He held her tightly and gently rubbed between her legs, enjoying each twitch and vibration her body generated. When her breathing leveled, she reached for him and drew him toward her, but he shook his head and whispered, "Not yet, you've more to go, and we'll get there together this time."

"I won't survive another one of those."

"Sure you will. Close your eyes and take a minute to relax. We'll go a little slower this time." He thought about her words as he reached into the nightstand drawer. She heard him open a condom. Seconds later, he treated her to a gentler caress, and this time she reciprocated. She relished each discovery as she explored his body. Her hands traveled across his chest and down his arms. They stroked up and down his back and drifted to his firm buttocks. She felt the difference between his leg muscles and the softness of the skin on his inner thighs, the contrast added to her excitement.

With his teeth, he gently tugged at the erect nipple on each breast and felt the response radiate down her body. A new craving grew inside her as she fondled him. When she opened for him, he eased into her slowly and enjoyed the feel of her body clamping itself around him. Supporting himself on his forearms, he stroked lazily between her legs while his mouth roamed her neck. Her breathing quickened and he increased the pace. Then he changed their position, moving to his knees and pulling her toward him. His heartbeat sped as he drove into her. When she closed her eyes, he demanded she open them.

"Look at me, Kate. It's just the two of us, right here and right now."

One hand gripped her hip and the other added to her pleasure. She arched her back and ran her hands down her sweat-soaked body. When she let out a soft moan, he clamped down on his need to come until he felt her spasm around him. After several strong thrusts, his torso arched backward and a low guttural sound rumbled through his chest. Then a loud clap of thunder drowned out the sound of their orgasms.

He straddled her and rested his head between her breasts as his breathing leveled. She slowly stroked her fingers through his hair. He kept his eyes closed and enjoyed being touched by her in such a casual yet intimate way. They stayed that way in silence, listening to the rain pelt the tile roof of the house. After a few minutes, she asked him if he knew when the rain had started.

"I haven't the slightest idea, darling." Then he raised his head and looked at her. "It's a good thing we made it to the bed. We'd have damaged ourselves on that hard floor."

She smiled and nodded.

"Have I told you that you're the most incredibly beautiful woman I've ever met?"

"You've hinted at it, but mostly when you were yelling at me."

He laughed as he rolled to her side and propped his back against a pillow. "You bring out the worst in me, Irish." She started to get up, but he stopped her. "Relax for a minute, I enjoy looking at you." She closed her eyes to ward off her apprehension and felt his fingers toy with her hair. "Why are you frowning?"

She opened her eyes. "I didn't realize I was." When she started to sit up again, he sensed her unease and didn't stop her. "Our sandwiches are sitting on the kitchen counter. You must be famished."

He grinned. "I wasn't until just now. It's a great way to work up an appetite." He looked around the room. "All our clothes are down there, too." Another gust of wind-driven rain pelted the bedroom window, followed by a flash of lightning and a clap of thunder. Devon pulled the covers over her and kissed her on the forehead. "Give me a minute, and then we'll go downstairs." She admired his butt as he walked toward the bedroom door.

After her turn in the bathroom, she found him waiting at the top of the stairs … in his skin with his arm bent. He bowed. "Shall we dine, madam?" His antics made her laugh and he enjoyed the sound of it. They walked arm in arm down the narrow staircase and into the kitchen.

She shivered as he helped her gather her clothes; then they both dressed quickly to ward off the chill that descended over the Low Country. Devon found a fat candle in a cupboard and set it on a saucer. They didn't need the light, but he lit it anyway and placed it on the counter near their sandwiches. "Candlelight suits you."

She started to say something but he held up his hands. "Just go with me on this one, Kate." He put their unopened beers back in the refrigerator and brought out two colder ones. After twisting off the caps, he placed his on the counter, picked up her glass, and poured her beer. Then he stood at the counter and started eating. She sat across from him and took a bite of her sandwich as she watched him eat. The image of a traumatized boy searching Dumpsters for food came to mind. Devon caught her gaze as he swallowed a bite. "Don't go there, Kate. That was a very different chapter in my life and I'm two decades past the need for pity."

"How did you know what I was thinking?"

"You had the same look you when you walked toward my bed last night."

"Why do you call me Kate instead of Katie?"

"You ask almost as many questions as that child we met on the beach." He took another bite of his sandwich, chewed and swallowed. "Katie sounds like a sibling name. It works fine for Eve or Nate, but I don't feel the least bit brotherly toward you. Doesn't anyone else call you Kate?"

"Some."

He wasn't going to ruin what they had just shared by digging into her past. At some point, he would. Something made her unhappy and intuition told him it wasn't bungled weekend with a percussionist from Boston.

XXV

Heavy, dark clouds blotted out the full moon. Rain, wind, thunder, and lightning enveloped the Low Country as the nor'easter formed. The summer and fall had been unusually dry, and the lack of rain from tropical storms or hurricanes made the salt content of the coastal estuaries unusually high. That didn't bode well for the production of oysters, crabs, and other crustaceans that depended on a delicate mixture of salt and fresh water, but this storm promised to restore the balance.

Despite the downpour, they got ready for the trip back to Sullivan's Island. Katie walked to the front door and grabbed the handle of a duffle bag before Devon could stop her. It took much more effort to lift than she had anticipated, and she put it down. Devon asked her to carry the other one. "Are we moving your rock collection, McLean?"

Devon thought of the man's first weapons ... probably rocks. "You're close."

After a brief stop at a grocery store in Mount Pleasant, they drove across the causeway to Sullivan's Island. The fast incoming tide and stage of the moon would create very high water. With onshore wind and rain added to the mix, the causeway might be flooded a few hours from now. When the Porsche hit a deep puddle on the highway, Devon adjusted his steering to overcome the pull of the water. The driving conditions and severe weather unnerved Katie and she felt relieved when they parked in her driveway.

Devon grabbed two bags of groceries while Katie took a carton of soda and pulled the house key from her pocket. Devon told her he'd come back for the duffle bags. The wind-driven rain pelted them as they hurried up the steps to the front door. Once inside, Katie quickly closed the door behind them. They spotted Nate and Eve sleeping soundly on the floor in front of a glowing fireplace. Eve's head rested on Nate's chest, their limbs intertwined, and neither wore a stitch of clothing. Devon and Katie exchanged a smile, and then walked quietly toward the kitchen.

When Devon came back inside with the two duffle bags, Nate woke up with a jolt. Training had taught them to avoid surprises, and Nate found himself caught without his pants.

Devon murmured, "It's me, Nate. Chill out." Devon lugged the two bags past the living room and placed them at the bottom of the stairs.

Nate shook the sleep from his brain, grabbed a throw cover from the sofa and draped it over Eve. Then he pulled on his jeans and followed Devon to the kitchen. He rubbed a hand over his face. "Man, I was dead to the world when you got here."

Katie looked up and smiled as she pulled groceries from the bags. "It looks like the two of you enjoyed your quiet evening alone."

"Hmmm ... we did. But, I feel as though I should have been more useful. The two of you did all the hard work tonight."

"You did your share." Nate missed the innuendo, but Devon gave her a wink.

Eve yawned as she walked into the kitchen wearing her jeans and Nate's sweatshirt; it hung long and loose on her smaller body. When Devon smiled at the combination, Eve explained that she couldn't find her shirt. Nate asked her if she had looked between the sofa cushions. She eyed the groceries on the counter. "That food looks good. I don't know why I'm so hungry." She opened a bag of cookies and bit into one while she got milk from the refrigerator. Nate's cell phone rang as she poured some into a glass. The tone indicated the call came from dispatch.

When he answered, the voice on the phone responded, "I need your code, Commander." Nate gave the dispatch operator a six-character code then listened to the message and thanked the dispatcher. He ended the call and quickly dialed another number.

Devon read the expression on Nate's face. Something unusual had occurred, and it wasn't good.

Isaac answered Nate's call on the second ring. "It's Nate. Give me the details." He spent a few minutes on the phone asking how, where, and when questions. Then he hung up. Everyone in the kitchen looked at him expectantly. "Three hours ago, someone in prison stabbed Wade Simmons with a handmade shiv. He's dead."

Eve's glass shattered on the kitchen floor.

Nate watched her face go pale. He gripped her arm, made her sit down, pushed her head toward her knees, and told her to breathe deeply.

Seconds later, Eve felt the blood return to her head. "Despite what he did to me, Wade Simmons should not have paid with his life. I know you agree. Otherwise, you would have killed him yourself." She paused and took another deep breath. "I'd hoped his incarceration would get him counseling and that someone would help untwist his mind. I even thought he might feel remorse some day."

Nate's feelings toward Wade Simmons were not as magnanimous. "I never expected his rehabilitation, so I don't mourn his death. As cold as this may sound, I'm glad he won't be haunting us at the end of his prison term."

"Who killed him? Why?"

"The FBI's involved with the investigation. Although there's no hard evidence, they suspect a connection to the SSBA." Nate reached for Eve's hand. "Why don't you and Katie go visit your parents in Ireland?"

She didn't take his suggestion well. "And do what? Worry about you being knifed or shot down by a fanatic with a warped view of the world?"

He knew her anger was misdirected, but he'd help her vent it anyway. "That's redundant, Eve."

She snapped at him. "What's redundant?"

"All fanatics have a warped view of the world."

"We agree on that point. So, what am I supposed to do? Let them destroy my life? Let them threaten the man I love and run away while they plot against him?" Her body vibrated with emotion.

Nate raised his voice. "How am I supposed to answer that, Eve? I'll do anything to prevent you or Katie from being hurt again."

Eve rose from the table as lightning flickered and thunder rumbled. Despite how much she hated their situation, Nate was right. He and Devon would deal with these crazy men more effectively if they weren't worried about Katie or her. "I understand your logic, but I also hate it." She started to leave the kitchen and stopped. "I want the men who threaten my home and those I love to pay dearly for it. They should spend the rest of their lives in a hellhole." She turned to leave. "I'll think about your suggestion."

Bootsie appeared from beneath the table and trotted beside Eve as she headed for the stairs. Katie looked at Nate. "How much trouble are they going to cause us?"

He shrugged. "I don't know, but plan on packing tomorrow."

Nate and Devon decided on three-hour shifts throughout the night. Nate would take the first and wake Devon at midnight. Katie settled at the piano and played quietly for the next hour. When she felt a wave of sleepiness wash over her, she took a pillow from the sofa and covered herself with the throw Eve had left on the floor. Devon found her curled in front of the fireplace when he came downstairs at midnight.

Katie heard him turn a page in his book and found him sitting on the sofa a few feet away. He looked almost studious, with a small pair of reading glasses perched on his nose. His cutoff sweatshirt left his arms exposed; they were a vivid reminder of his muscular body and the way he used it to drive her beyond sanity.

Devon watched as she sat up and stretched the kinks from her body. "I worried the floor would make you stiff, but you slept so soundly that I didn't want to wake you."

"I'm okay. What time is it?" He looked at his watch. "Just past two. Nate went to bed and Eve's still working in her studio."

"She must be inspired … in a foreboding way. I've known her to paint round the clock when she gets in a mood. We shouldn't interrupt her." She yawned and got up from the floor. "I need a glass of cold water. Do you want anything from the kitchen?"

"No thanks."

A moment later, Katie screamed and a door crashed open. Devon felt his heart jump into his throat as he grabbed his handgun and ran to the kitchen. In the split second it took him to get there, she was gone. He ran into the porch and found the back door swinging in the wind. Then he heard her cry out just beyond the deck. He pulled the back door shut with a loud slam, hoping Nate and Eve were alerted by the noise. When he sensed motion to his right, he spun with his weapon at eye level and saw a man dressed in fatigues raising a rifle. Without hesitation, Devon fired and his bullet penetrated the man's face. The shot echoed throughout the house and yard.

Eve looked out from her studio window as Devon ran past the pool and down the back stairs. A second later, she collided with Nate in the second floor hallway.

Devon sprinted along the wooden decking that connected the O'Connor property with the waterway. The faint sound of an idling engine warned him of a nearby boat. Then he spotted them on the dock—a man struggled to drag Katie toward the end of the wooden pier. A clean shot at her abductor wasn't possible. Before he reached them, Katie had thrown her weight and overbalanced her attacker. They both fell into the water. A second man pulled the boat from the side of the dock. Devon shot the man in the boat.

He focused intently on the water around him. The second he spotted motion, he shoved the gun into his waistband and jumped into the murkiness below. When her hair brushed his arm, he grabbed it. Then a hand gripped his other arm … it wasn't hers. Something hard hit him in the side. He put all his energy into his legs and torso, propelling toward the surface, dragging Katie and her assailant with him. The sound of a boat engine buzzed dangerously close as he battled his way upward. He broke the surface, sucking in a lung full of air, ignoring the flash of pain in his right leg. Nate jumped into the water next to him. When Devon was sure Nate had a firm grip on Katie, he grabbed the attacker by the shirt. Then he shoved his head beneath the water and held it under for a full minute. The man fought Devon's hold on him with all his strength. When he couldn't fight anymore, Devon hauled him to the surface and let him gasp air. Then he shoved his head under again. He repeated the dunking a third time. The half-conscious man vomited as Devon hauled him toward the muddy shore.

When he got Katie to the marsh, Nate waded back to the boat. He verified the driver was dead, cut the engine, and secured a line. Then he grabbed the AK-47 and a spare rope. Eve lay in the marsh alongside the dock and pointed a gun in the direction of the house. If anyone came toward them, Nate had told her to aim at the chest and squeeze the trigger. Katie was next to her, shaking fiercely and trying hard to breathe normally. Thick, marshy pluff mud coated the women from head to toe. Nate met Devon at the edge of the water. They hogtied the wrists and ankles of their captive behind his back. Then Devon loosened the pants of the bound man and pulled them down to his knees.

Staying low to the ground, Nate pressed the muzzle of the AK-47 against the man's exposed genitals. "Who are you?" Fear and exhaustion kept the man from speaking.

"Find your tongue soon. My hands are covered in mud and you never know when my finger will slip on this hair trigger. Who are you? Who else is with you?" The man didn't answer, so Nate pointed the weapon a few inches from the man's body and fired a short burst into the ground. The impact of the bullets splattered cold mud over the exposed penis of their prisoner.

Devon got on his hands and knees and leaned into the man's face. "Listen up, cocksucker. We can shoot your dick off right now or blow your balls off first. Either way suits me." He looked up at Nate. "Fire off a few more rounds. We'll see how loud he can scream when you put that hot muzzle against his balls. There's no need to rush. He'll be pissing like a girl soon enough."

The man screamed and his body jerked as Nate fired three more rounds into the mud just inches from the man's ear. Then he moved the weapon toward the man's testicles. "What's your name?"

The man wept as he answered. "Chad."

Heavier rain fell as Devon crabbed his way across the marsh toward the two women. He pushed away the pain that shot through his right leg. When he got to Katie, she was shivering but lucid. He tugged off his sweatshirt and pulled it over her head. Then he slipped her arms through the cutoff sleeves and rubbed them to get her blood flowing. Eve's arms trembled as she kept her eyes and the gun trained on the path that led to the house. Devon pulled the gun from his waistband. "Take a break, Eve. Have you seen any motion?" She shook her head. Devon wondered how many others were inside the house or searching the grounds. He overheard Chad plead with Nate.

Moments later, Nate wadded a piece of Chad's shirt and stuffed it in his mouth. He crawled through the mud toward the others. "There are six of them, Dev, including the one in the boat."

"Do you think he's telling the truth?"

"He didn't change his story … even after he pissed himself."

"Then that leaves three and under the circumstances, I don't like the odds." He looked at Eve and Katie. "We should get them out of here."

Nate agreed. "We'll use the boat and head for the Coast Guard station in Charleston."

Devon glanced at the small runabout. "It'll be a hell of a trip in this weather, but I don't have a better idea." He crawled across the mud into the water and stroked quietly until he reached the small watercraft. Then he used a line to drag it close to shore and pulled the dead man from the boat. Nate kept watch while Eve and Katie belly crawled across the mud and through the shallow water. Devon helped them over the side of the boat and instructed them to lie on the bottom, huddling close to each other for warmth. When he gave a signal, Nate crawled over to Chad and dragged him to the boat. With Devon's help, he hoisted him over the bow. Seconds later, Devon turned the ignition key. The boat engine sputtered and died. He adjusted the choke lever and tried it again. It sputtered longer but died again. On his third attempt, the engine kicked over.

As he navigated toward the Intracoastal Channel, an armed man charged onto the dock and fired in their direction. Nate aimed his weapon and squeezed the trigger as a bullet sliced through the sleeve of his shirt. The assailant dropped to the ground. Devon pushed the throttle forward and the boat picked up speed. Nate tore the sleeve from his shirt. Eve reached up and tied it tightly around the wound.

When they reached the Charleston Harbor, danger was still ahead. They had to cross a major shipping lane and fight strong seas. Nate told both women to stay low toward the back of the boat. Then he removed the gag from Chad's mouth. If they managed the swells without capsizing, they'd still have to avoid being run over by a freighter entering or leaving the busy port of Charleston. From the deck of a large ship, the small craft wouldn't be seen, nor would it appear as a blip on the ship's radar screen. Even the wake from a fast-moving tug-boat could put them at risk.

Nate kept his eyes focused on the activity in the harbor while Devon positioned their small craft to take each swell head on. The engine shuddered as they crested a large wave. Then brackish spray showered the vessel as it encountered the next swell. Almost an hour later, they reached calmer waters near the mouth of the Ashley River. Soon, they'd be docked at the Coast Guard station at the northwestern tip of the battery. Ironically, the station was only a few blocks from Nate's home, another house they would have to avoid that night.

XXVI

The volume of seafaring vessels around Charleston kept the Coast Guard busy on a normal day. They oversaw the movement of all commercial ships in and out of the busy port. Boaters of all skill levels navigated the Intracoastal Waterway and the ocean nearby, and they relied on the Coast Guard to bail them out when they got into trouble. Search-and-rescue teams saved lives or recovered corpses. When Devon maneuvered the boat within inches of the landing platform, the severe weather and endangered seafarers had already swamped the Coast Guard with problems.

Nate tossed the line to a young seaman. After securing the boat, the men helped Eve and Katie debark. Nate told the seaman who he was and that he needed to see the officer on duty. He said he knew the station's commander. The seaman saluted and excused himself to use the phone in the guardhouse. Seconds later, he pointed to a door and told them someone would be waiting for them. He asked about the man on the bottom of the boat and Nate told him he belonged in the brig.

When they reached the end of the dock, a young seaman hurried toward them with blankets. Commander Marsalis waited for them as they entered the building. Their condition surprised him. Besides being soaking wet, they were covered in mud from their hair to their bare feet. The women looked ill, exhausted, and very cold. But both seemed lucid and appreciative of the blankets wrapped around their shivering bodies. Blood had streaked down Nate's arm. Devon was shirtless and his torn jeans exposed an open thigh wound.

Nate raised his filthy hand and apologized for not offering it to his friend. He kept the introductions brief. The commander asked what they needed. Nate nodded at Eve and Katie. "They may be bordering on hypothermia. Can we have access to a warm shower? Hot coffee and dry clothes would help."

Commander Marsalis turned to a female officer, asked her to ensure the women's locker room was empty, and to post an emergency off-limits sign for thirty minutes. He said he would send a medic soon. Nate thanked him.

Within minutes, the officer returned and escorted them to the locker room. She asked if Eve and Katie needed any help. They declined, and let Nate and Devon guide them through the door. Lieutenant Worthy positioned herself discreetly on the side of the room, standing at ease with her eyes focused past the shower room. Her commander had ordered her to remain with the two women at all times, a procedure that would prevent allegations of sexual misconduct, a smear no commander wanted on his watch. Nate and Devon never questioned her presence.

Eve and Katie sat down wearily on a bench and Katie felt a new bout of shivers take over her body. Nate rubbed her arms to help warm her while Devon entered the communal shower and cranked on four showerheads. He felt the water temperature rise and breathed the moist, steamy air that built within the tiled room. He returned to the others and announced. "We don't have the time or the need for propriety. Everyone get in there now and start soaking up the heat. And breathe in as much of that steam as possible." He shared Nate's concern about possible hypothermia and wanted to prevent it.

No one argued. Fully dressed, they walked to the shower room. Katie's movements were sluggish and Devon caught her when she stumbled on the threshold. He picked her up and carried her to a stream of warm water. When she stood on both feet, Katie steadied herself by leaning two hands against the shower wall. The clean, warm water streaming over her stirred tears of relief and the numbness she felt for the past two hours started to dissipate. The increased blood flow in his own body caused Devon's leg to throb like a very bad tooth as he stripped to his skin. The mud and clothing made it difficult for him to judge Katie's injuries. He gently began to undress her. Nate and Eve did the same on the other side of the shower.

A burgeoning bruise on her jaw concerned Devon. Her abductor may have knocked her unconscious. After removing her clothes, he found several more bruises on her body. The one on her hip was big as his hand and worried him the most. He pressed gently near the bone and she flinched.

Katie looked down and saw the mark. "I think I did that when I fell on the edge of the dock. Then I don't remember much until Nate pulled me from the water." She carefully ran a hand through her hair. "God, even my scalp is sore." Using his fingertips, Devon helped her wash the mud from her long hair and carefully felt for bumps as he did. "I saw where you fell off the dock and searched the water. When I jumped in, your hair brushed my arm and I grabbed it. The bastard had a hold on my other arm so I couldn't get a better grip on you." He kissed her with tenderness that surprised both of them.

Eve unwound the makeshift bandage that covered Nate's arm. The water hit his wound and stung. Blood dripped to the shower floor and a second reddish stream ran into the center drain. Following the source, they saw blood running down Devon's leg.

Nate and Devon turned off the faucets while Eve walked out of the shower and picked up towels from a rack. The lieutenant pointed to dry clothing on the bench and announced the commander would be entering the locker room soon. She thanked the lieutenant, and carried the towels back to the shower.

The women were dressed in warm sweat suits by the time Commander Marsalis and a younger officer entered the room. The commander carried a bottle of bourbon and put it on the bench. He introduced Lieutenant Pollard, a physician assistant. Eve thanked the commander for the dry, clean clothing and the use of the shower. Nate pulled on a pair of sweatpants and then used his towel to wipe blood from his arm. When Devon started to pull on pants, Eve stopped him. "Not until Lieutenant Pollard looks at the wound on your leg. You'll have to be comfortable in your towel for now."

He grinned. "You just like looking at my legs, sweetheart."

"I looked at one of them in the shower and it's not a pretty sight."

The lieutenant inspected the wound. "Looks painful, sir. What caused it?"

"Propeller."

Paul Marsalis looked down at Devon's leg. "What happened tonight, Nate?"

"I'm involved in an FBI case, Paul. My phone sank and I need to make a call."

"You can do that when the medic is done. Why is a man sitting in my brig? Where did you come from in that small boat?"

Paul deserved an explanation, both as a friend and the station's commander. "We came from Sullivan's Island."

"You've got to be kidding me! In this weather?"

"It wasn't our idea of a spontaneous pleasure cruise … our lives were threatened. What's the status of the causeway?"

"The tide's going out, but sections of the road are still flooded. Few vehicles can get through."

Nate glanced at Devon and saw him flinch. Lieutenant Pollard finished cleaning the long, deep gash on Devon's leg and told him he needed stitches. Devon looked down at the injured leg resting on the bench. "You can handle that. Right?"

The lieutenant nodded. "In the infirmary, Commander. There's damage to the muscle tissue and you'll need a local anesthetic. You should use the leg sparingly for the next week."

The treatment had caused his leg to throb painfully. The bourbon sat unopened on the bench near Devon. After seeing the grimace on his brother's face, Nate walked over and opened it. He took a swallow then handed the bottle to Devon. Two swigs later, Devon put the bottle on the bench. "Wrap if for now. We can deal with the stitches later. Have you got a penlight in that bag, Lieutenant?"

"Yes, I do, sir."

"That's great." Devon pointed at Katie, who sat on the floor with a metal locker at her back. "I want you to shine it in her eyes and tell me if she had a concussion. Then I want you to check her hipbone. She has an ugly bruise. I want to know if it's serious."

Lieutenant Pollard stuffed the penlight in his pocket and approached Katie. He helped her stand up and saw the bruise on her jaw. "Someone clipped you pretty good there, ma'am." She agreed. He shined the penlight into her eyes then stuck it back in his shirt pocket. "The eyes look normal, sir." He placed his hands around the back and sides of her neck and asked to roll her head around gently. "Stop the instant you feel any pain." She rotated her head slowly and told him her neck felt stiff but not painful.

He pointed at her hips. "Which one is it?" Katie lowered the waistband of her sweats and revealed a massive bruise covering her hipbone. The medic carefully rested his fingers against the bruise. "When I press on the bone, I want you to give me a number from one to ten. One means you can barely feel my touch. Ten means you already passed out. Ready?" She nodded and the medic applied pressure to the bone. He stopped pressing when she winced and gasped. "What's the number?"

"Four."

He removed his hand and gently pulled up her waistband "That was a five on my scale. But the bone isn't splintered or you wouldn't be standing right now. It's a bad bruise and needs time to heal. Aspirin will alleviate the discomfort."

"It doesn't hurt that much unless it's touched."

"That's good." The medic turned around. "Who's next?" Eve pointed at Nate's arm. "Why don't you sit down, Commander? I'll be with you in a minute." Eve sat next to Nate and he wrapped his good arm around her shoulder.

Paul handed Devon a pair of sweatpants and asked him when the trouble had started. Devon stayed seated on the bench so he wouldn't put too much weight on the injured leg. He began pulling on the pants, stood carefully, hiked the pants over his hips, and removed his towel. He told Paul he had heard Katie scream shortly after two o'clock that morning. He looked at his watch and realized he was unclear about the episode that occurred just over three hours ago. "What happened in the kitchen, Irish?"

"I went to the porch to check the storm damage. I heard a cat."

"Please don't tell me you unlocked the back door."

"Sometimes Bootsie sneaks out to the veranda. Then she crosses the porch roof, goes to the tree, and climbs down to the ground."

"You opened the door, didn't you?"

"I was worried about the cat."

Devon looked at the ceiling and quietly begged an invisible deity for patience and understanding. Nate and Paul suppressed smiles but shared an amused look.

"Listen, McLean. I only cracked the door a few inches and the safety chain was on it."

His military training helped him keep control. "I was sitting in the living room, Irish. Why didn't you tell me you were concerned about the cat?"

She had braced herself for his anger. His calmness unnerved her more than yelling and her emotions bubbled to the surface. "Because I didn't expect a man in fatigues to kick the door open, grab me by the hair, and yank me from my house! Because I didn't expect to be punched in the face, dragged down the dock, and wrestled with until I fell in the water. I thought he would drown me." She covered her face with her hands.

Devon limped to her and murmured, "Fuck me and the horse I rode in on." He gathered her in his arms. Her attempts to push him away were useless, so she buried her face into his shoulder and cried. He whispered, "I'm sorry, Kate. I'm so sorry." He kissed the top of her hair and rubbed her back soothingly.

When she quieted, he put a finger under her chin and tilted her head. "It wasn't your fault those men came after us. Got it?" She used a sleeve to wipe her eyes and nodded. Devon grinned and she responded with a weak smile. Then he added, "But you didn't have to open the door for them." Her temper flared and she tried to shove him away. He didn't budge an inch. "That's much better, Irish. The color is back in your cheeks and so are those gold flecks in your eyes." Devon grabbed the sleeve of her sweatshirt and wiped it under her nose. He caught Lieutenant Worthy's gaze and winked at her.

When Lieutenant Pollard finished treating the wound on his arm, Nate pulled on a sweatshirt. He tossed one to Devon and asked Paul for a phone. Lieutenant Worthy escorted them to a small meeting room and waited outside.

First, Nate called his father and told him they were safe, despite reports by the local news. He answered several questions and suggested his father visit Olivia in New York for a few days.

Then he called Isaac. Within minutes, their conversation became heated, and the two men argued before Nate hung up. He tried to solve the puzzle, but some of the pieces were wrong.

Devon watched him focus on an invisible spot across the room. "Talk to me, Nate. What's bothering you?"

"After Wade Simmons was killed, a rumor circulated that I was the next SSBA target. Isaac knew I was on Sullivan's Island. Two FBI agents from Columbia were sent there. Even in bad weather, they should have arrived before the cause-way flooded. Where were they when the shooting started?"

"Did Isaac name the agents?"

"One of them was Charlie Potts. He worked with us on the Diana Weaver case. I didn't recognize the other agent's name."

Devon thought about his impression of Agent Potts. "Why weren't we told about a stake out?"

"When I asked, Isaac couldn't answer."

"Where are the agents now?"

"Again, Isaac couldn't answer that. The local police reported that three men we killed. I didn't tell him about Chad. Somehow, he knew I wasn't telling him everything."

"I don't want to think it, Nate, but the FBI may have a skunk in house. Until we know one way or the other, we don't know who we can trust in the Bureau."

Nate nodded. "Isaac suggested we go to an FBI safe house in Bluffton."

"Forget it! We won't be sitting ducks a second time. Let's contact Max and others that we *can* trust … the sooner, the better."

Nate agreed. "I'll ask Paul to hide Chad. I don't want the FBI to have him yet."

The two women had not uttered a word since entering the room. Nate turned to Eve. "You and Katie will be safe here. I'll ask Paul for a room in their barracks."

"No!"

Her response surprised him. "What?"

"Talk about sitting ducks. When you and Devon leave, whom do we trust? Suppose a man flashes a badge and tells us to go with him. What do we do?"

"Paul can prevent that."

"For how long?"

"I don't know."

Eve looked at her sister who had remained surprisingly quiet. "If you have an opinion, express it now."

"They saved my life tonight. I'm going with them."

"Looks like the two of you have traveling companions … like it or not."

Nate shook his head. "Go get those stitches, Dev. I want to see if Chad knows anything about those agents." He turned to Eve. "Don't be shocked if you wake up on a plane headed for Ireland."

Paul assigned a seaman who drove them to a diner on Route 21. Two blocks away was a rental car agency and a storage facility. When the driver pulled away, they walked. Nate approached the facility and disabled a security camera. The storage unit held valuable items including cash, credit cards, identities, clothing, weapons, and electronic equipment. Nate changed his clothes and his identity. His first stop was the car rental agency, which had opened twenty minutes earlier. He drove away in a comfortable four-door Buick sedan, returned to the storage facility, and they were gone before the attendant arrived to begin his workday.

XXVII

If a crow left Charleston, South Carolina, and flew a straight course southwest for ninety miles, it would land in Savannah, Georgia. Nate would have taken the slower and more scenic route to downtown Savannah, a route that went through Beaufort and past Bluffton before crossing the Talmadge Memorial Bridge. But today, they wanted a different course, a traffic-laden highway that would offer them more cover than the lesser traveled roads, many of which were only two lanes. Nate headed toward Walterboro and Interstate 95 South.

They drove in silence until Eve questioned Nate about the storage facility.

"It's for emergencies, just like our current situation. We keep another one near Washington." He reached across the front seat and squeezed her hand. "You should have stayed at the Coast Guard station."

"Could you leave us there and not worry?"

"No."

"And we feel safer with you and Devon. I guess we're in this together."

"My testimony in court put you and Katie in real danger. This is my fault."

Devon spoke up. "You did what was right at the time. Unless you have a crystal ball that I don't know about, second-guessing doesn't solve problems."

Nate caught his brother's gaze in the rearview mirror. "You're right."

Devon booted a laptop computer and made a phone call. "Max, we need help. Look for an e-mail." He typed a lengthy message, encrypted it, and then sent it into cyberspace. He tapped Nate on the shoulder. "I hate to admit it, but I'll function better if I can buy cheap reading glasses somewhere."

"No problem. Eve and Katie need different clothes so they don't stand out." He glanced over at Eve. To his surprise, she was sound asleep. "We'll stop when we hear back from Max."

By the time they reached Pooler, Georgia, they had a plan. Max had set them up in a place on Hilton Head Island. They'd dump the rental car in Savannah and catch a sightseeing boat on River Street; it would take them to the island. From there, they'd ride a trolley, which would stop within a quarter-mile of their version of a safe house. They just had to blend in with the tourists.

Eve woke when Nate decelerated on the Interstate 95 off-ramp. He pulled into the parking lot of a large discount chain store. Katie asked him why they were stopping there. "We need to do a little shopping. Dev and I had stuff in storage but we need other things. The two of you look like matching refugees. So you get to pick out new clothes."

Devon saw the look of horror on Katie's face. "You want us to shop here? Buy clothes here?"

He patted her hand. "Just close your eyes and pretend its Rodeo Drive." She shuddered.

When they got out of the car, Devon favored his injured leg.

Nate asked, "You okay?"

"Yeah. It's just stiff."

"How many stitches?"

"Twelve."

When they entered the store, Nate reminded everyone to shop quickly. He grabbed a shopping cart and pushed it toward Devon. "You stay with them and I'll grab what we need. I'll look for you in their clothing department."

Before he could object, Nate walked away. Devon murmured, "I'm being punished for something." Then he realized the shopping cart made walking easier.

Eve spotted a rack of clothes and started sifting through it. She pulled out black leggings. "Dibs."

Katie looked at her sister's choice. "Those aren't bad. I could even use them for running in this weather. Get another pair for me." Eve took purple leggings off the rack.

"Get real, Eve, you know how purple clashes with my hair color." She scowled at the tag. "Grape?"

Eve pulled a soft yellow tunic sweater from a nearby rack and held it up for her sister. "You look good in this color, and it will offset the leggings." She looked at the tag. "Banana."

"Good grief, I sound like a fruit salad."

Eve grabbed another tunic sweater and looked at the tag. "I'll get strawberry."

Devon spotted brightly colored hats and tossed two into the cart along with cheap sunglasses.

"You don't really think I'll wear those, do you?" Katie asked.

"It's part of your cover." He spotted denim cutoffs. "What size jeans do you wear?"

"That depends on the designer."

"The designer's C-H-E-A-P. What size, Irish?"

Eve responded, "Six … size six should fit both of us."

He tossed two pair into the cart while Eve added fruity-colored T-shirts.

Nate showed up and dumped a small basketful of items into the cart.

They stopped in the accessories department. Nate got two large canvas totes and told the women to get big purses with shoulder straps, emphasizing the bigger the better. Despite Katie's objection, Eve quickly pulled two from the rack. "They're ugly, but they'll do." Devon saw a rack of panties and picked two packages that had the words *small* and *bikini* on them. When he showed them to Eve, she nodded then added socks, moisturizer, and a few cosmetics to their purchases. Katie picked up the lip-gloss and cringed at the brand name.

Devon took her by the hand. "Your agony is over duchess." On the way to the cash register, he veered down an aisle and snatched a pair of reading glasses as well as the latest Grisham hardback.

Nate accelerated down the Interstate 95 on-ramp and asked Eve and Katie to change out of their sweat suits. They packed items into the large purses. Devon checked the laptop for the latest e-mail from Max then stored it in a canvas tote. He added packages from the discount store on top. They left the other tote empty until they removed a dismantled rifle from the trunk. It would be covered with packages as well. Both men still carried Mark 23 pistols, and Eve pulled a small Beretta from beneath the front seat, adding it to the contents of her purse.

They drove in silence for several miles and Eve felt the tension emanating from Nate. She turned so she could see her sister in the backseat. "Do you think Lieutenant Worthy recovered from her grueling assignment?" Devon saw the two women exchange smiles before Eve turned forward in her seat.

Katie replied, "She's one tough cookie. She barely flinched the entire time these two paraded around the women's locker room in nothing more than a towel. And you know she used her X-ray vision while we frolicked in the shower."

Nate glanced at Eve. "What are you two talking about? No one frolicked in that shower. If Lieutenant Worthy had seen any signs of misconduct on Dev's or my part, she'd have drawn her weapon and we'd be sitting in the brig with Chad. That's why she was there."

Katie laughed. "I guess stripping a woman in the shower doesn't fall under the category of misconduct." She remembered being numb to the bone, but not dead. Devon's touch had revived her as much as the warm shower. "I'm sure the lieutenant did her sworn duty, but she enjoyed it immensely. Her stoicism impressed me."

Eve agreed. "The lieutenant was attractive, but I didn't like her shoes."

Nate took her seriously. "She was in uniform. I imagine she wears very pretty shoes when she isn't on duty." Devon wondered how long his brother would pay for that remark.

Eve ignored it—for now. "I started to feel a little sorry for her, Katie, but she gave Nate another once over when he pulled on his sweatpants. I thought about scratching her eyes out to end her misery."

Nate looked at Eve in surprise. "The two of you must have been hypothermic. Lieutenant Worthy acted with total professionalism the entire time we were there." Devon closed his eyes. After years of watching his older sister toy with her boyfriends, Devon had learned an important lesson … the woman wins in the end.

Eve tapped Nate on the shoulder. "Listen up, Commander. I'm not blind … I see the way other women look at you. The lieutenant conducted herself professionally, but you and Devon were no hardship for her. With the right invitation, she'd have saluted her commander and followed either of you out the door. She almost lost it when Devon winked at her." Nate gave his brother a pained expression in the rearview mirror and Devon knew he was on his own.

Katie leaned forward in her seat. "I didn't know he winked at Lieutenant Worthy. When did he do that?"

Devon sighed. Until now, he had avoided the hot seat. "Are you sure I didn't blink? My eyes were scratchy from the brackish water."

Eve wouldn't let him off the hook. "Nice try, Devon. When I sat down next to Nate, we both saw you wink at her. You were hugging Katie at the time."

Katie's body swiveled in his direction. "You winked at another woman while your arms were around *me*?"

"What's the matter, Irish? Are you jealous of Lieutenant Worthy?"

"No, I'm not jealous of her. Why would I be?"

"If you aren't jealous, why do you care if I winked at her?"

"Actually, you might be perfect for Lieutenant Worthy. You drive me bonkers."

"That's because you're crazy about me."

"You're the one who's crazy, McLean. Just because we had mind-altering sex yesterday doesn't mean I'm declaring my undying devotion to you."

Nate raised an eyebrow and exchanged the *"ah ha"* look with Eve. That explained a lot!

"You're in denial again, Kate."

"McLean, you are the antithesis of any man I've ever known."

"That just shows your taste in men is improving."

"I don't think that for one moment. For heaven's sake, you walk around with a loaded gun stuffed in your pants."

He threw his head back and laughed aloud. "And I pity the man who doesn't!"

Nate and Eve cracked up.

Katie thought about her remark. "You know perfectly well what I meant."

He adopted a serious tone. "What else about me bothers you?"

"You're bossy, stubborn, and opinionated."

"And to think those are traits I use to describe you."

"Stuff it, McLean."

Devon enjoyed getting her riled. "I understand the problem, Irish. I'm not *intellectual* enough to fulfill your needs." He made air quotes around the word *intellectual.* Then he added, "I can accept that because you're too *prissy* to meet my needs." He repeated the gesture with the word *prissy* and waited for her to ignite. Nate laughed quietly and wondered if Katie had spontaneously combusted as she hissed the word.

"Did you say *prissy*? No one has *ever* called me that!"

Devon shrugged, "We're all entitled to our opinion."

Katie remained silent.

Moments later, Interstate 16 ended in downtown Savannah. When the two men had discussed a destination, Eve had been asleep. She asked Nate where they were going.

"Hilton Head Island. We're taking a boat from River Street."

She looked surprised. "That's a roundabout way to get to Hilton Head."

"You're right, but we avoided the Bluffton route because of the FBI safe house. We don't want to be spotted in that area."

XXVIII

In Savannah, the four refugees descended a steep stone outdoor stairway, crossed cobblestone side streets, and walked past old brick warehouses along River Street. Those historic structures had stored cotton, tobacco, and other commodities for more than two hundred years. Now they housed shops that sold T-shirts, souvenirs, frozen margaritas, and other tourist trappings. Devon spotted an Irish pub near the public dock and they ate a quick lunch before boarding the boat to Hilton Head Island. The remnants of the storm caused unseasonably cold and damp weather, so few other travelers embarked for the trip

Devon sat in the rear of the sightseeing boat with the brim of a baseball hat pulled low over his eyes and his injured leg propped on a chair. He had swallowed four aspirin when they got to Savannah, and the pain relief helped him doze. He needed the rest; Nate would take his turn when they reached their destination.

Nate sat a few feet away from Devon feigning interest in an area travel guide while scanning the boat and the surrounding waterway for any sign of trouble. He wished there were more tourists on board so they could blend in with the crowd. With their wardrobe, packages, and demeanor, they looked like out-of-towners visiting the Low Country. They also tried to avoid appearing like a constant foursome.

Eve and Katie stood near an open window and tried to let the view distract them from their worries. Tall, long-necked birds stalked the edges of the waterway while oyster harvesters explored the mud banks in flat wooden boats that had weathered decades ago. Katie pointed at the water a few feet from the boat. Eve signaled Nate to the side. Despite his preoccupation, he smiled when a pod of dolphin broke the surface. She watched the stress slip from his face for just a second.

An hour later, they landed on Hilton Head Island, walked past a striped light-house, and followed the signs for a trolley. Dozens of tourists milled past shops, and a long line waited at the trolley stop. Both men were glad for their anonymity among the crowd. Soon the foursome stepped off the trolley near a cluster of red and blue wooden buildings. Eve scanned the small village ... it reminded her of an old New England fishing town. Pleasure boats floated in the marina, shops and restaurants occupied the two-story buildings, and a friendly outdoor bar took center stage on a large deck that overlooked the waterway. Large logs burned in an outdoor fire pit. Bartenders served drinks to the people gathered around on stools, many of whom appeared to be locals.

Devon spotted a small wooden sign indicating the location of the local inn. He nodded toward the bar. "The three of you stay here while I register and get our keys. Order a beer for me." He and Nate put the tote bags under an empty table and the two women sat down. Nate took a position at the bar where he could watch the activity around them.

Ten minutes later Devon returned with an envelope and stood next to Nate. He saw the two women glance in his direction and he winked at them.

"That habit will get you into serious trouble one of these days, Dev."

"I'll pay dearly for that innocent twitch at the lieutenant."

"Hmmm. Your timing sucked, but I admired your comeback."

Devon took long swallow of beer. "Your lady started that little diversion just to break the tension." He saw the skepticism on Nate's face. "If you don't believe me, ask her."

The bartender turned up the volume on a football came that had caught everyone's interest. The sound drowned out their voices from those within ear-shot. "I have the keys to the house Max reserved. I'm registered as Michael O'Malley. We have less than a half-mile walk. The house sits on a point. The neighborhood is surrounded by water on three sides and is accessed by a single road. Max used a local service to stock some groceries."

Nate finished his beer. "We'll take all the small favors we can get. Let's split up and head over to this place."

Devon nodded. "I'll tag Kate and follow the directions the desk clerk gave me. You and Eve can walk through the marina and follow a trail to the Calibogue Sound. Turn right at the beach and walk until you reach a breakwater. I'll look for you." Nate left the bar and approached the table where Eve and Katie waited. He picked up a heavy tote as though it weighed next to nothing. Eve put a large purse over her shoulder and took the hand he extended.

Devon sat down at the table with Katie and waited until Nate and Eve were out of sight. "It's time to go." Without seeing the young boy darting behind him, Devon stood. He winced sharply as the boy accidentally ran into his bad leg. The frightened boy muttered a quick apology and ran off.

"You okay, McLean?"

"Yeah." Devon leaned down for the other tote bag and straightened up slowly.

Katie wrapped an arm around his waist. "Don't take this the wrong way. It's just part of my cover."

He smiled, wrapped an arm around her shoulder, and guided her to the short-cut that would take them to their next destination.

The gray, weathered house was one of many duplexes that sat on the farthest point from the island's bridge. From the rear of the house, Devon could see Dau-fuskie and several other barrier islands. Braddock Cove sliced through marshes to his right, and the tides of the Calibogue Sound flowed swiftly in front and to his left. Nate and Eve walked up the beach bordering the Calibogue Sound. Devon stood on the back deck until Nate spotted him. Then he went back inside. Soon all four were settled inside the home, away from the scrutiny of the outside world and those who might want to harm them.

Devon and Nate carried the totes to a dining table and began unloading. Eve went to a nearby counter and dumped the contents of the large purses. Nate pulled heavy metal parts from the bag. Within seconds, he assembled an M4 car-bine rifle, plugged an ammunition clip into the chamber, and sighted the weapon on the front door. Then he put it on the table.

Devon looked at his watch. "I'll get through to Max. You should catch some shuteye."

Nate thought about his SEAL training. During *Hell Week*, they were pushed to their physical and mental limits for five days with no more than five hours of sleep during the entire ordeal. The day he and Devon arrived on Coronado Island, they made a pact to endure anything the instructors could dish out. Fewer than half the recruits walk away from Coronado as SEALs. They had. He was eleven years older now and had to admit his body wouldn't handle that kind of punishment again. He looked at his watch. "I'll be awake in two hours. You need to check that leg and stay off it."

"I'm okay, big guy."

"Damn it, Dev. I've watched you. That leg feels like an abscessed tooth beg-ging to be pulled. For Christ's sake, take more aspirin."

Eve recognized sleep deprivation. She kissed him on the cheek and turned him toward the stairs. "Go upstairs. If Devon doesn't do what you ask, I'll nag him until he does. Trust me, he'll cave."

Katie yawned. "I'm going to take a nap too. Wake me if I'm needed."

Twenty minutes later, Devon read an e-mail from Max. He told Eve that others would arrive about eight o'clock that night. "That's good, Devon. Now let's check your leg."

"Give me a minute. I need underwear."

He grabbed a package from the counter and left the room. Minutes later, he came back wearing boxers and carrying his sweatpants.

Eve handed him a first aid kit and extra gauze pads. "Nate got this during our shopping spree today."

Devon sat down, propped his leg on the coffee table, and began unwrapping a heavy elastic bandage. "Our stop in Pooler wasn't your idea of a shopping spree, and I think it traumatized Katie."

"Deep down, she isn't like that. Growing up, Katie was genuine and well grounded."

He looked her in the eye. "You're a well-grounded woman, Eve, your sister pales in comparison."

She shook her head. "I know why you're saying that. Maybe working in the movie business has affected her. But I also believe someone hurt her."

"Are you referring to the infamous percussionist?"

"No. I think there was someone on the West Coast, someone much more manipulative than Rob Thornton."

He removed the layer of gauze that covered his stitches and Eve winced when she saw the long gash and bruising that covered his thigh. Devon inspected the exposed wound and grunted. "That propeller took a good chunk out of me. I heard the engine and tried to avoid the prop while I kept a grip on Katie's hair. It should have been idling; the driver must have bumped the throttle when I shot him." He looked up and saw the horror of the previous night reflected on her face. "Oh man, Eve, I'm sorry."

She shook her head to clear her mind. "I'm okay. Let's put a warm compress on your leg. Then we'll use the ointment and let the air at it. I'll get you some aspirin." She started to walk into the kitchen then added, "Thank you for saving my sister's life."

When Katie entered the room, she saw Devon sitting in boxers with his leg propped on the table and the computer in his lap. "Can't you keep your pants on, McLean?" Then she spotted his injury. "Ouch!"

Devon put the laptop on the coffee table and reached for a box of sterile gauze pads and adhesive tape. "You're awake sooner that I expected."

Katie watched as he bandaged the wound on his leg. "I slept for an hour, and then tossed for the last ten minutes. So I'm up now." She looked at her sister. "Why don't you crawl in with Nate?"

Eve thought about it—the strength and warmth of Nate's body always soothed her—but she hesitated. "I may wake him, and he needs the sleep." Devon and Katie glanced at each other. They knew she'd need just a little more convincing. Katie told her Nate was sleeping soundly when she tiptoed past the open door of his bedroom. Devon told her if Nate did wake up, he'd be glad to find her snuggled next to him. Eve smiled and acquiesced.

While Devon pulled on his sweatpants, he gave Katie a quick study. She had sleep-tousled hair and wore the pale yellow top and purple leggings with socks but no shoes. He tried to ignore her pert nipples poking at her top and remembered she hadn't bought a bra. The funny discussion between Eve and Katie came to mind.

"You look pretty good for a fruit salad, Irish."

She looked down at her outfit. "I tried to follow your suggestion and pretend I was shopping on Rodeo. I couldn't stretch my imagination quite that far."

He patted the sofa cushion next to him and invited her to sit down. Then he asked, "How did you end up in Los Angeles?"

Still groggy from her nap, Katie curled into the corner of the sofa with her knees drawn toward her and her feet tucked against her butt. She stretched her upper body and yawned. "During my senior year, a professor introduced me to a colleague. He taught at UCLA's School of Music. They convinced me to apply for a grant so I could get my master's degree there. I auditioned with several professors in the Department of Music and I got the grant."

"I'm impressed."

"Yeah, well, it helped, but I also had to earn a living. Professor Clark, the colleague from UCLA, helped me get a job with MGM Studios. The company subsidized my tuition in exchange for my employment. I signed a two-year contract and moved to Los Angeles. I ended up living there for four years."

"Is that when you and the percussionist split up? When you moved to the West Coast?"

She covered another yawn. "Actually, Rob and I were on shaky ground before I even applied for the grant. He chose performing as a career and had this dream of us working together in a famous symphony. We'd travel the world and wow audiences with our God-given talent."

"That sounds pretty romantic. Why didn't you go for it?"

"First of all, it was Rob's dream, not mine. Secondly, the earning potential isn't great unless you're in the top echelon of performers worldwide. I'm not that talented."

Devon looked at her in surprise. He never expected to hear self-criticism from Katie O'Connor. "I've heard you play and it sounded great to me."

She tilted her head and shrugged. "I play well, but I'm not good enough for the top symphonies. I dislike mediocrity. My strength is in composition, not performance. My professors agree with me. To make a short story long, Rob and I argued a lot during our senior year of college. He and I saw our lives taking very different directions and neither of us wanted to compromise." She shrugged. "When I got the grant, he got a new apartment. It just happened to come with a new girlfriend." She tried to sound nonchalant about the experience, but Devon suspected other feelings. The wound may have been old, but it had been deep.

"That's enough about me, McLean. Tell me about all the torrid affairs you've had in the line of duty. Surely, you've been forced to seduce several beautiful spies for the safety of our country. You're very good at seduction by the way."

"You're thinking of old war movies, Kate. The Middle Eastern women I've seen are covered in black from head to toe and never allowed outside their homes without a male relative escorting them. They could be stoned to death for bumping into an infidel by accident."

Katie shook her head. "I couldn't imagine living like that, but I guess they don't have any choice." Devon agreed then circled the conversation back to her. Katie was unusually relaxed and talkative, so he'd take advantage of the occasion to learn more about her.

"Tell me about the special man you met in Los Angeles."

She looked at him quizzically. "I met a lot of people there. What makes you think I met a special man?"

He watched her build the barrier and figured he'd just have to tear it down. "Call me psychic. A beautiful woman doesn't spend four years in the land of make-believe and not meet a man who becomes special to her. What did you do for MGM Studios?"

"I wrote music."

The abruptness of her answer told him she had put up a barrier about that period in her life. He'd have to start tearing it down brick by brick.

"What was his name, Irish?"

"Whose name?"

"The man you fell in love with." He held up a hand. "Wait." He closed his eyes. "I want to guess." Devon put his fingers against his temples and squeezed his eyes as though conjuring the answer to his own question. Then his eyes popped open and he shouted, "Fred!"

He looked so ridiculous that Katie couldn't help but laugh. "No, you goof. It was Antonio." She looked at him in disbelief. Devon not only wheedled the man's name, he had gotten her to admit that she had indeed loved him.

Not wanting the first two bricks to go back up, Devon switched into high gear. He repeated the name *Antonio* aloud as though studying its sound. "Where did you meet Antonio? Did you spend time in Europe?"

"We met in Los Angeles. The studio assigned me to a documentary. I helped create the score. He was the director."

Devon became the conjurer once again. "I see an attractive man in finely cut Italian suits. He drives a fast car and wears expensive sunglasses. He has a nice build, his hair is dark, and he wears it past his collar." With his eyes still closed, Devon paused then added, "Antonio likes expensive restaurants and his manners are impeccable."

"You're scary, McLean. But if you're so smart, tell me how old he is."

Devon had just described the typical European jetsetter. He had no idea about the man's age, but he'd get the answer from her. He pretended to conjure again. "He's fifty-eight years old, but you met him three years ago, so he was only fifty-five when you fell in love with him."

"He was forty-two, and I had just turned twenty-four. He treated me to dinner for my birthday." She gave Devon a serious look. "How do you do this, McLean? I've never told anyone about Antonio. Not even Eve."

"Why not? I thought you and Eve told each other everything."

Katie shrugged and remained silent. Devon kept digging. "Where did he take you for your birthday?"

Twenty minutes later, Devon had learned much about Antonio and the eight months he and Katie had been lovers. An experienced, sophisticated man swept a beautiful young woman off her feet and showed her how to live life in the fast lane—a classic story. Her discussion of the romance made Devon think of Antonio as a creative but selfish person. There was no question about the size of the man's ego—gargantuan.

"He sounds like a man who likes to be in control all the time, Kate. Knowing you, I'm surprised your affair lasted that long."

The term *affair* took her off guard. "He took charge, and I wasn't the same person I am now. As I look back, I realize that experience changed me. I was malleable then, too much so. He had a way of making me feel insignificant if I didn't please him, especially in bed."

Devon knew to tread lightly. "Was he a good lover?"

"I thought so at the time. I had only been with Rob until then. Antonio was more worldly, but he wanted total control. I did things for him even though I didn't want to do them. Looking back, I'll admit he wasn't a very generous lover."

"Sounds like shades of *Nine and a Half Weeks*." Devon regretted the remark as soon as he had said it.

Katie's eyes flashed. "He never played 'Mustang Sally' and forced me to strip, McLean." Her voice quieted. "But he did other things." She remembered her apprehension the first time Antonio suggested bondage. "He tied me to the bed several times. God, I can't believe I'm telling you about any of this!"

"Did he hurt you?"

"No. He abhorred physical violence. His games were mental. Sometimes he'd make love to me; other times he'd ignore me. There were times he'd just stare at me. Once he walked out of the room and left me there for an hour."

"Sounds a little sick to me. Do you still see him?"

She shook her head. "He told me right up front that he wasn't a monogamous man. I thought I could handle that." She added with self-mockery, "Why shouldn't I be a sophisticated woman of the world just like every one else involved in the Hollywood scene?" Her tone became sad again. "But I had fallen in love and was naïve enough to think I could change him."

"Didn't he love you back?"

"Oh, he told me he loved me, but his definition and mine were very different."

Devon heard both anger and hurt in her last statement. Katie figured she'd gone this far, so she might as well tell the rest of it. Devon would probably dig it out of her anyway. "He had business in Europe and he'd been gone for two weeks. When he returned, he called me while he drove away from the airport. I got the usual lines: 'I miss you. I love you. I can't wait to be with you.' He told me to take a long, luxurious bath; he even told me what scent of bath oil to use. Then I should wait for him on the bed, wearing nothing, and without any covers. All the top covers had to be taken off the bed. The bottom sheet had to be satin, white satin." She paused and looked up at Devon. "Do you believe that I actually did everything he asked?"

Devon's body surprised him with a response. The image she described had sparked a reaction his brain didn't expect. He got up slowly and limped across the room. With his back to her, he made a slight adjustment.

"Is your leg bothering you, McLean?"

"I'm a little stiff, Irish. I just need to move around." A minute later, he sat down. "I got the kinks worked out. Finish your story."

"Okay, but this next part is going to sound kinkier than your sore leg. I had done exactly what he asked. Antonio got to my place, used his key, and came into the bedroom. After giving me a very approving look, he told me we'd share a very special night together. He meant the word *share* literally." She paused for a second. "Another woman walked through my bedroom door. She was Marilyn Monroe gorgeous. Antonio had her stand in front of him and he unzipped her dress. Then he slipped it off her shoulders and it fell to the floor. She stood there wearing nothing more than a smile and her high heel shoes."

Devon coughed. Was she telling the truth or was she was punishing him for Lieutenant Worthy's wink? Then he heard the hitch in her throat.

"The man I loved brought a beautiful woman to the bed I wanted to share with him—only him. He wanted me to make love with her while he watched. Then he'd join us. I couldn't do it. I had never denied him before that night, but he pushed me too far. We had a horrible fight. In the end, he told me I was narrow-minded and prudish; he saw no reason to go on with our relationship. He helped her with her dress and they left."

A tear ran down her cheek. "I really loved him, Devon."

He reached out and wiped away the tear. "I'm sure you did, darling."

She scrubbed her hands briskly across her face and her demeanor became defiant. "The next three months were difficult but enlightening. I had to finish the score for the documentary; I was under contract with the studio and had no choice. Antonio and I found ourselves in each other's presence more times than I care to count. He treated his new girlfriend like a trophy. That's when I took a very hard look at myself and realized I had served the same purpose for him. I hated the thought of it. I'm not sure I've forgiven myself, even after all this time."

Devon pulled her toward him and wrapped his arms around her. He whispered. "Do you still love him?"

"No, I don't. I can honestly say I'm over him. But I still feel the hurt."

"That's a good sign, you know. It means your heart didn't freeze. A frozen heart can't feel any pain, but it can't feel any love either."

She pushed back from his chest and looked him in the eye. "You're pretty smart for a man. You got me to spill my guts about Antonio, and then you made me feel better about it." She repositioned herself into the corner of the sofa. "Have you ever had one? A *ménage a trois*?"

Devon thought for a moment. She'd been painfully honest with him, so he thought she deserved honesty in return. "I've been asked by two women."

"Were they attractive?"

"Yes, but I wouldn't put them in league with you or Marilyn."

"Did you do it?"

He thought carefully about his answer. "I gave it serious consideration. Then one of them mentioned a sex toy that caused me to hesitate." He smiled. "Do you really want to know what happened?"

She nodded.

"I grabbed my clothes off the floor and left."

XXIX

Shortly after nightfall, two cars pulled into the driveway of the adjoining duplex. Four men climbed out and unloaded suitcases and golf clubs. The conversation focused on which five golf courses they would play within the next three days and the amount of wagering for each round. Cutting remarks and insults flew among them.

Devon watched the activities of his new neighbors from an upstairs bedroom window. When the group disappeared inside the adjacent rental property, he went downstairs. Nate had gone out the front door to retrieve a bag of golf clubs the group had left in the adjoining driveway. After removing the bag cover, he extracted an M4 carbine rifle, a scope, ammunition, night-vision goggles, and protective gear. Within the next fifteen minutes, the four men from the adjacent house had made their way next door. Two meandered through the front, while two others wandered in through the back porch.

Firm hands clasped and greetings exchanged among the men. Nate introduced Eve and Katie to the former Navy SEALs. Devon added a short anecdote for each man. "Max is the third partner in DMG, Inc. and the three of us went through the SEAL program together. Tommy's parents were *Who* fans when he was born, so he's named after the pinball wizard—and he's lived up to his namesake on the machines. Chip's father was a navy frogman before they became SEALs. He got his nickname because he was a *chip off the old block* in the water. He swims better than any of us, so we blame it on genetics and massage our egos." He turned to the fourth man and grinned. "Watch out for Gabe—he's a sweet-talker. He also pulled me away from a fire on board a ship in the Persian Gulf."

Gabe returned Devon's grin. "Someone had to save that lily-white ass of yours."

Eve and Katie surveyed the men. All were strong, lean, and good looking. Max, at six feet, was the shortest, while Chip, at six four, topped Nate by an inch. Gabe was black and had a smile more dangerous than Devon's. Tommy resembled Devon in both size and complexion. Chip had a blond, boyish California surfer look, while Max had dark hair and features similar to Nate. Both women felt the strong camaraderie among the men.

Gabe reached for Eve's hand. "So you're the woman who toppled the mighty Dunlevy. His finicky taste in women has finally been rewarded." Eve smiled and told Gabe she wanted to hear more about Nate's taste in women.

Tommy had been mesmerized by Katie O'Connor since the moment he put eyes on her. After a few flirtatious remarks, he caught Devon's stare. His former commander smiled, but his eyes sent a different message. The look unnerved Tommy, just as it had years ago. Although Devon never spoke a word, he had communicated an order to *stand down.*

The pleasantries were over and the former SEALs got to work. After Nate explained the background, Max told them about the latest message he received from Tee-Jay. "Manfred and Everet Dodd are protecting assets by moving money to offshore accounts. Tee-Jay followed a trail and found a transfer to another offshore account. He traced it to an FBI agent ... one who helped us take down the camp in Georgia."

Nate asked. "Charlie Potts?"

Max nodded. "How did you know?"

"A good guess. He was supposed to be on Sullivan's Island the night the SSBA came after us. We never saw him."

"He has over one million dollars in this account."

"That could explain why we didn't know about a stakeout. The man we have stashed in the brig admitted the colonel sent six men to kill me. Three came by water, the others by land. When I questioned him about the FBI agents, he swore he never saw them, but he couldn't speak for the others."

"If Potts is on their payroll, why didn't he alert the ones who took Diana Weaver?"

Nate tossed out a theory. "The uproar over the senator's niece forced the colonel into hiding ... no doubt with his best soldiers. The caretakers had become loose cannons, so give them up. They get blamed for the niece, the FBI cleans up the mess, and Potts keeps his cover."

Devon spoke up. "I like your theory, Nate. It explains the absence of the colonel and others that morning. But why haven't they been found? Did someone else cross the line?"

Nate looked around the table. "Here's a difficult question. Do we trust Isaac?"

Devon remained silent. He and Nate were too close to be objective.

Max asked, "What makes you think we can't trust him?"

"His connection to Charlie Potts and this case—that's all."

"When was your last contact with him?"

"About fourteen hours ago, Max. I called him from the Coast Guard station in Charleston just before we left. He knew I held back on him, and he was pissed. I told him I'd contact him when I could do it safely. I also told him he'd put us at risk if he tried to contact me."

"Did he?"

"No ... he didn't."

Gabe interjected, "He might work for the FBI now, but he's a SEAL. I can't think of anything that would cause him to turn on you or any of us."

"I can." Devon's words drew immediate attention. "Do we know if Charlene and his two kids are safe?"

His remark hit home. When family members were in jeopardy, anyone could act out of character. Would they betray? They thought about the dilemma.

Gabe told them he would find out. "Our wives are good friends. I can call Isaac and small talk him without raising any suspicion. If he's concerned about his family, we'll know it."

Chip added, "We deal with the SSBA legally or we'll be sitting next to them in prison."

Nate agreed and asked Gabe to call Isaac.

Max set up equipment so Isaac wouldn't be able to trace the call. A speaker would enable everyone to listen, but Isaac wouldn't detect any audio feedback.

Gabe punched in Isaac's number. The call went through and the two men talked jokingly about their wives. Gabe asked about the kids. No one could hear any tension in Isaac's voice. Then Gabe told him about a poker game he was planning and asked Isaac what nights he'd be available. Isaac mentioned three nights during the following week.

His pleasant tone changed suddenly. "I can't play poker this week, because I'll be too damn busy wringing Dunlevy's neck! I know you can hear me just fine. I don't know where you are, but I probably know who else is there. Under the circumstances, I'd have put a similar team together. Now listen to what I have to say."

They remained silent.

"First, my wife and my children are safe. I appreciate your concern for them. As for the SSBA, we found Reverend Dodd and he's chirping like a songbird in exchange for clemency. His brother ordered the hit on Simmons and Dunlevy. I found out Charlie Potts is conspiring with the SSBA. Who knows how many others are paying him? The agent who went to Sullivan's Island with him was found shot to death. Potts cost a good man his life. I don't know where he is, but I swear he'll pay for it."

Nate looked around the table and stopped with his brother whose instincts he trusted the most. When Devon nodded, Nate spoke up, "How do we take these bastards down?"

Isaac's voice boomed. "You have no idea how many times I've wanted to hug you and then choke you, Dunlevy. That goes for you too, McLean. At least you're preparing me for teenagers. God help me when I have to face that every day." He continued, "You aren't safe until the colonel and his platoon are put away. With your help, we'll take these men. I'm sure Potts told them about the Bluffton safe house. I don't know where you are, but I'll bet my left nut that you aren't very far from there."

An hour later, Max set up a recorder in a bedroom for Eve and Katie. "You have a special assignment. Talk to each for the next few hours ... just girl talk and don't mention the SSBA." Gabe joked that sharing notes about sex would get them a commendation. When they looked at him skeptically, he brought them two large glasses of wine. They reluctantly began their assignment. Soon they were relaxed and enjoying their project.

Nate and Devon had a similar project. Max placed a recording device in another bedroom and the two men talked about sports, war stories, and other topics considered manly. They took a break from their recording assignment and found Max sitting at the laptop. He looked up and smiled at them. "I just got a message from Tee-Jay. A banking error eliminated most of the funds in Potts' offshore account. Tee-Jay wants to know what charities should receive the funds." He paused. "It's decision time. One of us leads, the rest follow. Who's running this op?"

Nate replied, "Give us five minutes." He turned to his brother. "We need to talk." They walked into the downstairs bedroom and closed the door.

When Even and Katie came downstairs and heard the muffled sound of their voices, they wondered what had triggered the private conversation. Both male voices got louder and the women exchanged surprised looks.

Tommy jokingly asked Max, "Think they're putting on the gloves?"

Before Max could respond, Eve said, "I've never heard them argue. Have you?"

He nodded. "It happens. Not often."

Tommy told her he'd seen them fight and he'd never forget it.

Eve was shocked. "You mean fight as in grapple with each other and throw punches."

"No, ma'am. I mean put on the gloves and go ten rounds in the ring."

Max told them about a boxing event that occurred in San Diego years ago. "It was a fund raiser and spectators had to pledge donations. The proceeds went to the families of two SEALs who had been killed in a helicopter crash. Nate and Dev signed up to fight each other."

Tommy went on, "Half the base showed up for the *Dunlevy versus McLean* match. I remember Colonel Dunlevy flying out to watch it. Besides the pledges, there were hundreds of side bets. They climbed into the ring and pummeled each other for the full ten rounds."

Katie asked him who won.

"Who cared? It was one of the best fights I've ever seen."

Max answered her question. "The referee raised two gloves and called it a draw. Most people felt the fight had earned their side bets, so they added the money to the funds collected for the families. I heard the match added more than twenty grand to the kitty. I went to the locker room after the fight. They were lying on gurneys while two med techs worked on them." Max shook his head and chuckled. "When one groaned, the other laughed. Neither one could remember who suggested they fight each other. We ended up in a bar that night, and no one would let them buy a drink. A few hours later, we poured them into bed."

While Eve and Katie heard about the match, Nate and Devon went toe-to-toe over another decision. Both men were in lockstep agreement that one of them would participate in the SSBA takedown at the Bluffton safe house while the other would remain in the Hilton Head house with Eve and Katie. The consensus ended there.

Devon pointed his finger at the closed bedroom door and spoke heatedly. "You've got a woman out there who's going to worry herself sick while you're gone."

Nate returned the heat. "People rarely die of worry." He pointed at Devon's leg. "You have a serious leg injury. It'll slow you down."

Devon shouted, "Fuck the leg!"

Nate shouted back, "Get a grip, Dev. I see how you're moving."

"I'll move just fine. Let's end this debate now." He reached for a coin.

Nate shook his head. "Not this time. We aren't on even ground."

"Okay, Nate, you want to base the decision on perfect health. Here's a good question. When was your last flashback?"

"Goddamn it, I should just flatten you."

"Try. After you pick yourself up off the floor, we'll still have to settle this."

"You're on shaky ground." Nate fought for control. "Despite my head problems, I never spaced out while I was in danger." He lost his restraint and shouted, "Including the days I rotted in a fucking cell with Eve's rapist!"

They were teetering on the edge of an unfair fight and Devon had pushed it far enough. "You didn't know *what* would happen. It cost me sleep while you were in there."

Nate started to calm down. "I have to end this nightmare and Eve has to be safe. I don't trust anyone else with her life more than I trust you."

Devon had lost the battle, but he went for a concession. "And because of her, you're not detached enough to run this op. If I stay, Max calls the shots."

"Agreed."

Devon cast his eyes toward the ceiling. "Give me strength."

Eve was imaging the two men hammering at each other in a boxing ring when they walked into the living room. She gave Nate a peculiar look.

"What?"

His voice snapped her back to the present. "Did you settle your disagreement?"

"We did." Eve and Katie saw the scowl on Devon's face. They weren't convinced.

Before daybreak, Chip and Tommy walked to the nearby marina, eased a boat out of its slip, and quietly cruised out of Braddock Cove. They crossed the Calibogue Sound and navigated the May River inland. When they got close to their destination, Chip slipped over the side of the boat and onto the sandy marsh. Tommy waited until Chip had taken cover. Then he guided the small craft forward until he reached the long wooden dock behind the safe house. He did not attempt to hide his arrival. Anyone who spotted him would mistake him for Devon McLean.

They had used a satellite view of the area to plan the operation. The neighborhood was separated from the adjoining community by a small bridge and a long gravel road. Other than the safe house, there were two other homes and FBI records showed they were summer residences. The location was a good choice for an FBI hideaway. The satellite image had shown no activity at the other two homes during the past twenty-four hours. Chip spotted a moving vehicle on the gravel road and radioed in. "There's a white van approaching. Does it belong to the FBI?"

Max responded. "Negative."

Chip watched the movement of the van until it stopped. "We have company at the first house on the right." He waited. "No one's getting out of the van."

Nate radioed back. "If they're SSBA, we'll give them what they're expecting."

After dawn, Nate, Max, and Gabe drove to the Bluffton safe house. Nate stopped the vehicle along the gravel road and Gabe slipped out of the rear seat. The other two men drove to the house and walked boldly through the front door. Inside the safe house, Max set up equipment to play the recordings from the previous night. Nate opened two windows to ensure the sound would carry beyond the reinforced structure of the safe house. Tommy settled into a surveillance position and remained silent.

Two men sitting in the white van picked up the recorded conversation between Nate and Devon. Max interjected his own voice. Soon after, the voices of the two women competed with the sound of a television.

One of the van occupants reported to Columbia. "We're monitoring the house. Dunlevy and two other men are inside. So are the two women." He listened and smiled. When the communication ended, he turned to his partner. "The colonel wants to take the house tonight. After the men are eliminated, the women become the spoils." From his position in the marsh, Gabe picked up the conversation from the white van and transmitted the information to Max.

While others prepared to do battle in Bluffton, Agent Potts stayed on Hilton Head Island. He had wasted an extra day collecting another payment from the SSBA because Dunlevy hadn't blindly gone to the FBI safe house. Now, his plans to leave the country had been delayed again because the money stashed in an offshore account had disappeared. His contact in the Cayman Islands confirmed that is wasn't just a banking error or a frozen account. Someone had tampered with the funds during the last twenty-four hours. He was sure the former SEALs knew the person who screwed up his bank account.

Throughout the day, the two men in the white van monitored the conversations coming from the safe house. Intermittently, they listened to the food channel playing in the background while the women talked. Then to pass the time, they tried following the football games watched by the men inside the house. Later that afternoon, an FBI agent watched two vans leave a church parking lot in Columbia. The group appeared to be a hunting party, but a source confirmed it was SSBA. Nate sent a message to his brother. Shortly after nightfall, he sent another message. The vans had reached the outskirts of Bluffton. He signed off asking Devon to keep everyone safe.

Nate and Max argued loudly over a contested football score and the men inside the white SSBA van listened with great interest. Meanwhile, Tommy belly crawled under the van, quietly ran a tube through the engine compartment until it reached the dash panel, and released an odorless gas that knocked out both occupants. Then he shut down communications inside the van. Nate helped him remove the two men and secure them inside the safe house.

A handpicked FBI team from Washington arrived. Isaac and two agents joined Nate, Max, and Tommy inside the safe house. Gabe, Chip, and four more FBI specialists took distant, well-chosen positions around the periphery. After checking weapons, equipment, and communications, they waited.

When the first van arrived, nothing happened. The arrival of the second van triggered the attack. Sixteen SSBA militants armed with AK-47 rifles emerged from their vehicles and surrounded the house.

Isaac issued a loud warning. "This is the FBI. Put down your weapons now."

A single shot hit the front door, followed by a barrage of bullets from the assault weapons. They did little to penetrate the bulletproof windows and reinforced exterior walls.

Those inside the house drew SSBA fire and returned it with M4 carbines and MP5 submachine guns. The SEALs and FBI specialists around the perimeter used M40A1 sniper rifles. With precision, they incapacitated an inferior opponent one-by-one. Their objective was to disable and not kill. Six SSBA soldiers stormed the back door of the safe house. Nate and Tommy stopped them. The conflict began to wane as injured militants called out in pain.

Isaac issued another order. "This is the FBI. Cease fire now."

When more shots were fired, FBI sharpshooters eliminated two more SSBA soldiers from the fray. Both were injured and called out to surrender. Nate shouted to them, "Move away from your weapons and stay down."

As the two men crawled away from their rifles, a line of fire hit the ground near them, one man screamed out in pain. When a voice shouted out, Nate spotted a man with the insignia of an army colonel standing in a dense stand of trees. He had fired at his own unarmed men and threatened to kill them. Nate aimed his weapon at the crazed imposter. "Drop it, Dodd." He watched a malicious smile form as the man turned and re-aimed his weapon in his direction. Then Nate squeezed the trigger.

The fight was over. Many of the SSBA militants were wounded and five were dead, including the self-proclaimed colonel. Without his threats, the troops gave up. One FBI agent had been wounded, but not critically.

Max grabbed Nate's shoulder. "We're out of here. *Now!*"

"What's wrong?"

"Trouble on Hilton Head. It's quicker by water." He and Nate ran down the dock. Tommy was waiting at the helm with the engine running when they jumped into the boat.

XXX

Early that morning, Charlie Potts had watched everyone except Devon McLean and the two women leave the house on Hilton Head Island. He had confirmed that the crazed colonel and his militants were headed for the Bluffton safe house with the goal of killing Nate Dunlevy and anyone who stood in their way. The SEALs and the SSBA could shoot it out all night long. As soon as his money was safe, he'd slip through the cracks and hide on a remote island in the Caribbean. That evening, the FBI agent overcame a locked window, hid in the downstairs bedroom, and waited for an opportunity to undo the tampering of his bank account.

Warmer daytime temperatures had returned with the passing of the storm, but the house on Hilton Head had cooled with the night air. Katie lit the *Duraflame* log that sat in the fireplace and hoped the fire's glow would brighten their moods. Devon found a deck of cards and challenged someone to a game of gin at ten cents a point. Katie accepted; Eve declined. Instead, she tried to engross herself in Devon's book, but even John Grisham couldn't keep her attention. Her mind kept going back to conflict in Bluffton. She couldn't imagine what might be happening there. When Nate left early that morning, there was no hugging or kissing. He gave her a penetrating look with those gray eyes, squeezed her hand, and promised to be back.

She gave up and put the book down. Devon glanced at her as he shuffled the cards. "He'll be fine, darling." He knew things could go wrong, but he sounded convincing for her sake. "Why don't you take a hot soak in the tub? It'll help you relax."

"I'll try that. At least I won't drive the two of you crazy by pacing the room."

"Use the downstairs bath and keep the doors partially open. I won't disturb you."

"Are you concerned about something?"

"I'm just being extra cautious." He smiled. "Humor me."

She tried to smile back and walked down a short hallway to bedroom. Devon had instructed them to keep the exterior bedroom dark and the interior bathroom lit. The light from the bath helped her see when she sat on the bed and toed off her shoes. She walked to the bath and cranked on the faucets. After tossing her T-shirt on the vanity, she unfastened her cutoffs and let them drop to her feet. Then her world went black.

When she regained consciousness, cuffs pinned her arms behind her back and a hand clamped firmly over her mouth. Someone pressed her body against the vanity cabinet. When her vision cleared, she saw her reflection in the mirror. A trickle of blood ran from her temple and she wore nothing but her panties. A strange man stood behind her holding a gun against her throbbing head. He put his mouth close to her ear. "If you make a sound, you're dead."

Devon's hearing alerted him. He grabbed for the rifle and jumped up, cursing the stiffness in his leg. His peripheral vision sent a warning to his brain. He shouted for Katie to get down and spun around with his weapon. Then he saw them. Agent Potts had Eve in a firm chokehold and held his gun to her head. "Place your weapon on the table very slowly, McLean, or I'll blow her head clear off her shoulders." He told Katie to crawl to the center of the room and lay face down on the floor. When she hesitated, he squeezed his arm against Eve's throat, causing her to choke. Katie reluctantly obeyed. He gave Devon another instruction. "Use one hand and put your cinch piece on the floor, then kick it under the table." He kept pressure on Eve's throat. "Do it now or she's dead!"

Devon slowly removed his handgun and followed his instructions.

"Now keep your arms in front of you, McLean." He shoved Eve to her knees and made her lie face down on the floor near her sister. The agent tossed a pair of nylon handcuffs to Devon and pointed at Katie. "Cuff her." He kept the gun trained on Eve's head as Devon secured Katie's wrists. "Now stand up with your arms on top of your head. If anyone flinches, you'll take your last breath."

"What do you want from us, Potts?"

"Someone has tampered with my bank account."

"What am I supposed to do about it?"

Potts pointed at the laptop that sat on the coffee table. "The FBI didn't make those funds disappear and it sure as hell wasn't some idiot from the SSBA. I have no doubt that you know who caused my problem. Now fix it."

"I'll see what I can do."

"Don't play fucking games with me. I have someone waiting to make a size-able withdrawal. Kneel down and get busy. Keep your hands where I can see them."

Devon knelt slowly, trying to disguise the pain that shot through his leg. Potts kept the gun trained on Eve and Katie while he watched an e-mail screen display on the computer. He didn't see Devon tap a function key, one Max had pro-grammed before he went to Bluffton.

"This could take awhile. I'm waiting for a response."

"I had planned to be long gone by now, McLean. You have thirty minutes to make something happen. Then I'll flip a coin and decide which woman to shoot first."

When the laptop beeped, Potts said, "Don't touch the keyboard yet. I'm going to tell you what to type. Don't make a mistake, and don't send the message until I say so."

Devon carefully entered the message dictated to him. It instructed the recipi-ent to correct a banking error that occurred within the last twenty-four hours and listed the bank name and account number. He added that the transaction must occur within thirty minutes. Potts told him to turn the computer screen in his direction so he could scan the message. "Hit send. If I don't receive a phone call from the Caymans within thirty minutes, someone is going to die."

The rogue agent tossed two pair of nylon cuffs at the former SEAL. "Open that closet door and loop one cuff around the upper hinge and through the other." He waited. "Now put the other pair on your wrists and pull them tight." When Devon obeyed, he pointed to the cuff dangling from the hinge. "Now loop that one around your right wrist and make it snug." Devon's hands were restrained above his head. To be sure the cuffs were tight, Potts picked up the fireplace poker. He swung it like a bat and hit Devon on his injured thigh. Devon's breath left him in a whoosh, his knees gave out, and the nylon cuffs tore into the skin of his wrists.

Charlie Potts looked down at the two women and glanced at his watch. Then he told Eve to stand up. Without the use of her hands, getting to her feet took work. She stood and faced him in her bikini underwear. Devon shook his head to clear his vision and tried to overcome his pain. "Leave her alone, Potts."

He ignored Devon. "I should thank you for starting this ruckus. Setting up your lover added nicely to my retirement fund. The minute he walked into the safe house, I collected another payment." He glanced at Devon. "It's in a differ-ent account." He reached out and grabbed Eve's breast.

She moved backward abruptly and almost tripped. After regaining her balance, she took another step backward. "Keep your filthy hands off me." The remark earned her a punishing backhand. She toppled over a chair, hit the ground hard, and lost her wind.

Devon wanted Potts focused on him. "How did you find us?"

"I picked up your trail at the Coast Guard station and followed you to Savannah. Then I lost you when you boarded the boat, but I knew you'd land on Hilton Head. I questioned a few trolley drivers and one of them recognized the beauties." He nodded at the women. "He remembered dropping them at the marina. I got a room at the inn and figured I'd stumble across one of you soon enough. Then by dumb luck, I looked out the window last night and I saw a man getting out of an SUV. You can take the man out of the military, but you can't take the military out of the man. I followed his car on foot. There's only one road in and out of here. Two vehicles drove up to a house and when they unloaded, I knew my hunch was right. Four men moved with military precision. I had trouble seeing their faces in the dark, but I recognized Max's voice."

Devon ignored the pain pulsing through his leg. He had to keep the man occupied. "You have a good eye and a sharp mind, Potts. Was it worth your career?"

"I've been working toward early retirement for several years. I could have a different job if the Sovereign Church's candidate for lieutenant governor is elected, but the man is an asshole. So are the rest of them, but their money's green."

"Did you kill a fellow agent?"

"He wasn't supposed to die. Even I draw the line somewhere. The SSBA wackos screwed that up. I was there to confirm Dunlevy was dead when the FBI came to investigate. I have to admire the way you slipped away from that attack."

When the laptop beeped, Devon said, "That may be my contact with information about your account, but I'll have to decipher it." He counted on Potts's greed to cloud his judgment.

Potts had to make a decision. He wanted his money back and he wanted to disappear. McLean was too dangerous a man to unleash. Killing them was a last resort. If anyone suspected him of the crime, there'd be no place to hide. Every living Navy SEAL would hunt him down for the rest of his life … one that would be short-lived … his death would be very painful. He tapped Katie with his foot and told her to roll over. Then he reached down, grabbed her by the shirt, and yanked her to her feet. The T-shirt ripped open and Potts stared at her exposed breasts.

She shouted, "Stop looking at me like that!"

He laughed. "You're a prissy one, aren't you?" The man had struck a raw nerve and Devon worried she might do something stupid. Katie thought about a well-aimed foot directly into his shinbone, but she made eye contact with Devon and saw him shake his head.

Potts instructed Katie to position her cuffed hands behind her back so she could hold the laptop while Devon read the screen. When Potts set the laptop in her outstretched fingers, she fumbled with it. She turned asking him for help, her breasts bumped him twice as though by accident, and her antics maneuvered him closer to Devon. With feigned confusion, she turned in his direction, dropped the laptop, and swung her foot sharply into his shinbone. The surprising and painful impact threw him off balance.

Devon kicked out with his good leg and slammed it into the agent's kidney. Potts was propelled forward, landing hard on his knees, and losing the grip on his gun. It hit the floor a few feet from Eve. She crawled to it and covered it with her body. Katie took another hard kick at the man, but he grabbed her leg and dropped her to the floor. Potts slowly got to his feet and stood bent in pain for several seconds. Then he straightened and returned Katie's kick, his own foot landing solidly against her bruised hip. The pain forced her to cry out and he kicked her again.

Meanwhile, the three SEALs arrived at the southern tip of Hilton Head Island. Tommy quietly beached the watercraft on the Calibogue shore just past the entrance to Braddock Cove. After Max and Nate jumped into the surf, they pushed the boat back into deeper water. Max had instructed Tommy to wait for thirty seconds then race the boat into the cove.

Inside the house, Potts picked up the fireplace poker. "I'm done fucking around here, McLean." He held the iron rod with both hands and swung it with full force. Although Devon tried to lessen the impact by turning his torso, the force of the poker slammed into his unguarded rib cage. Potts swung again and landed a second blow to the ribs. Devon struggled to regain his vision, his breath, and his footing as he hung by his wrists from the door hinge.

They heard a fast boat speed through the cove near the house, its wake slap against the shoreline, and then silence. Potts carried the poker to where Eve lay on the floor. He leaned down, grabbed her by the hair, and told her to stand up. She resisted, so he let go of her hair and swung the poker sharply across her back. Then he reached down and pulled his backup weapon from an ankle holster.

Max kicked open the front door and came in low. Nate stood in the open doorway and sighted his weapon on the agent. "Give it up, Potts." Two guns discharged. Agent Potts fell beside Eve and she stared at the gruesome hole in the man's forehead.

The second he had squeezed the trigger, Nate felt his chest implode. The impact threw his body backward before he fell to the ground. Every ounce of breath was sucked from his lungs and there was unspeakable pain in his chest.

When Tommy got there, Max was stripping the gear away from Nate's body. "I've got this covered. Go help the others."

Tommy freed Devon, cut the restraints on the two women, and checked their injuries. Devon asked him to get blankets for Eve and Katie and make sure they weren't going into shock. Then he limped outside and lowered his damaged body to the ground next to Nate.

"The hit broke the skin, but the bullet didn't penetrate far, Dev. He's still dazed."

"Kevlar doesn't stop the impact, Max." He took his brother's pulse and felt reassured. "Stay with us, big guy. Try taking a deeper breath even though it hurts like hell."

Nate heard their voices then he heard Eve cry out. His lungs begged for more air and he fought to stay conscious.

Eve dropped to the ground. Devon felt her shaking when he put his arm around her. "Don't worry, darling. His vest stopped the bullet. He's mostly stunned."

Nate opened his eyes and saw her beside him. He whispered, "You okay?"

She nodded. "Are you?"

"Hmmm ... just need a minute." With effort, he raised a hand and wiped a tear from her cheek. The streak of dirt he left on her face reminded him of the day she had planted flowers on Sullivan's Island. The memory made him smile. He murmured, "I caused a real mess, didn't I?"

She choked back a sob and tried to return his smile. "It was our mess. Is it over?"

"It's over, baby."

EPILOGUE

Nate walked to a monitor in the Charleston Airport. "It looks like your flight to DC is on time, Dev." He glanced at his watch. "But, we've got time to grab a beer."

"Sounds good to me."

They ordered two beers at the airport lounge and talked about the heightened concern for security at U.S. ports. Devon reiterated his support for DMG contracts along the southeast coast, work that Nate could spearhead from Charleston. He tossed a twenty on the bar when the server brought their beers. "Keep it open, please." The server nodded and walked away.

Devon lifted his bottle. "Before we left, Eve and Katie badgered me one more time about what happened in Bluffton."

Nate put his bottle on the bar with a loud tap. The bloody images were still fresh. "What did you tell them?"

"Nothing."

"Good. What happened in Bluffton is history and so is the SSBA. Eve and Katie went through enough with Potts." He paused. "Max told me he'd set up a hot button on the laptop. I can't describe my fear when he told me you used it and Tee-Jay confirmed you were in serious trouble." He shook his head. "I never saw it coming."

"I've done enough self-flagellation over that night for both of us. It doesn't change what happened and we survived." Devon watched Nate unconsciously rub the dent in his body. "How's the chest?"

"It only hurts when I breathe, but dropping that bastard was worth it."

Nate thought of the hours everyone spent at the hospital that night and was grateful their injuries only required Emergency Room treatment. He remembered a conversation between Eve and him while they waited for x-rays. "Is something going on with you and Katie?"

Devon shook his head and laughed quietly. "God knows." He finished his beer. "You heard her mention our single episode of mind-altering sex. I won't argue with her description and I won't deny I'm drawn to her. But she's going back to California. Maybe we'll stay in touch." He looked at his watch and signaled the bartender for another round. "It's my turn to be nosy. Where are you at with Eve?"

"Hang on to your barstool, Dev. I want to marry her ... have a family with her. But I can't think of either one right now. During the next year, the admiral will tap us on the shoulder and we'll disappear. I've been honest with her about that."

Devon thought about his brother's predicament. "A year's not forever, but marriage should be and kids are. For what it's worth, I think you and Eve would make great parents."

"Hmmm. I have to fulfill my commitment to the admiral. If she can handle this next year, then we've got a chance."

"She's stronger than you think."

"You're right."

Both men focused on their private thoughts while they finished their beers. Moments later, Devon checked his watch. "It's time for me to head out."

Nate didn't miss the tender step his brother took when he moved away from the stool. "How's the leg?"

"It stiffens up and I'm taking the antibiotics they gave me at the hospital." He rubbed his side. "The ribs hurt more than the leg. Eve made me promise to call her within the next few days." He shook his head and laughed. "I'm not accustomed to a woman worrying about me."

"She cares about you, Dev. So do I."

They stopped near the security checkpoint and grasped hands. "I can't describe how much I owe you, so I'll just say thanks."

"You don't owe me damn anything, big guy." He started to walk away then turned around and grinned. "But you could name your first kid after me."

Nate smiled, shoved his hands in his pockets, and watched Devon clear security. When his brother disappeared from view, he turned and left the terminal.

978-0-595-41271-6
0-595-41271-8

Printed in the United States
94904LV00004B/1-24/A

9 780595 412716